This is a work of fiction. N
businesses, places, even̅s, ̅o̅c̅a̅l̅e̅s̅, ̅a̅n̅d̅
incidents are either the products of the
author's imagination or used in a fictitious
manner. Any resemblance to actual persons,
living or dead, or actual events is purely
coincidental.

To my wife, Marna Ross, the heartbeat of my life. Your love is the melody that inspires every word I write, the suspense that keeps me on the edge of my seat, and the twist in every tale. You are the romance in my drama, the vivid color in my world. This story is but a mirror reflecting the beauty and mystery of our love. With all my heart, this book is for you.

SHADOWS OF DECEIT
IWAN ROSS

Siren,
In ancient lore, a call from the deep,
A sea nymph's song luring mariners to sleep.
Their sweet melodies echo 'round their isle,
Drawing the unsuspecting to their guile.
Siren,
A woman, irresistible in her allure,
Her charm, her mystery, impossible to ignore.
In her presence, hearts beat a little faster,
In her absence, they yearn for her laughter.
Beware, dear reader, of the sirens' song,
For in this tale, right blurs with wrong.
- Iwan Ross

1

The weight of the long day takes its toll on Alice, and her face shows deep lines of exhaustion. Despite this, her emerald green eyes remain sharp and alert, peering out from behind a pair of elegant reading glasses. She rests a notepad on her lap, and her gaze falls upon the page filled with neat, crossed-out questions written in a legible handwriting. The scratching sound of her pen on the paper echoes around the small consultation room as she erases the questions.

A far-off expression clouds her eyes as she studies the notepad, her mind consumed by the task at hand. The smell of coffee lingers in the air, having been her constant companion throughout the arduous day. She bites her lip in concentration as she twirls a strand of raven hair around her finger. Her forehead creases as she reads and rereads the questions on the notepad, deep in thought. With a stoic expression, she raises her head and intently peers at her clients over the rim of her glasses.

"Are you satisfied with your physical intimacy?" Alice asks, her tone soft yet firm. The therapist's voice, soothing and calm, fills the room, occasionally interrupted by the rustling of papers and the gentle hum of the aquarium.

The Granger's, a married couple, sit closely on a plush leather couch, their eyes trained on their therapist. They look at her with a pleading gaze, as if she holds the key to freeing them from an unseen malevolent force. She can feel their desperation and the weight of their expectations bearing down on her. They exchange a nervous glance, eyes darting away before meeting hers, and remain silent.

Mrs. Granger's middle-aged frame sits rigidly upright, with her knees pressed together and her hands clasped in her lap. Her tightly permed hair, which gives her a few extra inches of height, complements her pursed lips. The green jumpsuit she's donning clings to her like a second skin. Despite her uptight demeanor, there's a sadness in her eyes that's hard to ignore. It's as if she's carrying a heavy burden that she can't quite shake off.

Samuel Granger is a man who carries the vitality of youth in his stride, a stark contrast to his wife, Madison. Dressed in fitted blue jeans and a crisp white t-shirt, he exudes an effortless cool that belies his age. He completes his ensemble with a classic blazer and rugged boots, adding a touch of sophistication to his casual attire. His eyes, bright with the spark of life, hold a vibrancy that seems untouched by the passage of time. Beside him, Madison appears as a timeless beauty, her maturity adding a depth to her allure that's hard to ignore. The contrasting hints of their outfits subtly reveal a difference in their ages, adding to the enigma of their bond and creating a magnetic pull that draws people into their story.

Meanwhile, Mr. Granger wets his lips as he ogles the therapist's shapely legs beneath her snug miniskirt. His wife scowls at him, and he winces as she jabs him sharply in the ribs. Flushed, he turns his attention to the aquarium. The blue light casts an otherworldly glow on his face as he feigns interest in the colorful assortment of tropical fish swimming within. Alice's lips curl into a smile, barely containing her amusement at his childish antics.

The scent of lavender wafts through the air, emanating from a small diffuser on the therapist's desk. Mrs. Granger's hands fidget nervously in her lap, the leather couch creaking with her movements.

Mr. Granger shifts restlessly in his seat, his fingers tapping a nervous rhythm on his knee. The soft fabric of Alice's miniskirt brushes against her legs as she adjusts her position, the sight of her, a guilty pleasure sending a roguish smile to his lips. Her poise and magnetic presence leave him completely mesmerized and unable to look away. She meets his sultry gaze and can almost feel the heat emanating from him. The low hum of the aquarium is the only sound in the room, adding to the stifling atmosphere.

Alice's gaze flicks to her notepad, and the scratching of her pen fills the room. She crosses out the answered questions and lifts her chin, looking Mrs. Granger straight in the eye. "What are your concerns about Mr. Granger?" Alice removes her glasses and wipes them clean, revealing her bright, shining eyes. Mr. Granger's face lights up with a beaming smile, captivated by his therapist's gaze.

Mrs. Granger's eyes dart around the room, filled with contempt. She sneers as she speaks, and her voice is sharp. "He always comes home late—playing golf with friends, he says. He brushes me off when I confront him. I can't live with a man like that." The room falls silent as her blunt remark hangs in the air.

Alice furrows her brow, deep in thought. "Why are you so dependent on your husband? Don't you have your own life and friends?" Alice jots down the term 'co-dependency' beside Mrs. Granger's name as she takes notes.

Anger clouds Mrs. Granger's face, her eyes narrowed with fury. Her nails tap against the leather armrest as she speaks. "Yes, I do, but I must account for my expenses, unlike him." With a menacing expression, she jabs her thumb in her husband's direction. "He does whatever he wants."

Alice exudes an air of smug confidence as the room fills with tension. She asks, "Do you want financial freedom?"

Mrs. Granger's jaw is tight and her fists are clenched so tightly that her knuckles turn white. With anger in her voice and the scent of her sharp floral perfume filling the air, she asks, "Who would want a man who's never home, anyway? Would you live with someone like that, Doctor What's-her-name?" Her husband jumps as she slams her hand down on the armrest.

Alice ponders the question, her pen clicking repeatedly. "Is it a want or a need?" she asks, meeting Mrs. Granger's hostility with a stern gaze.

Mrs. Granger is fuming as she grabs her bag and storms towards the door. Her footsteps are heavy and purposeful as she makes her way. "Come along, Samuel! I can't listen to this nonsense any longer."

Samuel raises his hands in surrender, trying to reason with her. "No, Madison, it's not nonsense," he says, leaning in closer. "We have to do this. If you leave now, you lose everything and you know that." In search of support, he quickly glances at his therapist.

Alice shrugs, seemingly indifferent to the discussion at hand. "It's your call whether you stay or go," she tells Madison Granger, her gaze unwavering. "Either way, it doesn't matter to me. It's your assets on the line, so the decision is yours to make." With a quick glance, Alice checks the cassette recorder's red light, making sure it's blinking.

Madison Granger sighs heavily and slumps into her seat, the leather creaking beneath her. Her husband's hand draws near, but she recoils and frowns, causing a rift between them. Alice's piercing gaze bores into them over the rim of her glasses, making them feel uneasy. The silence is deafening, broken only by the occasional creak of the leather chair as Madison shifts uncomfortably in her seat.

Alice commands, "Let's lay down some ground rules," in a voice carrying an undeniable air of authority. "Doctor What's-her-name doesn't exist here. In this room, I am simply Alice." Her gaze sweeps over the couple before her, unwavering. "I want to clarify—I'm not your savior. I won't swoop in and magically fix your problems," she continues, her tone resolute. "The court has tasked me with assessing your relationship, not mediating your disputes. The legal system will take care of dividing assets and distributing wealth post-divorce. I stand apart from that process."

She inhales deeply, her eyes never leaving the couple. "Can we agree on this?" A palpable tension hangs in the air as the Grangers' nod their agreement, their eyes wide and filled with newfound respect. They recline in their chairs, a sense of relief washing over them as they relinquish control. The musky scent of Mr. Granger's cologne permeates the air, intertwining with the comforting aroma of freshly brewed coffee wafting in from the next room.

With her heels clicking on the hardwood floor, Alice stands up and says, "Please excuse me for a moment." She hastens to the entrance, steps out, and closes the door behind her, muffling the sound of the Grangers' conversation.

Samuel Granger shifts on the couch, and the old leather groans in protest. He turns to face his wife. "I know this is hard on you," he says. "But the end is near. After today, we only have five sessions left. Can you please try to be more flexible and understanding?" His frustration seeps into his voice as he speaks.

His wife ignores him, her eyes fixated on her hands as she studies her perfectly manicured nails. The lines on Samuel's forehead deepen as he scans the room, his gaze settling on the wall adorned with framed copies of their therapist's degrees and graduation photos. He fixates on Alice's beaming smile in the images.

He rises from his seat and takes slow steps towards the wall; the frames rattling slightly. Two photographs of a younger Alice, clad in a black gown and academic cap, take center stage in the framed collection. A picture on the right captures her, tossing her cap into the air, her smile radiant and triumphant.

Desire surges through his veins like a wildfire, igniting an uncontrollable fire within him. His heart thumps loudly in his chest, like a drumbeat resonating through the room. A flush spread across his face, the heat almost palpable. He inhales deeply, trying to calm himself, but the image of her lingers in his mind, stoking the flames of his desire. He lets out a dramatic sigh before quickly composing himself and scurrying back to his seat.

As Samuel sits, the office door flies open. In walks Alice, her perfume's seductive scent of caraway and jasmine wafting in the air and leaving Samuel spellbound. He watches in wonder as she takes her seat, smoothing out the fabric of her dress over her legs and pulling up a drooping sock with a gentle tug. The room is awash in a warm, golden light as the sun's last rays filter through the window, illuminating the elegance of her silhouette.

Samuel's intense gaze meets Alice's as she straightens, causing a playful smirk to spread across her lips. Her sudden movement stuns him, and he leans back in his chair, crossing his legs. His fingers tap restlessly on the armrest, and he looks up at the ceiling, his face twisted with a mixture of guilt and curiosity. Alice's gaze meets Madison Granger's, who responds with a fierce glare and an insincere smile that doesn't quite reach her eyes. Samuel rubs his side to soothe the pain where his wife nudged him for stealing an eyeful of his therapist's cleavage. His cheeks flush an angry red as he attempts to calm himself down.

The air in the room is still, and each breath feels like a struggle. The gentle rap on the door is a welcome sound, momentarily breaking the oppressive silence. A young woman enters the office, her long, tightly braided cornrows swaying slightly with each step. A broad and open forehead frames her deep-set eyes. Her vibrant clothing mirrors her joyful demeanor, and her dazzling smile lights up the space. Carefully, she sets down a tray of steaming beverages on the low coffee table.

"Good afternoon, my name is Natalie, and I'm Alice's personal assistant," she says, pointing to the items on the tray. "Decaf, filtered coffee, apple juice, orange juice, warm milk, cold milk, and—oh, Lord have mercy—chocolate chip cookies."

Madison Granger's eyes flash with wrath as she shoots Natalie a hostile glance. Her voice grates on the nerves, sending shivers down the spine as she demands in an ear-piercing screech, "I don't drink coffee. Bring me black tea."

Samuel Granger speaks up, softening the tension. "Hi, Natalie. I'm Samuel Granger, and this here is my wife, Madison. You can call me Sam." He stands, puts on a disarming smile, and holds out his hand.

Natalie's eyes widen as she fixates on the large, callous hand in front of her. Her eyes light up with excitement as she eagerly shakes Samuel Granger's hand. "Oh my, it's such a pleasure to meet you, sir. Your handsome face is all over the television." With a graceful bow, she backs up towards the door. The tantalizing scent of freshly brewed coffee mingles with the sweet aroma of oven-fresh treats, filling the air with an irresistible allure.

Samuel lets out a deep, rumbling laugh that reverberates off the walls, and slaps his knee with glee. "Wow, can you believe that?" he asks. "Her soul seems to resonate with mine," he exclaims, letting out a chuckle.

His wife's mouth twists into a frown, and she rolls her eyes in annoyance. "You, a handsome face? Don't make me laugh!" she retorts.

Samuel glares at his wife, his eyes piercing like daggers, before settling into his seat. Alice prepares her questions while she waits for him to pour his coffee. The sound of the clinking of the spoon against the cup echoes in the room. He offers his wife a cookie, but she raises her hand in refusal and wrinkles her nose. He puts two cookies on his saucer and reclines, his jaw snapping as he chews the crunchy treats.

His wife moves to the edge of the couch, her arms crossed in annoyance. Alice jots down her observations and faces Samuel. "Is there a reason you don't seem to pay attention to your wife like you used to?" The tension in the room is palpable, and the air feels thick with unspoken anger.

Samuel fidgets in his seat and places the half-eaten cookie on the saucer. He responds cautiously, his voice barely above a whisper. "My wife has my full support in her decision to seek a divorce. I feel neglected, and I need you to understand—"

The clinking of silverware interrupts him as Natalie saunters in, the sound of her heels echoing through the room. She delicately places a silver tray with a gleaming teapot, sugar cubes, serviettes, and antique-looking teacups on the coffee table. "There you go, ma'am," she says and straightens, momentarily eclipsing Madison's view. The comforting aroma of freshly brewed tea fills the air. "Y'all need anything else?" Natalie murmurs softly, barely audible. Madison cranes her neck around Natalie, seeking a clearer view of her therapist. She wears a deep frown and shoos Natalie away with a dismissive wave before pouring herself a soothing cup of tea.

The moment Natalie is gone, Samuel resumes speaking, his voice competing with the clatter of his wife's teacup. "What was I saying again?" He inhales deeply, taking in the scent of freshly baked cookies.

"I remember you telling me you felt neglected." Alice gives him a subtle nod, her sleek hair brushing against her shoulders.

"Yes I said, if I can get attention somewhere else, I'll take it. Madison is free to go if she so chooses." His sorrowful voice is heavy with emotion.

Alice scribbles the phrase 'projected blame' next to Samuel's name, her pen pausing in mid-air as she studies her list of questions. "And what about your children?" She asks, her voice tinged with caution.

Madison Granger sputters out a wet cough, the sound harsh and grating. "God!" she exclaims. "Who said anything about children? He has an air rifle that fires blanks. No can do." She puffs out her cheeks and makes a popping sound as she exhales. Despite Samuel's scarlet flush, he maintains his composure and bites into a cookie.

Alice sucks her teeth as she plans her next question, and the tension in the room thickens. She gazes up at Mr. Granger with a curious glint in her eyes, her playful smile countering his sultry gaze. Mr. Granger's wife glares at him, her expression stony and unyielding.

"Why did you leave it up to your wife to start the divorce proceedings?" Alice asks, her voice soft and measured.

Mr. Granger's eyes dart to his wife, his panicked expression betraying his attempt at a lie. He shifts in his seat, tugging at the sleeves of his blazer. Alice notices the subtle signs of Mr. Granger's discomfort—the sweat beads forming on his forehead, the way his hands tremble slightly. She can tell that he is struggling to find the right words to respond, his mind racing with excuses and justifications. His body language speaks volumes, revealing the guilt and shame that he is trying to conceal. Alice waits patiently, giving him a chance to compose himself and speak the truth.

Minutes pass in tense silence, punctuated only by the gentle hum of the fish tank and the rhythmic whir of the filter. A tranquil blue glow from the aquarium illuminates the walls, while the bubbling water provides a soothing backdrop. Silence blankets the room, each person avoiding eye contact and fidgeting in their seats. The sound of the ticking wall clock fills the room, adding to the growing tension.

Alice pulls her hair into a high ponytail, feeling the strands tightly grip her scalp. She reviews her notes, the crisp sound of paper rustling filling the room. Madison looks down, her eyes heavy with emotion. Mr. Granger's gaze lingers on the delicate features of his counselor's face—her aquiline nose, narrow eyebrows, and glossy cupid's bow lips. His gaze lingers on her sensual mouth, and Alice can feel the intensity of it on her skin.

A sharp nudge in his side startles him out of his lustful gaze, and he shoots an irritated glance at his wife. Their commotion catches Alice's attention. She raises an eyebrow as she meets Madison's solemn gaze, noting their hands tightly clasped together in a show of apprehension. Alice's eyes widen in surprise as she notices Mr. Granger's wedding ring, while his wife's left hand is completely bare.

To support her claims, Alice chews on her lip and savors the minty taste of her lip balm while meticulously noting down her observations about their wedding bands. The distant chime of a clock in the house reverberates through the room, marking the hour. Alice closes her eyes and lets out a sigh of relief, feeling the tension slowly leaving her body.

Alice's emerald eyes flit back and forth between the spouses, taking in the details of their appearance and body language. The sound of Samuel's heavy breathing echoes through the room, along with the rustling of papers on Alice's lap. The heavy scent of lavender mixes with Mr. Granger's musky cologne, filling the room.

Alice sits still as Samuel's eyes devour her from head to toe, and she can't help but feel a tinge of satisfaction at the sight of his cheeks turning a rosy shade of pink. She gives him a playful grin and teasingly puts the base of her pen in her mouth, savoring the icy feel of the metal plunger on her tongue. He quickly averts his gaze, glaring at the books stacked on the shelves behind the shiny, dark-brown cocobolo desk.

Alice furrows her brows as she studies Madison's expressionless face, quickly scribbling down the words 'narcissistic personality disorder' next to her name. Madison leans in and strains her eyes to glimpse at Alice's scribbled notes. Alice remains composed, grinning as she lifts the edge of the paper to conceal her personal notes.

Mr. Granger looks back at his counselor and offers a charming smile that warms his face. Alice narrows her eyes, holds his amorous gaze, licks her lips, and shoots a fleeting glance at his wife. She trows her off guard by asking, "What do you want to get out of this?"

Madison's eyebrows shoot up in surprise, and her face contorts with deep frown lines. "First, let me be clear: I don't want to be here," she says with a pensive sigh. "After being married to this man for twelve years, I think I deserve a just reward for the pain and suffering he's put me through. What I want is out."

A mix of anger and confusion clouds Samuel's expression as he scowls at his wife, deep furrows creasing his forehead. "What pain and suffering?" he asks in incredulously. "I gave you everything you ever wanted. Yes, I worked hard, and I know I neglected you. I'm sorry about that. But to call it pain and suffering is something else entirely. Many—"

Just then, Natalie walks in and places the empty cups and saucers on the trays. The sound of the porcelain cups clinking together fills the room. Madison shoots Natalie a furious glance, exasperated by the interruption. "For crying out loud!" she snaps. "Can't you see we're busy?" With a dismissive gesture, she shoos Natalie away and adds, "Get out and come back later. Shoo now."

Natalie's eyes widen in disbelief as she stares at the haughty snob. She glances at Alice with a silent plea for help. Alice's face flushes red with anger, and her hands tremble as she stands and takes the trays from her assistant. Her heels click on the hardwood floor as she walks towards the door. "Thanks for your help, Natalie," she murmurs. Natalie walks away with heavy steps, her shoulders slumped in resignation.

Mr. Granger glares at his wife, his eyes burn with fury, and he warns her through gritted teeth, "I'll deal with you later," as his fingers curl into fists. Madison furrows her brow in disapproval, adding to the palpable tension in the atmosphere.

From a safe distance, Alice watches the tense confrontation between Madison and her husband, noting the underlying issues in their marriage. Madison's fingers fiddle with the delicate necklace around her neck, the sound of the gold chain clicking against the metal pendant filling the air. Alice's hand glides over the paper as she scribbles down line after line, her eyes scanning her arsenal of inciting questions eagerly before she fires away. "Mrs. Granger," she begins, her voice low and measured, "what would you call this problem of not paying attention to your husband?" The silence is almost tangible, only broken by the sound of her pen scratching against the paper.

The scent of hairspray makes Alice's nose sting as Madison runs her fingers through her permed hair, a sinister glint in her eyes. "How can I pay attention to someone who's never at home?" she complains.

Her partner interrupts, his voice thick with frustration. "Now c'mon, that's not fair. Even when I am home, you ignore me and watch TV with that flea-infested mutt of yours. You only prepare dinner for yourself and feed your overweight dog. Tell me something. When's my birthday?"

In the dim-lit confines of the consultation room, words laced with anger and resentment escape her lips, each syllable dripping with venom. "You might as well have married your mother, for all the attention you pay me, you mommy's boy!" Her voice, raw and bitter, reverberates through the room. "How can I remember your birthday with all the endless chores and demands in my day? The date should be a permanent memory, imprinted on my soul, not just a fleeting entry on a calendar!"

As she lashes out, her fingers absentmindedly twine through her permed hair, the strands whispering a soft sizzle as they rub against each other. The sound is faint, but in the charged silence that follows her outburst, it crackles like distant thunder—a storm brewing beneath the surface of their strained relationship. Her words are like daggers, cutting through her husband's resolve as he cringes beside her.

The tension between them is palpable, a tangible entity that threatens to shatter the fragile peace they've clung onto. Their once secure marriage now hangs in the balance, with despair looming close.

Alice watches with a satisfied smile as she takes detailed notes, observing the husband's face turning red with fury. His eyes flicker with rage, burning like an inferno. "Let's not bring my late mother into our troubles," he sharply rebukes his wife, "She knew how to care for my dad, unlike..." But before he could finish, Alice interrupts their bickering with a raised voice and directs her attention to Mr. Granger. "Let's focus on your wife," she says, briefly inspecting her notes. Turning to the sneering woman, she asks, "Are you taking a stance for or against not caring?"

With a glint of excitement in her eyes, Madison claps her hands slowly. "You're on the right track, doctor," she says. "Why should I waste my time on a man who can't give me children? I'm getting older every day. If I leave now, I still have time to find a man who is fertile. Unlike this man who is shooting blanks," she adds, making a wanking gesture with her hand. Alice winces at the harsh comment, feeling a sharp jolt of pain course through her heart.

Samuel Granger's frustration boils over and he lets out an exasperated sigh before shooting his wife a withering glare. "Okay, Madison, you seem to have the moral high ground. But tell me, is there anything you won't use against me?" He then issues a stern warning, "Let me make one thing clear. You will not walk out with everything I worked for. Remember, never bite the hand that feeds you." He delivers his words in a booming, authoritative voice.

Mrs. Granger challenges her husband with a frosty glare, shakes her head, and brushes off the threat. Their words rise in volume, becoming more and more passionate, tainting the air with a noxious fog.

Alice allows them a moment to vent their frustrations before scanning over her list of questions. She checks off all but one, then turns to face the smirking Madison. "Do your reasons for a divorce have a deeper meaning?" she asks.

Madison scoffs at the suggestion. "What are you trying to imply? I've already given you my reasons for leaving my husband. I won't repeat myself."

Alice's smile remains subtle as she responds, "Thank you for your honesty, Mrs. Granger." She takes her time recording her conclusions, while Madison's repeated sighs serve as a constant reminder of her discontent.

As Alice looks up, she feels her stomach knotting at the sight of her clients' somber expressions. Her gaze shifts between the couple, and she hesitates before speaking. "Do you both agree that you cannot resolve the issues in your relationship, Mr. And Mrs. Granger?" Alice's voice wavers as her eyes dart back and forth.

The wife shows her enthusiastic agreement through a nod of her head. Her husband says something but then decides against it, shaking his head instead. Alice notices his silence and asks, "Mr. Granger, is there anything you'd like to add?"

Samuel's face softens with compassion as he faces his wife. "Madison, know that I fully support your decision. I only want what's best for you, and I love you." His sincerity shines through as he continues, "Remember, if you ever change your mind, I'll always be here for you."

He reaches out to touch her hand, but she recoils instantly, delivering a swift and powerful slap to the back of his head. "Don't you dare touch me, you slimy bastard," she seethes, her voice venomous. "Go screw your tramp instead!" Samuel Granger winces at her words, his wife's menacing palm looming threateningly near his face. He instinctively raises his hands in defense, a pitiful shield against her wrath.

Alice flinches as the sound of the slap echoes through the room, the sharp crack ricocheting off the walls. Her eyes widen in disbelief as she takes in the scene before her. The tension in the room is palpable, a tangible entity that fills every corner, every crevice. The smell of anger and bitterness hangs heavy in the small room, a cloud of acrid smoke that cloaks everything in its suffocating grip. She writes the word 'adultery' with a sharp, angry stroke next to his name, punctuated by a question mark.

Despite the hostility, Alice feels a sudden surge of pity for Samuel. Under the constant barrage of his wife's petulance, he appears less like a man and more like a puppet, controlled by her strings. His enthusiasm and joy are being smothered under the weight of her resentment, just like a heavy, damp blanket that stifles any possibility of happiness.

Alice gives them a stern gaze, determined to make another attempt. She insists, "I need to hear a straightforward answer from both of you. Can you admit that the issues in your marriage are beyond resolution, Mr. And Mrs. Granger?" Her tone conveys a sense of conviction and confidence, leaving no room for uncertainty.

Mr. Granger nods his head in confirmation and says, "My heart says no, but my mind screams yes."

As he sits there, his wife's piercing gaze drills into the side of his head. In a cold and unfeeling tone, she declares, "I stopped caring for him a long time ago." With one last strike, she delivers the finishing blow. "It's a yes from me."

Alice notices the tension in the room as soon as Mrs. Granger speaks. The air seems to grow thicker, and the silence is deafening. She can see the pain in Mr. Granger's eyes, and his body slumps slightly as if he's being punched in the gut. Mrs. Granger sits up straighter, her chin held high in defiance. Alice can almost feel the anger emanating from her. Alice feels suffocated by the emotional atmosphere in the room, and her mind races with worry about their divorce. She smirks at Madison's cruel remark, and responds with a mocking grin, enjoying the thrill of the verbal sparring, "Oh, music to my ears. Thank you." Madison Granger winces as she picks up on the sarcasm and shoots her therapist a withering death stare.

Alice pauses, basking in the surrounding silence before making her final notations. She observes Madison's seemingly stony expression, noting the tension in her body, the clenching of her jaw, and the curling of her fingers into tight fists. Her husband wears a mask of concern and confusion, his eyebrows knotted together, lips pursed in silent contemplation. Despite Madison's stoic façade, Alice knows there are underlying emotions that need addressing before they can make any headway in their counseling sessions.

With meticulous care, Alice weighs her observations, ensuring she has overlooked no crucial details. Under the assessment heading, she writes 'irreconcilable differences'. Studying her conclusion paints a gloomy picture of the couple's marital troubles. The risk of her court report being rejected for such commonplace notions looms large. The thought of divorce attorneys dissecting her work for banal perceptions sends an icy shiver down her spine.

Lost in thought, she twirls a lock of hair around her finger, her brow furrowed in deep concentration. Suddenly, her eyes light up, and she snaps her fingers in a moment of revelation. With newfound conviction, she scratches out 'irreconcilable differences', replacing it with 'irreparable damage', marking it with a firm check.

The writing pad slams onto her desk with a resounding thud that reverberates throughout the room. The abrupt noise startles her clients, causing them to flinch in their seats. A self-satisfied smile plays on Alice's lips, content with her choice. She takes a deep breath, inhaling the musky scent of Mr. Granger's cologne, and feels a wave of relief and accomplishment wash over her. As she glances out the window, the sun sets in a beautiful canvas of orange and pink hues, mirroring the end of this chapter of her professional day.

Alice rises from her chair, her fingers delicately tracing over the fabric of her dress, ironing out creases that have formed during the tension-filled meeting. "Time's up," she announces. Her words fill the room, echoing ominously like a judge delivering a verdict.

The Grangers' faces register disbelief as they process her words. They slowly stand, their eyes locked onto Alice, reflecting a mix of confusion and curiosity.

Suddenly, Madison is on her feet, her eyes sparkling with an emotion that she keeps hidden. "Be right back," she declares, her voice carrying an air of nonchalance that starkly contradicts the charged atmosphere in the room. With a casual toss of her hair over her shoulder, she adds, "Just going to powder my nose." Her words hang in the air as she exits the room, leaving behind a trail of her floral perfume that mingles with the lavender scent of the room.

In response to Madison's departure, Alice throws open the window, welcoming the cool evening air that rushes in to caress her skin. The distant hum of the city serves as a constant reminder of life beyond this intense confrontation.

Samuel's restless hands betray his mounting anticipation. He waits for his partner's return, his visible impatience a silent testament to the suspense that continues to build within the room.

The nervous energy radiating off Alice is almost tangible as she absentmindedly fiddles with her wedding ring until it slips, clattering loudly against the floor. She swiftly retrieves it, catching Mr. Granger's impish grin.

His cheeks flush a rosy hue as he awkwardly scratches the back of his head, attempting to mask his embarrassment. "You're married?" he asks, his voice laced with surprise. Alice's heart skips a beat, the intensity of his captivating hazel gaze sending a thrill coursing down her spine. Beneath his charming facade, she detects a hint of danger that speeds up her pulse.

"Yes, happily married. Thank you very much, Mr. Granger," Alice responds, her voice trembling with a cocktail of excitement and apprehension.

Samuel's face darkens with regret, his eyebrows arching in surprise. "Please call me Samuel, or Sam, whatever works best for you," he replies, his voice infused with gratitude. "I can't thank you enough for what you've done for us." He extends a hand towards her. As Alice takes his hand, the warmth of his grip sends a jolt of desire sparking through her veins. Their eyes lock, and for a fleeting moment, everything else blurs into oblivion. The spark of attraction between them is undeniable, a secret whispered only by their intertwined gazes.

Madison re-enters the room, her triumphant expression faltering as she registers the electrified atmosphere. Her voice slices through the tension like a cold steel blade. "Oh, Sammy. There you are, ensnared by another one of your sirens." With a tap on her wristwatch, she announces, "It's time to go."

Her presence casts a long shadow over the room as she hastily gathers her belongings and heads towards the door, Samuel reluctantly trailing behind her. His slumped shoulders and anxious backward glances betray his reluctance to part from Alice.

Alice watches their departure, her brow knit together in confusion. She silently mouths "Sammy?" towards his retreating back, receiving only a shrug and a sardonic half-smile in return. As the heavy front door slams shut behind them, Alice sinks into her office chair, releasing a sigh of relief that fills the now empty room.

The tension lingers like an unwelcome guest as Natalie's heavy footsteps echo ominously across the wooden flooring. Each step sends a shiver of anticipation through the office, causing the stationery on Alice's desk to tremble in response. As Natalie draws nearer, she throws Alice a look steeped in contempt, her brow furrowing into a tight knot of disapproval.

"Cher, that woman, she dissed me for nothin'. Thanks for savin' ma behin'. You're da bomb," Natalie breaks the silence, her words enveloped in a thick layer of gratitude.

Alice reclines in her chair, her feet propped up on the desk, her face a mask of fatigue mixed with relief. "If only you knew, Natalie. I'm glad it's over now. I don't want to see them again. Why do I always end up with the hopeless cases?" Her voice trails off, her mind wandering amidst thoughts.

Natalie stifles a laugh, her hand covering her mouth as she shakes her head in amusement. "Are they too far gone? Did you check out all that bling on her arms and around her neck? Gawd have mercy. Gold and silva. Ya don't go mixin' it up like that. It ain't funky, she is a magpie who loves them shiny things," she muses, her laughter ringing through the room. She busies herself with her chores, closing the windows, feeding the fish, and turning off the diffuser. The silence descends suddenly, filling the room with an eerie stillness.

Alice turns to Natalie, her eyes glinting with a spark of mischief. "It's the same with all the couples I see. Love starts in the mind," she taps her temple with her finger, "and marriage happens in the heart," she gestures towards her chest. "But eventually, it all ends in the bedroom," she points towards her privates with a sly grin.

Natalie scoffs, playfully wagging a finger at Alice. "Nah, there is no marriage my dearest pastor can't fix. He can unite a wolf with a sheep and make 'em have babies. For the low price of a bottle of sherry." Their shared laughter fills the room, a moment of levity amidst the lingering drama.

Their laughter gradually subsides, and Alice's eyes well up with grateful tears. "Thank you for your help today, Nat," she says softly. "Would you mind canceling my appointments for tomorrow and rescheduling them for another time? You can use the free time to transcribe the notes and recordings from today's sessions." She gestures towards the notepad and cassette recorder, a silent plea for help.

Natalie claps her hands together, her smile as warm as ever. "Aww, thanks Alice. Now, y'all have yourselves a good night and rest well, cher." Her words linger in the air, a promise of a calmer tomorrow after the stormy day.

As Alice ascends the grand staircase, her heels echo with a rhythmic clatter against the polished wooden steps. Each step she takes is a journey back in time, each creak of the wood a whisper from memories long past. To her right, a gallery of framed wedding photographs graces the wall, each one encapsulating a moment of joy and love frozen in time.

She pauses on the landing; her gaze drawn to one picture that stands out from the rest. A radiant bride in a white lace gown beams beside her handsome prince, clad in a sharp black tuxedo. The chapel doors stand ajar, revealing a jubilant crowd of family and friends surrounding the couple. Alice's heart is still ringing with the sound of exuberant clapping and cheering that fills the air.

The newlyweds bask in the warm glow of a thousand twinkling smiles, their shared happiness radiating like the sun at its zenith. Colorful paper confetti flutters around them, dancing in the wind like autumn leaves caught in a whimsical dance. The sight fills Alice's heart with joy, the echoes of their wedding vows still ringing in her ears.

Suddenly, Natalie's voice booms through the stillness, shattering the tranquility of the moment. "Goodnight, my darlings. See you in the morning!" Her chortles ricochet off the walls, fading into the quiet night. The front door closes with a resounding bang, returning the house to its previous silence. The abrupt disturbance startles Alice, pulling her out of her reverie and back to the present with a jolt.

Caught between the echoes of the past and the silence of the present, Alice stands on the landing. The whispers of her memories and the hush of the night envelop her, wrapping around her like a comforting shroud.

When the pandemic reshaped the world outside, Alice's husband James transformed their home into a sanctuary. A spare bedroom evolved into an elegant, spacious office—a haven of productivity amidst the chaos. The air hums with the gentle lullaby of a classical composition, its enticing notes weaving an invisible path that Alice instinctively follows.

The door to his office stands slightly ajar, a tantalizing invitation to peek into his world. James swivels in his chair, his deep blue eyes darting across the trio of monitors on his desk. The glow from the screens casts a mesmerizing kaleidoscope of blue squares onto his glasses. His furrowed brow reveals a mind lost in concentration, and his foot bounces rhythmically under the desk.

A small flat-faced dog, with a short black and white coat and large, round expressive eyes, lounges on a plush carpet near his feet, a silent observer to his master's dedication.

Alice taps a cheerful rhythm on the doorframe, puncturing the intense silence. James turns his head, greeting her with a charming smile that flaunts his deep-set dimples. "Hey Spid, what a pleasant surprise. Are you done for the day?" he asks, leaning in with interest.

As Alice approaches, a subtle masculine scent wafts from him, causing her heart to flutter with excitement. She nods, letting out a deep sigh. "Hi James!" she exclaims, her eyes lighting up. "I'm so relieved this cruel day has turned around. Dealing with those horrible clients was a nightmare. By the way, I won't be home for dinner tonight. It'll just be you and Sparky, having a boys' night at home." A bright smile illuminates her face, painting a picture of relief and anticipation. The moment Sparky hears his name, his tail wags excitedly.

James chuckles at the eager dog while running his fingers through his thick, graying hair. "Sure thing, thanks for reminding me," he says. "Robert is coming over, and we'll probably end up binge-watching romcoms. Don't worry about Sparky; he has everything he needs." With a twinkle in his eyes, James gives her a playful wave and a "Cheers."

Alice throws him a playful kiss, pivoting on her heel and lifting the back of her skirt in a flirtatious gesture. The sight elicits a roar of approval and wolf whistles from her husband. "Nice peaches. Slap you later, Spid," he teases, causing Sparky to bark with delight.

"See, Sparky thinks you're sexy."

"I wish! He barked because you whistled," she fires back over her shoulder, her laughter echoing through the corridor as she struts away, leaving behind a trail of intrigue and unspoken promises.

Wall-to-wall wardrobes tower over Alice's room, a testament to her sophisticated taste. The sleek, white doors of the wardrobes gleam in the sunlight that streams in from the large windows. With high ceilings and plush carpeting, the room is spacious and airy. The scent of freshly cut flowers fills the air, adding a touch of elegance to the already sophisticated space. Alice sinks into the soft velvet armchair by the window, enjoying the warmth of the sun on her skin. She feels content knowing that her room reflects her refined taste and impeccable style.

As the soft glow of dusk sneaks through the windows, Alice's phone buzzes with an incoming message. It's not a regular text, but a notification from Wickr—the encrypted messaging app that her agency uses for all their communications. The app, cleverly disguised as a mundane weather forecast tool, is Alice's secret gateway to her other life.

The message reads: *FYI: Hera. LOCATION: Confirmed. Tap pin to view. TIME: 07:30 pm. RSVP: Reply YES to confirm, NO to cancel. CLIENT: Mr. Vesper.* Her heart skips a beat at the sight of the familiar code name. A single tap of her French-tipped nail reveals a digital map pinpointing a nearby hotel. A wave of nostalgia washes over her, tightening around her heart.

With purpose and determination, she taps out each letter of her curt 'Yes' response. The phone chimes, and a small vibration alerts her to the new notification displaying a reference number. In just thirty seconds, the Wickr app will automatically erase the message, leaving behind no record of the dangerous assignment she has accepted. With a quick glance, she commits the reference number to memory, her eyes scanning over the digits effortlessly.

Her sports watch reads five-twenty-five. Plenty of time before her rendezvous with Mr. Vesper. A shiver of excitement courses through her. She can't wait to see what the night has in store.

Alice sets vanilla candles around the tub, their sweet aroma permeating the bathroom. Their gentle flicker casts a warm glow on the beige walls, setting a tranquil, romantic ambiance. As she sinks into the warm embrace of the water, bubbles tickle her skin, and the scent of the sea breeze transports her spirit to a serene oasis. She closes her eyes, inhaling deeply, allowing the calming scents to wash over her senses. The soft lapping of water and the crackling of the candles create a peaceful symphony, leaving her utterly relaxed.

Alice rises from the plush seat, catching her reflection in the vanity mirror—a satisfied smile gracing her features. She turns to face the towering wardrobes, their grandeur concealing an array of outfits for every occasion.

Her heart flutters in anticipation as she opens one, revealing meticulously arranged rows of clothes. Her fingers caress the cool fabric of a short, sleek black dress, its subtle shimmer captivating under the room's soft lighting. The dress hugs her figure, highlighting her toned legs. She pairs it with sheer black stockings, adding an extra layer of allure to her ensemble.

Her choice of footwear is a pair of black stiletto heels—sensual, yes, but also practical. She twirls in front of the mirror, watching as the dress swirls up and settles gracefully around her.

As she applies the final touch of crimson lipstick, her hand remains steady. She's been here before, each rendezvous bringing its own set of challenges and rewards. Alice thrives on this thrill, the adrenaline rush that keeps her coming back for more.

Before leaving, she glances at her sanctuary one last time and grabs her purse. The clock ticks closer to the appointed hour, but Alice remains composed. She steps out of her room, leaving behind the safety of her world for the uncertainty of the night.

Her heartbeat syncs with the rhythm of her heels against the wooden stairs. Every step she takes brings her closer to Mr. Vesper, and the promise of an unforgettable night.

James and Sparky are lounging on the leather couch, the sound of the television filling the room. She blows them a kiss before stepping outside, the bustling city streets alive with the sound of traffic and chatter. From the edge of the sidewalk, she hails a cab—the sound of honking cars and the aroma of sizzling street food fill the air.

A yellow cab pulls up beside the bustling sidewalk, and Alice walks around the back, sliding into the cozy rear seat, charging the air with seductive amber scents that mingle with the scent of leather. She grimaces at the sight of the driver's bald patch gleaming in the roof light, which casts a warm glow on his wrinkled face.

Taking a deep breath through his nose, the cab driver savors the scents and then adjusts the rearview mirror to get a better look at his passenger. "Good evening," he says in a deep, gravelly voice. "You give off an ambiance of heavenly bliss. Where to, miss?"

Alice meets his gentle gaze with a shy smile and sinks comfortably into the soft leather seats. "Thanks. I'm headed to Sky Bridge Fusion in Queens."

The shiny-headed man punches the details into his GPS and drives off, following the directions of a female navigator. Alice gazes out of the window, mesmerized by the passing skyscraper lights and neon billboard signs that cast a rainbow of colors on the street. The sound of honking horns and the chatter of the crowd outside fills her ears, making her feel alive.

As night falls, the bustling city transforms into a sea of people and vendors. The taxi comes to a screeching halt at a busy intersection, and Alice looks up to see a statuesque woman striding down the sidewalk. Tattered tights peek out from beneath a tight-fitting black miniskirt that encases the woman's long, slender legs as she strides down the sidewalk. Her ruby-red lips pop against her jet-black leather jacket, and a purse swings from her shoulder as she saunters past the throngs of passersby. With every step, she sways her hips and tosses her hair with a playful flair, grinning and winking seductively at anyone who catches her eye. The scents of street food waft through the air, mingling with the sounds of honking cars and the constant hum of chatter.

A flashy black sedan pulls up beside the leggy lady, flashing its headlights. The driver rolls the window down, and his thick, bushy mustache and long, wavy locks dangle in the wind. Lady Long Legs leans against the doorframe and exchanges words with the driver, nods her head, and hops into the back. Zoom, they're off. Alice's heart wrenches with a sudden pang of pity for the lady of pleasure.

Alice meets the cab driver's dreamy gaze through the rearview mirror. The warmth of the car and the softness of the seats envelop her, and she feels a sense of comfort. The driver notices her gaze and asks, "Is everything okay, miss?" His gentle baritone voice carries a hint of worry. The sound of the bustling city streets outside the cab window fills the air, making it difficult to hear him. The smell of exhaust fumes and street food waft in through the open window, mixing with the scent of the driver's cologne. His voice is like a soothing balm to her soul, and she takes a deep breath, feeling the tension in her shoulders ease. She puts on a fake smile and feigns enthusiasm, replying, "Yes, thank you."

The cabbie nods and focuses on the road ahead, deftly navigating through the chaotic traffic. The city is a whirlwind of activity, with the constant honking of horns and the chatter of people adding to the cacophony of sounds.

Within a short time, the female navigator's voice echoes through the cabin, informing them of their arrival at the destination. The cab comes to a stop with a sudden jolt, and she feels her heart skip a beat. She takes a deep breath, trying to calm her nerves, and reaches for her purse.

The dazzling sight of an exquisite cocktail lounge welcomes Alice as she steps out of her cab. Its name, Sky Bridge Fusion, glows in elegant cursive neon letters, with a dancing martini glass replacing the letter 'y'. The sound of her heels clacking against the sidewalk echoes in the air, creating a rhythmic beat that resonates within her.

As she approaches the entrance, an usher dressed in black greets her with a snooty once-over, his dark eyeshadow matching his attire. Alice feels a chill run down her spine as she meets his disapproving gaze, but she puts on a brave face and forces a smile. "Good evening. Table for one," she says, emphasizing the last word with a confident tone.

His eyebrows arc upwards as he gestures for Alice to follow him. The pounding bass drum sets the tone as he walks with purpose, his footsteps creating a syncopated rhythm. The surrounding air is thick with the scent of luxury and sophistication, a blend of exotic perfume, and the rich aroma of expensive cigars. Promising singles of the city's upmarket cocktail scene fill the lounge. A lively atmosphere of cheerful banter, clinking glasses, and upbeat house music fills the air.

As they make their way towards a small table at the back of the lounge, Alice notices a duo of young beauties sitting at a nearby table. The twosome curl their lips in distaste and give Alice a stink eye with an air of superiority, while the loud chatter and clinking of glasses fill the air in the background. Alice can feel their judgmental gaze running over her from head to toe.

Putting on a feigned smile, Alice challenges them with a death stare, her eyes wide and alert. The sudden confrontation causes the girls to jump, and they quickly bury their faces in their phones, feigning intense interest. Alice can feel a sense of satisfaction bubbling inside her as she savors the sweet aroma of victory.

The aloof usher pulls out a chair for Alice and prompts her to take a seat. "A server will be with you in due course. Enjoy your stay," He says half-heartedly.

Alice drapes the strap of her shoulder bag over the corner of the backrest and sinks into her chair. "Thank you," she says. "By the way, where is the ladies' room?"

With a flourish of his hand, the usher points her toward the bathrooms. With a flick of his wrist, he beckons a server over and saunters back to his station with a flourish of his hips. A flock of servers rushes over, vying for the chance to attend to the beautiful lady who showed up solo. Alice's heart swells with amusement as they quarrel like seagulls fighting over a scrap of bread, their voices rising in a chaotic chorus. One individual asserts his point so convincingly that nobody dares to challenge him. His statement is that he witnessed Alice disembark from the taxi.

With a proud grin, as smug as a bug in a rug, the winning server introduces himself. "Good evening," he says, "My name is Rick and I will cater to your every demand. May I get you something from the menu?" He rubs his hands together eagerly, anticipation written all over his face.

Alice studies the menu with great interest, savoring the colorful names and detailed descriptions of the dishes and drinks. She turns to Rick; her charming grin is reminiscent of the Mona Lisa. "Rick, could I order the crab cauliflower and cheese fritters, please? And would you be so kind as to pair it with a delicious strawberry daiquiri?"

The server's eyes become distant as he fixates on her lips. The sound of his breathing is like a freight train rumbling through a tunnel. Alice raises her eyebrows in confusion and gives him a puzzled look before asking. "Anybody home?" To emphasize her point, she snaps her finger in his face, creating a sound that resembles a whip cracking through the air. He blinks rapidly, trying to shake off his lustful trance as he looks around, momentarily stunned. With a jolt, he turns around and hurries to his station.

While she waits for her order, Alice takes in the view. The lounge is modern and eclectic, with a fusion of different styles and cultures. Dim lighting creates an intimate atmosphere, while neon signs add flair and contrast. Her gaze lingers on two young women, their voices bubbling with excitement as they try to captivate a suave gentleman. They hang on his every word, their laughter fueling his already inflated ego. A smug smirk stretches across his face, making Alice's stomach churn. As she watches, a rush of heat engulfs her chest, her cheeks flushing with a tinge of red. He exudes an unmistakable air of arrogance. Alice fixes him with a gaze that could cut through steel. She can't believe how oblivious everyone is to his antics. "Don't they see he's just playing games?" she mutters to herself, her voice brimming with disbelief. The server arrives, interrupting the vexing scene, and places her order on the table.

Alice's eyes widen as she takes in the array of tempting delicacies on the table, and her mouth waters. The aroma of spices and herbs fills the air, causing her taste buds to tingle with anticipation. She lifts the crimson cocktail to her lips and savors the coolness before taking a long sip, the sweet, tangy, and smooth liquid filling her mouth.

The golden crab fritter beckons to her with its enticing color and aroma. She adds a splash of fresh lemon juice and dips it into the parsley aioli. The sweet crab, nutty cauliflower, and creamy cheese flavors dance on her tongue, creating a delightful sensation.

Suddenly, her server appears beside her, interrupting her moment of bliss. "Do you need anything else? Extra condiments or utensils, another cocktail maybe?" he asks, eyeing her food.

Her eyes water from the spicy cayenne pepper and her cheeks puff out like a balloon. Alice must swallow before she can speak, but the mountain of mashed crab cakes pins down her tongue, making it difficult. Her face flushes red with indignity, and she lifts a thumb to signal that everything is good. The server senses her distress and quickly disappears.

Eyes wide, she swallows hard, flushing her mouth with a long sip of daiquiri. She uses the last crab cake to soak up the remaining aioli left in the bowl, savoring every bit of the delicious flavors.

Her server returns with a smile, the clinking of dishes and silverware filling the air as he clears the table. "The food is good, eh? Can I get you anything else?" he asks, his voice friendly and warm.

"Can you watch my stuff while I visit the ladies'?" Alice asks and wipes her hands on a soft napkin. With a nod, he clears the table and wipes down the condiments. The sound of chatter and laughter echoes off the walls as she makes her way down the hallway to the bathroom.

Alice returns and hands over two crisp three-figure bills to the server. He snatches them with a grateful nod, his eyes lighting up as he shoves the money into the back pocket of his jeans. "Thanks so much!" he exclaims. "I hope we see you again soon."

His eagerness brings a smile to her face, and the sound of his gratitude fills her with warmth. "Do you have a business card? My hubby will love this place." The experience has heightened her senses, and she gathers her belongings to follow the server to the counter. With a clatter, he clears the tray and tells her, "Sure, you can grab one on your way out from the counter at the door," gesturing towards the entrance.

Alice slides a couple of business cards into her wallet, taking a deep breath before leaving. The sound of chatter fades as she steps outside, replaced by the honking of cars and the hustle and bustle of the city.

2

The blood moon rises over the towering hotel, casting a crimson hue over the city skyline. Alice stands outside Sky Bridge Fusion, her eyes fixated on the grandiose hotel where she is about to rendezvous with Mr. Vesper. The hotel's towering glass windows reflect the bustling city around her, making her feel small in comparison. A white limousine pulls up smoothly under the porte-cochère, and two elegantly dressed passengers step out before it drives off. With a nod of his cap, the doorman greets the approaching duo and pulls open the heavy door for them. The elegant pair make their way across the lobby. The man, tall and imposing, casts a long shadow over his partner, their silhouettes merging and morphing in the warm, amber light. Their chic attire stands out in stark contrast to the relaxed vacationers milling around them.

Alice cranes her neck to look up at the towering skyscrapers, their sharp edges glinting ominously in the moonlight. The smell of exhaust fumes and street food wafts through the air, mingling with the aroma of freshly cut flowers from the nearby floral shop. She feels a mix of excitement and apprehension, eager to meet her assignment.

The sound of traffic whizzes by as Alice waits nervously, tapping her foot on the sidewalk. Some drivers wave a friendly hello while others blare their horns, startling her. Her presence attracts the attention of nearby pedestrians, who grin and wolf-whistle at her.

Suddenly, all the cars come to a silent halt, as if under an invisible spell. She turns her gaze towards the approaching traffic and spots a mounted police officer raising a gloved hand at the approaching vehicles. The sound of the horse's hooves clacking on the sidewalk creates a steady rhythm that matches his calm demeanor. He greets a crowd of curious onlookers with a friendly salute and raises a hand to halt the vehicles.

Alice takes advantage of the opportunity and hurries towards the median, the clacking of her heels echoing on the asphalt. The officer steers his chestnut horse in the opposite direction, creating a path for her to cross. She can feel the adrenaline pumping through her veins as she runs across the road and blows the officer a kiss as soon as she reaches the safety of the sidewalk. The officer lifts his cap, revealing a head of sweaty hair, and points towards the sky. Alice follows his finger and discovers a sky bridge that links the hotel to the building with the cocktail lounge. Her face grows hot with embarrassment, and she tries to hide her smile behind her hand.

A sleek, black sedan glides to a stop in front of Alice, the purr of the engine fading to a low hum. The window rolls down, revealing a handsome man who raises his eyebrows in greeting. The scent of expensive cologne wafts out of the car as he speaks. "Hey, beautiful. Want to join me for a ride?"

Alice flashes him a guarded smirk and lies. "No, thanks. I'm meeting my hubby." The man snorts in disgust, and the sound of the engine roars as he puts his foot down. With a sudden burst of speed, the sedan leaves behind a cloud of acrid smoke and the smell of burning rubber.

Two majestic fountains stand guard on either side of the hotel entrance, their gentle sprays of water sparkling in the sunlight, casting a rainbow of colors over everything nearby. As Alice approaches the entrance, the doorman nods his head in greeting and holds the door open for her.

Alice approaches the tinted glass doors and catches a glimpse of her reflection. Her eyes widen in surprise at the image staring back at her. With every step, her leather shoulder bag catches on her short dress, exposing her smooth legs and curvaceous bottom. She hurriedly straightens her skirt, feeling her cheeks flush with embarrassment.

The doorman's beady eyes follow her every move as he opens the door, his expression inscrutable. She smiles sheepishly and mutters, "Oh, shoot!" as she claws at the seam of her dress, willing it to behave against the gusty draft. Upon entering the grand hotel, a symphony of sight and sound greets Alice. The murmur of guests weaves a soothing tapestry of conversation, while the soft glow of chandeliers and natural light pouring in from the domed glass roof paint a picture of elegance and warmth. A rich scent of sandalwood and the faintest aroma of blooming flowers fill the crisp air—a sensory cocktail that brings back memories of cherished moments.

As she gazes up at the elegant crystal chandeliers dancing overhead, their golden light casts a nostalgic glow on the luxurious surroundings she once knew so intimately. The familiar melody of the piano playing in the background serves as a gentle lullaby, pulling her deeper into the sweet embrace of her memories.

Alice strides towards the reception desk, and her eyes light up as she sees that the guest clerk's counter is free of a waiting line. In contrast, two snaking lines of optimistic visitors, engaged in lively conversation in a foreign language, patiently wait in front of the reservation clerk counters.

The young woman, clad in a uniform as crisp as the autumn air, her hair slicked into a sharp part echoing the hotel's impeccable lines, greets Alice. Her smile is friendly, yet holds an undercurrent of curiosity. "*Bonjour, madame, bienvenue à l'Hôtel Grande Truss,*" she says, her words wrapping around Alice like a velvety cloak. "*Comment puis-je vous aider?*"

Alice's eyes widen in surprise. "Excuse me!" she exclaims, her voice cutting through the silence and causing nearby people to give her a curious glance.

The clerk's speckled face shows defeat. "Apologies, ma'am. I thought you were French. I meant to say, good day and welcome to the Hotel Grande Truss. How may I be of help?"

Alice confidently recites the reference number, followed by a warm smile and the introduction. "Mrs. Vesper's the name".

The clerk suddenly changes her demeanor, standing up straight and donning a professional expression on her face. "One moment, please, Mrs. Vesper," she says before disappearing momentarily. When she returns, she's holding an envelope. "Mr. Vesper is waiting for you in suite 519, ma'am. The envelope has the key in it. Should you require help, a bellhop is available upon request," and points towards a man dressed in a maroon Taormina Jacket, with whistle braids, gold and silver trimmings, and double braided epaulets.

Alice's mind races to come up with a plausible excuse. "Oh, I only have my overnight bag with me," she quickly lies. To make her story more convincing, she places a hand on the clerk's shoulder, adding a personal touch.

The clerk's face lights up with delight. "Oh, thank you, Mrs. Gra—Uh, I mean, Vesper," she exclaims, her eyes sparkling with joy.

She almost called me Mrs. Grande, Alice muses inwardly. A smirk plays at the corner of her lips, adding to the confidence that exudes from her every step. The elevators are beautiful, with ornate details that suggest a bygone era. When a considerate guest holds the elevator door open for her, she smiles in gratitude and steps into the car. The velvet carpeting under her feet is soft and plush, making her feel like she's walking on clouds.

As the doors close and the bell chimes, Alice can't help but notice how quiet it is inside the elevator. The only sounds are the hum of the elevator's motor and the soft rustling of clothing as people shift their weight. Alice takes a moment to breathe in the elevator's scent, which is a mix of old wood, metal, and a hint of something floral. The car moves up smoothly, and Alice can feel a slight pressure in her ears as they ascend.

Alice keeps her eyes fixed on the reflection of her fellow commuters in the mirrors. She notices a man behind her leering at her backside. Instead, she focuses on the other passengers, who are all engrossed in their phone screens. She can hear the tapping of fingers on screens and the occasional beep of a notification.

As the elevator continues its ascent, Alice reaches into her coat pocket and removes her wedding ring. She can feel the cool metal against her skin as she tucks it away.

The elevator doors part, and a soothing robotic voice announces, "Fifth floor." The sound of a vacuum cleaner hums in the distance, filling the air with a rhythmic buzz. Alice steps out of the elevator, feeling the plush carpet beneath her feet. She turns right and follows the glow of the white candles lining the walls. The candles emit a delightful aroma of lavender and vanilla, filling her nostrils with a sweet fragrance. Along the walls, chic paintings hang in ornate frames, adding a touch of elegance to the corridor. Vases of fresh flowers stand beside the hotel room doors, their vibrant colors adding to the luxurious atmosphere.

Alice slides her card key over the reader, and a soft beep echoes through the hallway as the door unlocks. Her heart flutters with excitement as she steps inside, her eyes scanning the empty room in wonder. The pristine walls and freshly laid carpets emit a faint scent of pine and adhesives, evoking a sense of new beginnings. She can't quite place the hints of perfume that linger in the air, but it's sweet and floral, almost like jasmine. She removes her overcoat and shivers as a cool breeze slithers through her dress.

"Hello," Alice calls out, her voice echoing through the empty corridor, "is anybody there?" An icy stillness meets her words. To her right, an archway frames a cozy living space, while dead ahead lies a long, dark passage illuminated only by a single light shining through the crack of a door on her left. The warm, inviting light beckons her forward, and a cloud of steam escapes through the ajar door, carrying with it scents of vanilla and honey. As she approaches, the sound of an electric shaver buzzing and scraping against stubborn stubble fills the bathroom.

Alice greets the man inside. "Hello, Mr. Vesper. I'm here. I'll wait for you in the bedroom." The buzzing sound stops, and the man interjects with a non-committal "Uh-huh" before resuming shaving.

As she walks down the dimly lit passageway, the soft glow at the end draws her closer. Her breath quickens in anticipation as she steps into the grandiose bedroom. The plush, broadloom carpets feel like a dream beneath her feet, and she can't help but run her hand over the ornate carvings of the furniture. The scent of polished wood and sumptuous fabrics fills her nose, and she inhales deeply, relishing the luxurious aroma.

In a secluded corner of the suite, a private bar beckons with its karaoke system, promising hours of entertainment. The floor-to-ceiling mirrors that adorn the wardrobe doors reflect her image back at her, and she can't resist twirling around to admire the incredible detail of her surroundings. She feels like royalty in the opulent room that reminds her of a presidential suite from a TV show. The enormous windows offer a panoramic view of the airport and its surroundings, leaving her speechless. She strains to hear the hum of planes taking off and landing in the distance—her lips curve up into a confident smile.

Alice takes a deep breath, trying to steady her shaking hands, and looks around to make sure no one is watching her. She meticulously searches her shoulder bag, extracting a small bag of piano wire, carefully concealing it in her stockings to avoid detection. Her heart races, pounding against her chest as she tries to calm herself down. She feels a mix of fear and excitement as the adrenaline courses through her body.

Alice walks over to the enormous windows, gazes out and scans the scenery, taking in the sights and sounds of the bustling airport. The distant thunderclouds loom on the horizon, glowing ominously crimson under the spell of the blood moon. The sound of airplanes fills the air, a constant buzz of engines and whirring turbines. A vibrant procession of airplanes taxi towards the runway, their tails adorned with bright colors and designs.

A large passenger jet glides towards the runway, flaps down, landing gear lowered like an eagle's outstretched talons. It touches down smoothly, the sound of the tires hitting the asphalt like a muffled squeak. Thick patches of smoke shroud the landing gear and wreath upwards. The plane lowers its nose and speeds along, the sound of the engines fading into the distance. Suddenly, it comes to a stop, turns left off the runway, and heads straight towards her. As the airplane approaches, Alice beams at the two pilots and waves her arms excitedly. She feels a sense of awe and wonder, watching the massive machine in action.

Her joy is short-lived when a man in a deep voice startles her. "They won't even know you're here," he says, his words piercing through the cacophony of the airport.

Alice jumps, and the sudden movement causes her raven hair to fan out behind her like a dark halo. It startles her to find Samuel Granger standing right in front of her, and she lets out a dramatic gasp of surprise. "You're the mark!" she exclaims in a shrill voice, quickly covering her mouth as she realizes her mistake.

Samuel Granger's eyes bore into her, disbelief etching on his face as he scans her from head to toe. His eyes linger on her toned legs, clad in silk stockings and peeking out from beneath the snug, flared black dress. He sucks his teeth and exhales sharply, the sharpness of his breath filling the air with a pungent smell.

Alice's heart thumps against her ribcage, coursing steaming blood through her throbbing veins. She cups her trembling hand over her eyes, feeling her breath quicken as she tries to control her anger. The sound of her mark's labored breathing fills the otherwise silent room. "Mr. Granger, what the fu—" Alice begins, but Samuel interrupts her with a mischievous smirk.

Surprise spreads across his face, and he speaks with a playful lilt, "Doctor What's-her-Name?" Alice shoots him a fierce look, her knees trembling as she sinks into the empty chair. He adjusts the towel wrapped around his waist, the soft cotton brushing against his skin. Her gaze travels over his toned, muscular body, the sight of him causing her heart to race. The scent of honey and vanilla fills the bedroom, emanating from his dark, graying, and wet hair as he brushes it aside.

Samuel's deep, even breaths are like a soothing balm amid the charged atmosphere. The sight of him pours oil on the fire raging in Alice's guts, sending a rush of warmth through her body. She discreetly composes herself, her heart racing from the electric chemistry between them. His piercing hazel eyes remain fixated on her chest, where the subtle rise and fall of her breathing betrays her innermost desires. A sudden wave of excitement washes over her and she feels an unexpected chill. Almost instinctively, she folds her arms across her chest, not for warmth but for a sense of modesty. She momentarily drops her gaze to the floor and mutters, "I have to leave... right now." Alice collects her things and storms out.

Samuel Granger chases after her, the sound of his footsteps echoing in the empty hallway. In search of the room card key, Alice's trembling hand delves into the depths of her shoulder bag, her fingertips grazing over the rough canvas interior. Her eyes remain locked on the doorknob, as if willing it to unlock on its own. Her clammy hands jiggle the handle with a loud rattle, startling her assailant. He takes her from behind, his muscular arms coiling around her shoulders like a python. Alice's heart races as she feels his warm breath on the back of her neck.

In the heat of the moment, Alice's fingers close around the cold, hard metal of her mini stun gun. Samuel's fingers clench tighter around her shoulder, but she squirms free with a sudden twist of her arm, the sound of her bones popping muted by the rush of blood in her ears. The smell of sweat and fear permeates the air as she steps back, her heart pounding against her chest. She feels the rough texture of the wall against her back, her skin prickling with goosebumps as Samuel advances towards her again. But she stands her ground, ready to defend herself once more if needed, her eyes blazing with adrenaline-fueled fury.

Wide-eyed, Samuel wills himself to run for cover, but Alice is faster. She lunges at him and thrusts the prongs of the stun gun into the soft flesh of his neck, activating the trigger. Deafening crackles cut through the air, filling the room with the acrid smell of ozone. As the stun gun connects with his neck, her assailant's lips part and a high-pitched shriek pierces through the air. His eyes widen with shock, and a sheen of sweat glistens on his forehead. The acrid smell of burning flesh fills the room, and the sound of the stun gun crackling echoes off the walls. He clutches his neck, and his body convulses with agonizing pain. His plea for mercy turns into a stammer, like that of a bleating lamb. He drops to his knees, sways, and then falls forward, his body hitting the floor with a sickening thud.

Alice's mind races as she reflects on her actions, and a sudden shock causes her to gasp aloud. "Oh sugar," she says to herself, "what have I done?" She kicks off her shoes, sinks to her knees beside his sprawled frame, and checks Samuel's pulse. She places her finger on his wrist, feeling the strong, rhythmic beat of his pulse, like a bass drum. Thoughts swirl around in her mind like a hurricane. She quickly reaches for the bag of piano wire tucked in her stockings and shoves it and the stun gun into her shoulder bag. She fumbles with her phone, her hands trembling as she opens the Wickr app to send a message. Samuel's eyes snap open, and he looks at her with suspicion. "What are you doing?" he asks, his voice rough and uncertain.

With her heart pounding, Alice frantically searches for a convincing excuse. Finally, she blurts out, "I need to call for an ambulance." She delivers her lie with such conviction that it sounds almost believable.

Samuel protests and props himself up on his elbow, insisting, "No...no ambulance!"

With expert precision, Alice adopts a poker face and bluffs like a pro. She effortlessly slips the phone into her shoulder bag and responds with a nonchalant tone, "Okay, suit yourself." Her voice is impersonal, devoid of any emotion

Samuel's finger trembles as he points towards his sore neck, and a pitiful whimper escapes his lips. Alice senses the satire behind his brave facade and says, "Well, serves you right. It's just not right to treat a lady with disrespect."

Samuel rises to his feet, and the words "I'm sorry" escape his lips with a tinge of regret. He then adds, "I didn't want you to see..." However, as he tries to regain his balance, he sways like a drunkard who has just received a powerful punch to the head.

With an inquisitive tone, Alice asks, "What didn't you want me to see?" She then wraps her arm around his shoulder, and together they take baby steps towards the bedroom, moving like two intoxicated lovers.

He speaks with a reassuring tone, clarifying, "I just don't want you to draw attention." His eyes drift towards her hand resting on his shoulder, then linger on her plump, lustrous lips.

Alice furrows her brow in wonder as she squints her eyes in thought, eventually conceding with a resigned, "Okay, if you say so." She helps him sit down on the edge of the king-sized bed, and he sinks into the plush mattress.

Samuel gestures to the minibar and demands, "Scotch, double on the rocks, pronto," in a deep, raspy voice. Alice's scowl quickly fades as she notices the twinkle in his mischievous eyes. While she prepares his whiskey, the sound of the ice clinking against the glass fills the room as she pours herself a double vodka soda. She holds the glass with trembling hands, causing the ice to clink against the sides. Her eyes dart back and forth between Samuel and her shoulder bag, her heart pounding in sync with the silent rhythm of impending doom. Tucked away amidst her assortment of deadly tools is her secret weapon, a vial of Morpheus's tear. Named after the Greek god of dreams, it is a substance as beguiling as it is lethal. Just a single drop can send even the mightiest Titan into an eternal slumber. As an agent of the Greek Goddess Guild, she understands its power all too well—it is not just a tool, but a divine mandate, a tear shed by Morpheus himself. With this, she is confident that she will accomplish her mission—Samuel Granger won't stand a chance.

Her eyes gaze off into the distance, lost in thought as she weighs her options. The room is silent except for the soft hum of the air conditioning. She knows herself well, but she can't quite pinpoint what's stopping her from taking the opportunity. Perhaps it's the thought of Samuel Granger, a man of power who undoubtedly has security personnel watching his every move. Inhaling deeply, she takes a moment to ponder her next move. It's too risky to go through with it, but the curiosity gnaws at her. She imagines the security personnel lurking in the shadows, watching her every move, and a shiver runs down her spine. Despite the fear, she knows there's only one way to find out, and she decides to take the chance.

She looks at Samuel, her eyes twinkling with amusement, and their gazes meet in a dreamy exchange. Drinks in hand, ice cubes tingling with her steps, she sidles up to him and reclaims her space at his side. He takes a long mouthful of his whiskey with a trembling hand, and the popping and tingling sounds of the ice cubes in the tumbler put a smile on her face.

With his eyes fixed on the glass, he smacks his lips thoughtfully. "Oh boy, that was good," he exclaims, his face now free from anguish. "You have the magic touch. Another one, please." His eyes gleam with a kindred essence, revealing his sincere appreciation for the drink.

The plush carpet beneath Alice's feet muffles the sound of her footsteps as she glides towards the minibar. The air is thick with the scent of expensive cologne mixed with the aroma of freshly poured whiskey. As Samuel's gaze locks onto her, Alice feels a thrilling shiver run down her spine. Her cheeks flush with warmth, and she nervously bites her lip before asking, "Do you feel better?" The dimly lit room exudes a soft glow that creates a romantic ambiance, while the soft jazz music playing in the background adds to the alluring atmosphere.

Samuel's eyes widen with awe as he takes in the incredible sight of her playful spirit. He points to the two red puncture marks on his neck and says, "Shit happens." Alice's laughter fills the room, a sound that's as sweet as honey as she skips back to his side.

He impersonates an angry father and wags a finger at her, saying, "Go ahead, yuk it up. I'm glad you think my misfortune is so hilarious." Despite his teasing nature, the way he holds her close with a tender, fatherly touch melts her heart. She pulls him into a tight embrace, the warmth of his body enveloping her. She lingers for a moment before finishing with a gentle peck on his cheek. Inhaling sharply, she savors the masculine aroma of his fresh tobacco aftershave, a scent that seems to encapsulate the warmth of the moment.

Samuel takes advantage of the moment to put his hand on Alice's knee, but she quickly moves away from him, biting her lip and twirling her hair around her finger. With his eyes wide open, Samuel stares at her, desire radiating from his eyes. She asks with a frown, "What is it?" Her eyes instinctively move to his mouth. "Close your mouth before you swallow me whole," she playfully taunts, her voice dripping with seduction as she adds a sultry chuckle. The air is thick with anticipation and the heat of the moment is palpable.

Samuel takes a slow sip from his highball glass, his eyes wandering up and down the curves of her legs, accentuated by the short black dress. His eyes come to rest on her lips, which glisten in the dim light of the room. He takes a sip of his drink and savors the complex flavors before clamping his jaw shut. "It's that fidgety thing you do," he says, "you bite your lip and you, uh, that thing you do when you roll your eyes." He pauses, amused. "Whoa, you are priceless. I just may keep you around." He raises his glass, and she clinks hers against his before taking a generous sip.

With a warm and inviting gesture, he raises his hand and says, "Let's start over. My name is Sam, short for Samuel. Whatever works for you." Alice recoils slightly as she notices the stark absence of their wedding bands, a sight that stabs her heart with a sharp pang of guilt. The stillness of the air is palpable, interrupted only by the distant hum of an airplane flying overhead.

Alice meets his gaze with intensity and shakes his hand with a firm grip. "Spid, short for Spider. Anything but doctor," she replies, her voice laced with a hint of playfulness.

Samuel holds on to her hand and sputters out a wet cough before speaking. "Nice name, Spid. Your jokes will kill me. Where did you get that name?" he asks, his eyes roving over her legs once again.

Alice lifts his chin with a curled finger, fixing him with a stern gaze. "My husband gave it to me," she says, placing particular emphasis on the second word.

Samuel scoffs, and Alice playfully slaps his shoulder, the sound echoing in the hushed bedroom. Chuckling, he remarks, "Sounds kinky," and then looks mischievously at her. "He calls you a spider for one reason only, Spid," he taunts.

With a playful twinkle in her eye, Alice gazes at Samuel and feigns confusion. "Wrong!" she exclaims, flashing a mischievous grin. "I am a bouldering zealot," she proudly declares. She holds his gaze and adds, "My hubby says I move like a spider between the holds." Finally, Alice asserts with a confident tone, "So there!" Sticking out her tongue, she lets out a playful giggle.

Samuel's eyes widen with awe as he takes in the incredible sight before him. Hera—no, Alice—is a vision of playful spirit and lethal grace. Her laughter is a melody that dances upon the evening breeze, her smile a beacon that can outshine the moon. Yet beneath that captivating facade lurks a danger as old as the gods themselves. Her movements are so smooth and graceful that he can't help but compare her to a dancer. She's a riddle he can't figure out, and yet he's drawn to her like a magnet. When he reaches out to touch her, her resistance feels like a mirror of his own unfulfilled desires.

A youthful grin spreads across Samuel's face as he indulges in his lustful reverie, leaving Alice feeling a tug at her heartstrings. As he leans in for a kiss, she gently stops him with a finger on his lips. "Hold on, cowboy," she says with a mischievous smile. "I have something better planned for you." She reaches into her bag and pulls out a black lace item, holding it up for him to see. Samuel's face crosses with recognition as he sees the blindfold, and he lets out a delighted laugh. "Now we're talking," he exclaims, leaping up.

Alice stands on her tiptoes, her eyes closed, savoring the feeling of Samuel's solid, desirable body pressing against hers. She inhales deeply, taking in the musky scent of his cologne mixed with the smell of his sweat. She can feel the heat of his breath against her ear as she tugs the blindfold over his head.

Her heart races with anticipation, and she feels a tingling sensation spreading throughout her body. The sound of Sam's quickened breath fills her ears, and she can feel the gentle puffs of air warming her cheeks as she leans in closer to him. She runs the tip of her tongue along the edge of his lips, feeling the softness of his skin against hers, and she can taste the faint hint of mint from his lip balm.

Samuel puts two skillful hands on her sides, and she shivers at the warmth of his touch through her thin dress. Lifting her heels off the ground, she imagines the soft glow of moonlight filtering through the window, casting shadows on their entwined bodies.

Alice's skin prickles at the touch of his growing arousal against her soft skin. She feels her body stiffen up in response. As she pulls away, she catches a glimpse of movement beneath the towel. The sound of Samuel's excitement fills the air, making her pulse quicken with anticipation. On impulse, Samuel buries his face in his hands, and Alice can feel the heat radiating from his body.

The texture of the towel against her fingertips is rough, and she feels her heart pounding in her chest. A mischievous glint dances in her eyes as she playfully tugs at the knot of the towel, revealing the tempting secrets beneath. The towel flutters to the floor and snags on his flagpole, dangling like a pendulum on a grandfather clock. Alice cups a palm over her mouth to muffle a shriek, frees the towel, and gazes in wonder at his circumcised hotrod. The musky smell of his arousal fills the air, and it charges her senses with a craving for his manhood. She feels her heart racing as she takes in the sight before her, the glistening hotrod standing tall, throbbing with desire. The sound of her own breath echoes in her ears as she leans in closer to see the object of her desire. Her fingers tingle with anticipation as she reaches out to touch him, feeling the heat radiating off his manhood.

Alice is in awe of the meticulously trimmed foliage that blankets the launchpad of his rocket, running her fingertips over the soft, velvety hair. The scent of lust and desire fills the air, making her feel more alive and aware than ever before. She marvels at the sight, taking in every detail and wondering about the person who takes care of such beauty. Alice knows that only someone who enjoys giving and receiving oral pleasure could have taken such care. The memory of his uptight and unpleasant wife, Madison, flashes through her mind, reminding her of the limits of her desires.

Alice wraps her arm around Samuel's waist, and he shivers with eagerness at her touch. As her fingers graze his skin, she feels a surge of adrenaline, and her senses awaken. His body shimmers in the moonlight, resembling satin, with distinct tan lines on his arms and legs separating the sun-kissed skin from the paler areas. Alice's hands itch with an urge to caress his firm, perfectly rounded, pale buttocks, and she imagines the softness of his skin against her fingertips.

She digs deep into her bag, rustling through its contents until she finds the bottle of massage oil. The intoxicating scents of almond and jojoba wafts from the bottle as she places it within easy reach. Samuel's heart races with anticipation as he eagerly awaits the pleasures ahead. The control panel on the wall beside the bed immediately draws Alice's gaze. Its green lights flicker like a beacon, daring her to explore its magic. She approaches the panel, her fingers dancing over the smooth surface of the switches. The hum of electricity fills the air as she flicks a switch, intending to dim the lights, but suddenly all hell breaks loose. She can't help but let out a sly smile as she waits patiently for the consequences of her mischievous actions.

Lightning seems to strike, sending all the devices into chaos. Thunderous rock music slams out of the sound system, causing the room to vibrate. The curtains swing violently, alive with the whirring of the electric motor. The bedroom lights flicker, casting wild shadows that dance across the walls in sync with the screeching siren that resonates throughout the room. Alice is under the spell of the magical control panel, and now she must face the consequences of her curiosity.

With a sudden jolt, her eyes widen in alarm as she feigns surprise and lets out a deafening shriek. The smell of electrical discharge fills the room, and her skin tingles with the static electricity in the air. The bed springs creak like rusty hinges beneath Samuel's weight as he collapses onto his stomach. Alice's heart races with excitement, and she feels the heat of desire wash over her. "Oh, fudge!" she exclaims, caught between fear and arousal.

With a whirring sound, the bed slowly adjusted into a sitting position, startling Samuel. His legs wobble as he attempts to stand, but the sudden movement disorients him. In a moment of confusion, he inadvertently bangs his head against the wall, the mortification surpassing the pain. Stumbling from the impact, he ricochets off the bed with a resounding thud, causing the lamps on the nightstands to rattle before he lands face down on the floor.

Alice's heart races as she feigns panic and searches for the elusive red reset button. Abruptly, a phone on the bedside table starts ringing, its sharp shrill adding to the deafening cacophony of noises inside the room. She flails around, trying to find her phone in the darkness, but only knocks it off the stand, causing it to disconnect and the ringing to stop. Sam crawls on the floor, oblivious to her watching eyes, his movements slow and unsteady because of the blindfold. She can't help but let out a mischievous chuckle.

Alice quickly drops onto all fours and crawls around, her hands and knees skittering across the warm, plush carpet. Sam crawls beside her, and a sudden surge of relief washes over her as they fan out in opposite directions. The loud banging on the front door is sudden and jarring, causing her to freeze in place. She strains her ears, trying to catch any sound, but the only thing she hears is the faint creak of a nightstand drawer and the rustling of hands.

Suddenly, the wailing siren subsides, and the lights flicker back on, illuminating the room in a warm, golden glow. Alice feels a surge of relief flood through her, grateful for the sudden reprieve from the darkness. However, as her eyes adjust to the light, she stares at two indistinct objects swaying back and forth in front of her, like pendulums. Squinting and tilting her head, she strains to bring them into focus, and to her astonishment, she realizes she is staring at Sam's dangling family jewels, which are hovering mere inches from her nose.

She gasps in surprise, her senses suddenly overwhelmed by the faint scent of citrus and herbal body wash that emanates from Sam's body. She stares at the size of his gonads, her eyebrows furrowing in confusion as she tries to process what she is seeing. Entranced by the suspended sack, her cupped hand hesitantly reaches out, almost as if drawn by a magnetic force. However, she shakes her head in dismay and rises to her feet, her mind racing with a million different thoughts. "Let me get the door," she says, her mind racing with possibilities of what could wait on the other side.

Alice's heart pounds in her chest, a frantic drummer setting the rhythm of her rising fear. With each tentative step toward the front door, her hand trembles slightly. As she peers through the peephole, her breath hitches. On the other side of the door stand two massive bodyguards, their towering figures amplified by the fisheye lens. Their presence is imposing, an unwelcome intrusion in her sanctuary. The low rumble of their murmured conversation reverberates through the door, adding to the growing tension. The bodyguards look sharp in their crisp, black uniforms, exuding an aura of power. Despite the distorted peephole view, Alice can see the glint of their designer sunglasses and feel their intimidating glare. It lends them an air of mystery that only heightens her anxiety.

Alice recoils in shock, her body stiffening as she stumbles away from the door. She manages a shaky greeting, her voice barely above a whisper. The silence that follows is deafening, punctuated only by the deep, commanding voice of one guard. His words echo through the hallway, sending a shiver down Alice's spine.

In her panic, Alice realizes she doesn't have the room card key. She turns around, searching frantically for Sam, who stands just behind her. His smirk is infuriatingly calm, his voice smooth and confident as he reassures the guards.

The tension escalates as the bodyguards ask for a password. Alice looks at Sam, her eyes wide with panic. He seems unperturbed, a knowing smile playing on his lips as he delivers the unexpected password: "Thompson Twins". Alice watches him, her confusion apparent in her furrowed brow and crossed arms.

The leader of the bodyguards confirms the password over his radio, his voice carrying a faint, indistinguishable accent. Alice watches him curiously, wondering about his origins and how he came to work for Samuel. However, her curiosity remains unsatisfied, her questions unasked.

Without the bodyguards around, Alice can finally release the tension in her muscles and take a deep breath of relief. The sound of their footsteps fades into the distance, leaving the room quiet except for the soft hum of the air conditioning.

But Alice's relief quickly turns to excitement. She knows that her original plan to eliminate Samuel Granger is no longer an option, but the thrill of the adventure ahead still sends shivers down her spine. The night is young, and Alice is ready to play her role as Sam's unsuspecting high-end escort.

She takes a deep breath, feeling the cool air fill her lungs. Her heart races with anticipation, and she can feel the adrenaline coursing through her veins. This is it, the moment she has been waiting for. The game is just getting started, and Alice is determined to win.

Alice's blunder with the control panel didn't go unnoticed. Samuel Granger stands there, the towel wrapped tightly around his waist, his legs planted firmly on the ground. His eyes flash with a stern look, like that of an angry father.

Alice's heart races as she looks up at Samuel, feeling a wave of embarrassment and shame wash over her. She can feel her face growing hot as she tries to stammer out an apology. Samuel's stern expression doesn't waver, and Alice can feel the weight of his disapproval in the air between them. Her hands shake slightly as she tries to regain her composure, feeling small and foolish in front of this powerful man.

His thin smile is like a ray of sunshine, giving her the courage she needs to win back his trust. Her lips pucker up, and her doe-like eyes meet his smoldering gaze as she slowly undresses, teasing him with every movement. He responds with a roguish and cheeky smile, admiring her openly with his gleaming eyes. Alice's eyes widen at the sight of his erection straining against the towel, and she eagerly unties the knot to set it free. Alice grins mischievously as the towel falls to the ground with a soft thud.

Sam chuckles before turning to face the bed, a smirk playing at the corners of his mouth. "Let's give it another shot," he says, "just try not to kill me this time." Alice winces as she realizes the irony in his words.

She takes Sam by the hand and leads him to the bed, where she gently ties the blindfold over his eyes. With a mischievous grin, she playfully slaps him on the behind and salutes him from behind his back. "Yes, siree, Mr. President. You know what to do. Make yourself comfortable before your guards arrest me," she quips.

Sam laughs as he crawls onto the bed and flops onto his stomach, causing the mattress springs to emit a playful squeak. Alice expertly adjust the control panel, dimming the lights to create a soft cascade of moonlight that fills the room through the glazed windows. Ghostly shadows dance across the mirrors and walls, enhancing the ethereal ambiance. The hazy glow highlights every curve and muscle of Sam's toned body, captivating Alice. She eagerly climbs onto his back, finding comfort on the rise of his lower back.

Alice dispenses a generous amount of massage lotion into her palm, rubbing her hands together until they become warm and slippery. She massages the oils into Sam's back with gentle, circular motions, feeling the tension gradually dissipate under her skilled pressure. The soothing scents of the almond and jojoba oils fill her nose, and she feels a sense of calm wash over her. She uses her fingers like a pianist, easing the stiffness in Sam's muscles. His sides become a source of ticklish delight, causing him to flinch and burst into laughter each time her fingers graze them.

Alice leans in close and teases him with a whisper. "It looks like someone's got a thing for tickles." As she wiggles her hips against him, he shivers in response and feels a chill race down his spine. His skin prickles with anticipation as she moves closer still, her breath tickling his neck. With a mischievous smile, she watches him quiver as each feather-light touch sends waves of pleasure across his body. The intensity of the sensation is palpable, and they exchange knowing touches that linger, cherishing the timeless moment together.

In a realm of imagination, Alice gracefully lowers herself into a mystical stance reminiscent of a cowgirl, her movements fluid and enchanting. With an air of magical allure, she sways her hips in a rhythmic dance, seeking a connection with the rugged form of his back. Sam, drawn by the mystic energies, lifts himself from the ethereal bed and sways his hips in a mesmerizing sideways motion. Their combined energy resonates like the breath of a fantastic steam engine, filling the air with huffs and puffs. With increasing intensity, Alice's hips seesaw, a surge of power coursing through her very being. Yet, just before the imminent climax, she pauses, momentarily capturing her breath and brushing aside tendrils of hair that cling to her glistening, perspiring brow.

Assuming a cowgirl stance, Alice fixes her gaze upon his feet and exudes an air of authority. In a flawless British accent, she asks, "Pray, inform me, why does Mrs. Granger harbor such ire toward her spouse? Has he, by any chance, strayed from the path of fidelity?" Tempting him with her words, Alice displays an impressive command of language. As she speaks, Alice's eyes narrow slightly with curiosity and her lips curl into a subtle smile, revealing just a hint of mischief.

Samuel freezes in surprise, his body rigid and unmoving. Just as he readies himself to reply, she abruptly interjects, delivering a firm thump upon his backside, leaving a lasting handprint in its wake. A whimper escapes his lips, and he wriggles with excitement like a playful puppy. As he tries to shift his weight and turn onto his back, she grips his wrists tightly, her fingers digging into his skin and keeping him firmly in place.

Alice elevates her tactics, her voice taking on a determined tone. "Could it be that Mrs. Granger's anger stems from her suspicions of an extramarital affair on your part?" The room fills with a heavy silence, prompting her to deliver another well-placed thump to his posterior, trying a different approach. "Perhaps Mrs. Granger believes she has a financial claim because she possesses incriminating information." Sam's response is only a pained groan.

With a sudden flick of her wrist, Alice snatches off the blindfold, revealing his striking features in the dim light. Settling in beside him, her fingertips caressing his skin as she gazes deeply into his eyes. Her emotions are palpable, and the intensity of her gaze leaves no doubt that she means business. The sound of Sam's ragged breathing fills the air as the scent of his musky cologne lingers in her nostrils. His body heat envelops her, sending shivers down her spine.

The air in the room crackles with tension, causing goosebumps to ripple across Samuel's skin. Alice bites her lip, her eyes gliding across the room before settling back on him. Sam lifts his head off the pillow, longing to kiss her, but she resists his fervent advances. He swallows hard, his eyes wide with anticipation, and his parted lips betray his eagerness. A bead of saliva escapes from the corner of his mouth as he remains captivated by her presence. Inches away from a confession, he cannot tear his gaze away from her. Like a coiled snake, his arm encircles her waist, drawing her nearer. Their lips hover tantalizingly close, but she resists his advances once more. Sam gasps, his warm breath washing over her face like a gentle summer breeze. With every growl, the veins on his neck bulge, and his throat sounds hoarse. Alice knows how to push Samuel to his breaking point and employs her ultimate trick. She bites her lip, her eyes gliding across the room, before she flutters her eyelashes. Fixing him with a seductive gaze, she adopts a posh British accent and says, "There's something that troubles me. I am convinced you have a mistress. Why did you invite someone like me over? Isn't she enough for you?"

Sam's face lights up with a smile as he concedes defeat. With a resigned chuckle, he raises his head and props himself up on his elbow, a loud cry of excitement escaping his lips. "Blair! That's her name," he exclaims. "Boy, you really know how to get me going. Now kiss me, dammit," he leans forward, mouth open, waiting for Alice to meet him.

As Alice leans in to pretend to kiss him, she feels the heat emanating from his body and smells the musky scent of his cologne, a heady mix of sandalwood and spice. Instead of a kiss, she surprises him with a playful spanking, delivering two solid blows to each of his butt cheeks. The sound of her hand connecting with his skin echoes through the room, followed by a sharp intake of breath from Sam. "The truth will set you free, Mr. Granger," she exclaims, lifting her hand to pretend to whack him again. Sam holds his arms up in surrender. "Please, her name is Blair. She is my PA. Are you happy now?" Alice can't help but smirk at his response, feeling a sense of satisfaction wash over her.

Alice rewards his honesty with a gentle peck on his lips and pulls the blindfold over his eyes. She rises from the bed, gets the pitcher, and pours more drinks into their tumblers. She takes the cold ice cube and glides it slowly down Samuel's spine, causing him to shiver with delight. "I wonder if Mrs. Granger knows about Blair?" she says, smacking him on his bottom, causing him to groan, but he doesn't utter a word.

Alice straddles him, facing his feet, and lands a forceful blow to his reddened and hand-stained buttocks. She demands, "Where is your mistress tonight?" His backside muscles tense up as he roars in agony, but the swift whack that follows silences him. The thud resonates through the room, making Alice's ears ring.

Samuel winces in pain as he raises his waist. "Ouch!" He then exclaims, "She...she is in...I don't know where she is!"

Frustrated, Alice raises her hand to strike him again, insisting, "I said, where is your mistress? And why am I doing her work?"

Despite the silence, she puts her weight behind the next blow, shaking the bed with its force. "I said, where—"

"Wait, wait, please," Samuel pleads. "She doesn't know how to please me in the same way you do, okay?"

Alice whacks him again, then pauses. "Is that a hint?"

Samuel tries to reason with her. "Why do you think you're here?"

Alice applies almond and jojoba massage oil to her palm, filling the air with a sweet, nutty aroma. She kneads his sore bottom with smooth, circular motions, feeling the warmth of his skin and the tautness of his muscles. Suddenly, with a scoff, Alice breaks the silence and asks, "And yet, your wife thinks you're out playing golf. Does she know about Blair?"

Samuel moans in ecstasy as the expert massage works its magic. He raises his head and with a cocky grin asks, "So, where do you tell your spouse you are when you come here?"

Alice winces at his question. She snaps back, "That's not something you need to know," before delivering another stinging smack. Laughter fills the room as she strikes him, and the slick massage oil splatters over her face and chest.

As they interact, the air in the room crackles with an intense energy. He eases his body down, a mixture of satisfaction and reluctance in his sigh. In the distance, thunder rumbles, and a sudden flash of lightning brightens the room, creating eerie shapes that dance along the walls. Alice raises her gaze toward the heavens, her eyes fixed on the roof above. She watches as the fat raindrops splatter against the domed glass roof, leaving winding paths as they trickle down. Another bolt of lightning cuts through the night sky, its branches reaching out like grasping roots. A veil of dark clouds shrouds the moon, casting an eerie shadow over everything.

As darkness envelops the room, Alice leans in close, her lips brushing against his skin in a gentle kiss. With a playful touch, she leaves a mark on his sore bottom, a delicate imprint of her lipstick. "Answer my question: Where does your wife think you are?" she playfully smacks him on the backside.

Samuel chuckles and says, "I'll tell her I got tied up."

Alice giggles softly to herself at the irony in his words. "Nice one, but you better hurry if you don't want to break your curfew," she retorts.

Sam remains quiet, and Alice takes charge to maintain the rhythm of the conversation. "Would you enjoy it if Blair were here to witness our little escapade?" Alice hits a nerve. In an instant, Sam raises his head from the pillow and then lowers it again. The hairs on the back of his neck stand on end.

"What do you mean? It's just the two of us here," he says with a tremor in his voice.

Alice furrows her brow, trying to make sense of his words.

Sam senses her sudden silence and continues, "Yes, I wish Blair were here. Standing there, burning with envy."

As she teases him, she suggests, "Why not call her and invite her over?" With a playful grin, she lands another smack on his backside. As the blow connects, a bolt of lightning illuminates the room, casting dancing shadows on the walls, followed by a thunderous roar.

Samuel lets out a deep sigh of resignation and says, "Maybe another time. Right now, I'm just enjoying the ride—and the scenery."

Alice's frown deepens as she scans the dimly lit room, searching for something that catches her eye until she spots Sam's reflection in the mirror. A sly grin plays at the corners of his mouth, his eyes twinkling with mischief. Alice's laughter echoes through the air, carried by the cool breeze scented with perfumed candles. Her arms wrap tightly around his shoulders as he shifts under her weight, the muscles in his back rippling like waves on the ocean. The sensation of her breath on the back of his neck sends shivers down his spine, like a jolt of electricity. The sudden flash of lightning illuminates the room, casting a ghostly reflection of themselves on the mirrors. Together, they resemble a seasoned cowgirl atop a bucking bronco, poised and ready to conquer the thrilling ride.

Alice's eyes widen with excitement as she watches him in the mirror, her heart pounding with anticipation. She can feel the heat emanating from his body as he moves his hips sideways and back-and-forth. His eyes light up, and a smirk spreads across his face as he matches her rhythm perfectly. The sound of their charged breaths fills the room, punctuated by the hypnotic rhythm of their movements. Sam pants like a steam engine, his body tense with desire, and Alice feels her own heart racing in response. As they stare each other down, the smell of sweat fills the air, and Alice's chest rises and falls with each breath. Beads of perspiration glisten on her forehead, and she can feel the intensity of the moment building between them.

Alice repeatedly slaps Samuel on his backside, the sound echoing in the dimly lit room. "Faster, faster, faster," she gasps between breaths, her voice husky with desire. He picks up the pace and then suddenly stops. His body trembles with a rapid succession of convulsions. He groans and buries his face in the pillow to muffle the deafening grunts. The tremors in his body excite her, sending shivers down her spine. She stops, closes her eyes, and savors the surge of pleasure coursing through her veins with a hearty huff, feeling every inch of her body come alive. The musky scent of sweat mixes with the lingering smoke from the candles and the aftermath of sex hangs heavy in the room, making her head spin. As they lie there, spent, she can feel the warm sweat trickling down her back and the cool air brushing against her skin, sending goosebumps all over her body. Sam's lips emit a sharp hiss as a twinge of pain shoots through her thigh, interrupting their intense moment together.

Alice rises slowly, feeling the weight of her own body as she catches her breath. She fixes her gaze on their reflection in the mirror and winces at the sight of her disheveled hair and smudged makeup—remnants of an unforgettable night. With a deep frown, she reaches up to run her fingers through her hair, feeling the tangles and knots. Suddenly, a blinding flash of lightning illuminates the room, casting a haunting silhouette of a young woman in the mirror's reflection. Alice's ears ring with the deafening sound of thunder, and her heart skips a beat. She sits bolt upright, feeling the cool sweat on her skin and the goosebumps rising on her arms. Her eyes dart around the dimly lit corners of the room, searching for any sign of the mysterious figure.

Fear creeps into her voice as she shakes Sam's shoulders, desperately pleading, "There's somebody here, Sam!" With a sense of urgency, she pulls the blindfold off his head, hoping to find answers.

Confused, Sam sits up and rubs his eyes, struggling to comprehend the situation. "What do you mean, there's somebody here?" he asks, his tone betraying a hint of concern.

Alice points at the mirrors, her finger trembling as she tries to steady it. "There, right there, I saw her!" Her voice quivers with a mixture of fear and disbelief.

Sam sighs, his body sinking back onto the bed, causing it to shake slightly. "The excitement must have gotten to you," he says with genuine sincerity. "Please fix us a drink. I'm dry."

Annoyance etches across Alice's face, but she reluctantly complies, her gaze shifting between the mirrors, her mind still preoccupied with the foreboding image she witnessed. She walks numbly to the minibar; the ice clinking in the glasses as she refills their drinks, heightening the anticipation in the room. She can't help but steal a quick glance at her enchanting artwork on Sam's backside, the vibrant colors and intricate details captivating her senses A medley of handprints, lipstick stains, and half-moon nail marks are all signs of the recent good times with a thrilling finale. A coy smile plays on her lips, momentarily distracting her from the mysterious presence that lingers in her mind.

Alice glides into the spacious bathroom, her steps echoing off the marble floors. As she steps inside, she admires the opulent surroundings. The skylight above her illuminates the clawfoot tub, casting intricate shadows on the walls. With its irresistible features, the grand glass-enclosed shower calls to her, and she breathes in deeply, savoring the refreshing aromas of aromatherapy products. Her fingers tremble with excitement as she tinkers with the control panel, activating the jets and releasing a surge of steam. She closes her eyes and lets the warm water cascade over her body. She can feel the tension melting away as the warm water jets work their way over her skin, leaving her feeling refreshed and invigorated. The sounds of the water and the hum of the jets create a soothing melody, and she hums along, shampooing her hair, and luxuriating in the sensation. After indulging in the blissful experience, she wraps herself in an oversized, fluffy towel, relishing the comforting embrace it provides.

The calming sounds of deep breathing and light snoring fills the bedroom. Alice carefully tucks Sam under a soft satin sheet, dresses herself, and prepares a double vodka soda. With a resigned sigh, she opens the Wickr app and begins typing out a message; *Operation terminated; Intimate familiarity with target detected. Compromise imminent.* Sam suddenly snores, and she jumps as she hits the send button. She shoots a quick glance at him, and then hurriedly shoves the phone into her bag

Settling into a plush chair facing the large windows, she gazes out at the airport. Outside, the raindrops delicately patter against the glass, and the soft moonlight casts a shimmering glow on the wet asphalt. The tranquil stillness of the early hours envelops the airport. Alice's eyes roam the scene outside and land on a pilot smoking a cigarette near a large passenger jet. After stubbing out his cigarette, he picks up his briefcase and climbs the airstair into the doorway. Alice strains to see him and spots him entering the cockpit. Inside, the pilot sinks into a comfortable chair and carefully examines a notepad attached to a clipboard.

Suddenly, the door to the pilot quarters opens, and a well-groomed young flight attendant walks in, carrying a tray of beverages. The pilot jumps up from his seat, beaming with joy, and envelops her in a warm embrace. They exchange a few words before the pretty attendant leans back, and they share a deep and passionate kiss. Her spider-like fingers unbutton his jacket, and they both sink into a reclining chair at the aft of the cockpit. Their skins glisten with sweat as they breathe heavily, their bodies intertwined in a passionate embrace. The cockpit windows fog up, creating a hazy veil that blurs the outside world.

Alice stands, squinting her eyes and craning her neck to see through the foggy cockpit windows. A blurry figure moves in the distance, and suddenly the cockpit plunges into darkness. Alice's jaw drops in disbelief, and a bemused expression crosses her face. "Oh, come on! What the heck?" she exclaims, eager for more of the tantalizing cockpit action. Her hand flies to her mouth as she tries to contain her surprise.

Sam lets out a low, guttural grunt before turning onto his back and resuming his rhythmic snoring. Suddenly, the sound of a squeaky door hinge pierces through the silence, followed by a sharp click as the door slams shut. Startled, Alice's eyes widen with curiosity as she quickly glances over her shoulder, searching for the source of the sound. An icy shiver races down her spine, and she can feel the hair on the back of her neck bristle. With a sudden burst of energy, she springs up and dashes after the sound, the soles of her feet slapping against the cold, hard floor. As she nears the door, the faint smell of burning candles fills her nose. She peers through the peephole, her eyes darting back and forth as she scans the empty hallway, faintly lit by dim nightlights. She can hear her own heart beating in her chest as she wonders what could have caused the door to slam shut.

The moment Alice steps inside the living space, she's struck by the vibrant colors and intricate patterns of the illustrations. The fish artwork on the walls seems to come to life as she walks through the room, searching for the source of the sound. A refreshing and unique aroma fills the living space—a blend of eucalyptus and the faint scent of chlorine. She inhales deeply, feeling the coolness of the air against her skin, causing goosebumps

to appear on her arms. She shivers involuntarily and rubs her arms to warm
herself up. Lost in thought, Alice absentmindedly navigates back to her seat,
feeling the cool condensation on the glass as she takes a sip of her drink.
Outside, a pushback tug with its flashing emergency light emits a brilliant
yellow glow, gradually maneuvering the large passenger jet backward.

Her eyes widen in surprise as she checks her watch and sees the early
hours of the morning staring back at her. Alice jumps up and gathers the
empty glasses. With a clink, she sets the glasses on the counter; the sound
echoing in the still room. She then snatches a bottle of still water from the
fridge. Sam's snoring echoes, a deep rumble that fills the room. Every time he
exhales, his lips flap together like a horse snorting, causing Alice to stifle a
giggle. She pours the water into a glass, and a drop spills on her hand, sending
a shiver down her spine. Alice places the glass on the bedside table next
to Sam, whose phone lies nearby. Its screen brightens to display a message
preview. Overcome by curiosity, Alice notices the sender's name: Blair T.

Unintentionally, she reads the preview: 'Hey, hope you enjoy your
business trip. Goodnight and sleep tight and remember...' Alice's face
scrunches in confusion. "Business trip, my foot!" she mutters, causing Sam to
stir and babble in his sleep. The smell of Sam's breath fills her nostrils, and she
covers her mouth as she looks at Sam and then back at his phone. A sudden
wave of inspiration washes over her, and an impish smile plays across her face.

She snaps a photo of her masterpiece decorating Sam's bottom. The
camera's bright white light fills the room, making Sam mumble quietly. Alice
examines the photo, her face illuminated by the soft blue glow of the phone
screen. "Take that, Blair," she murmurs, capturing several more shots from
different angles before locking the phone and placing it back on the
nightstand. Her lips curl into a sly grin.

Sam's peaceful expression tugs at Alice's heartstrings, and she leans
forward to give him a soft peck on his cheek before gathering her belongings
and leaving. As she closes the door behind her, she takes one last look at the
room. The scent of Sam's cologne lingers in the air, and Alice's eyes scan the
plush carpet, taking in the intricate patterns and soft texture beneath her feet.
A frown creases her forehead, and she walks back to the minibar, noticing
the cool metal of the handle as she opens it. She takes a glass inscribed with
the logo of the swanky hotel, and slips it into her shoulder bag, feeling the

weight of it against her side. She closes the front door softly behind her and follows the dimly lit hallway to the elevators.

A soft shriek escapes her lips as she turns the corner and faces the elevators. Two bodyguards flank the elevator doors. The taller one presses the down button, and Alice hears the faint beep of the elevator arriving. Ding, the doors slide open. He beckons her into the car with a wink, and Alice's heart races as she steps inside. The towering protector follows her inside and takes up position behind her. Sensing the heat of his eyes on her back makes her skin feel like it's crawling with bugs, and Alice's hand sinks into her shoulder bag. She grips the stun gun between her fingers, feeling the cold metal against her skin. The soft hum of the elevator fills her ears as she keeps her eyes locked on the descending numbers. When the car finally stops and the doors open, she lets out a quiet sigh of relief.

As she rushes out of the elevator, the guard speaks to her back. 'Good night, Ms. Vesper. Take care now,' he says in his distinct accent, smirking knowingly. She scowls at him, feeling the anger rise in her chest. Her heels clack against the marble floor as she breaks into a run. She quickly pushes the oscillating doors open, and a rush of cool air hits her face. A postcard-perfect night sky greets her as she steps outside. Alice inhales deeply, savoring the cool breeze and the scent of wet earth after the rain.

Alice watches as the three blue dots on her ride-sharing app slowly inches closer to her location. A sassy white stretch limo pulls up as she waits for her request to be accepted by a driver. Alice's eyes shift from the phone to the nearby limo, and the bright lights of the hotel illuminate the shiny windows, distorting her reflection. The soft breeze caresses her hair, making it dance around her face.

The limo stops, and the driver gets out and walks around the back towards her, wearing a blue suit with sneakers. Alice comes into view, and the man's eyes widen in surprise as he covers his mouth. *"Magnifico!"* he exclaims, his eyes bright with excitement. "Signora Alice, my name is Mattia. I am the driver for Signor Granger. I can take you home now. Please, get in the car." He opens the back door, gesturing for her to enter. Astonished, her eyes widen as she looks back and forth between the phone in her hand, the luxurious interior, and the stubby little bald man at her side.

Alice hesitates and cancels her ride-sharing request before finally getting into the limo and sinking into the soft leather seat at the back of the cabin. The chauffeur closes the door behind her and gets into the driver's seat. With a soft mechanical hum, the tinted glass partition rolls up behind him, the ceiling lights dim, and the car pulls away. The soft hum of the engine and the subtle scent of leather wraps around her like a cocoon. Outside, the city lights streak past in a blur, but inside this space, time seems to slow, the outside world held at bay by tinted windows. A slim glass, with an open champagne bottle in an ice well, tempts her from their vantage point on a wooden shelf.

Alice's slender fingers reach out for the crystal champagne glass. But before she can lift it to her lips, a loud voice blares over the intercom, making her heart skip a beat. Her eyes scan the dimly lit cabin, and her eyebrows furrow in confusion. The smell of the bubbly drink fills her nostrils as she takes a sip, hoping to calm her nerves.

"Should I take you home, Signora Alice? Or perhaps make a detour?" The voice booms again, echoing in the spacious cabin. Alice's hand trembles slightly as she sets down the glass.

"How do you know my name? Have we met?" she asks, her voice barely above a whisper.

The silence stretches out for what seems like an eternity before the voice speaks again, this time more softly. "Signora, press the talk button if you want to speak with me."

Alice hesitates for a moment before pressing the red talk button, her fingers brushing against the smooth surface. "No detour, Mattia. Just take me home, please. And forgive me for asking, but have we met before? How do you know my name?" she asks, her heart pounding in her chest.

Mattia's response is calm and measured, and Alice can almost feel the tension in her body dissipating. "I have never met you, Signora. Miss Blair, assistant for Signor Granger, called me and shared your details with me."

Alice nods absentmindedly, lost in her own thoughts. The soft hum of the car engine fills the air as she takes a sip of her bubbly, savoring the sweet and tangy taste. She gazes out through the tinted windows, captivated by the mesmerizing city lights and the dazzling billboard signs.

Mattia expertly maneuvers through the quiet traffic, and the car comes to a halt at the base of the stairs leading up to Alice's house. As she gathers her belongings, Alice takes a deep breath, inhaling the crisp night air. She fumbles for the door handle, and as if by magic, the door opens, flooding the car with a warm and inviting glow. Mattia offers his hand, and Alice takes it, feeling the reassuring strength of his grip.

As she steps out of the car, she takes a deep breath to steady her nerves and put on a facade of confidence. The cool night breeze brushes against her skin, sending a shiver down her spine. Alice looks around, expecting to see curious onlookers peering out of their windows, but the street is quiet and still.

She feels a slight dizziness from the effervescence of the bubbly, causing her to wobble unsteadily on her feet. "Thank you so much, you are far too kind," she says, leaving a smudge of crimson lipstick on the crown of the stubby man's head. His round face turns a vivid shade of scarlet, and he quickly turns and walks away. She stands at the top of the staircase, the sound of the departing limousine echoing in her ears as she waves goodbye. "I hope you check yourself in the mirror before heading home, my dear little man," she whispers to herself with a sly grin.

3

Late in the morning, Alice stirs from her sleep, feeling the weight of exhaustion on her limbs. The stale air in her bedroom assaults her nose, and she quickly covers it with a sheet, trying to block out the wretched smells that linger from the night before. Outside, the birds chirping create a serene ambiance that engulfs her senses. She lies on the bed, staring at the ceiling, trying to recall the details of her dream. The stubborn dreams refuse to emerge from behind the obscure place where they go into hiding. An unsettling foreboding lingers in the back of her mind. Her face crinkles as her deep memory of the sensational events from the night before comes into focus—the good times with Samuel Granger, the reflection of the girl in the mirror, and at last, the memorable drive home.

A flood of memories overwhelms her, causing her to jolt upright and shiver involuntarily. She winces in pain as a splitting headache pounds in her head. The throbbing feels like a drill boring into her skull. She covers her eyes with her palms and mulls over her conversations with Sam, and.... Yes, that's it! She furrows her brow, trying to remember, until the chauffeur's words come back to her in a sudden realization. *Mr. Granger's PA, Blair, shared your details with me.*

In the silence, Alice's voice rings out, and she wonders to herself, "Was Blair there? And how did she know I was there?" Her loyal companion, Sparky, responds to her distress, wagging his tail as he bounds into the room and leaps onto the bed. She strokes his head tenderly, her fingers brushing against his soft fur. Her phone on the nightstand plays a cheerful melody, and she picks it up. She can't wait to see what the message says, so she taps on the preview with anticipation. As she reads the message, her eyes widen and her cheeks flush with excitement. *Thanks for the fun,* Sam writes, adding, *Impressive butt pics, by the way.* The message is clearly striking a chord with her. She can't help but feel a bit flattered by the compliment. Sam's message is certainly leaving a lasting impression on her.

Alice's face lights up with a beaming smile, causing her cheeks to flush into a deep shade of crimson. Filled with uncontainable excitement, she springs out of bed, takes two aspirins, and makes her way to the bathroom.

The sound of water gushing down the showerhead echoes through the room, creating a peaceful ambiance. The steam from the shower gradually fills the bathroom, carrying the sweet scent of coconut shampoo with it. Alice takes a long, relaxing shower, the sensation of the warm water running down her body leaving her feeling rejuvenated and invigorated.

The bedroom is in a state of chaotic disarray as Natalie goes upstairs to check on her boss. She hears her boss singing and turns her attention to the bathroom. She watches Alice through the hazy veil of the shower door, a smirk playing on her lips. Alice's voice echoes through the room as she sings the lyrics to "Uptown Funk" by Mark Ronson while performing some impressive hip shimmy and slide movements. Even though the vocals might not be the best, the performance is still awe-inspiring. Natalie can't help but clap her hands in time with the tune and sing along.

Alice steps out of the shower, feeling exposed under Natalie's intense and unsettling stare. Natalie stands with her arms on her hips, watching Alice and exclaims, "You're killing it, girl!" Alice's cheeks flush an even deeper shade of red as she dabs her face using the corners of the towel and greets Natalie with a shy smile, "Good morning, Natalie. I wasn't expecting company."

Alice steps off the cold tiles and onto the soft carpets. She catches a glimpse of her reflection in the full-length mirror. The tantalizing aroma of sizzling eggs and toasty bread wafts through the air, making her stomach grumble. Alice checks her watch in anticipation and suggests, "Fried egg sandwich on rye?" to Natalie.

Natalie nods her head with a bright, sincere smile. "Of course," she replies before walking out. The sound of her merry whistling fills the air as she descends the stairs.

Alice gazes at her reflection in the vanity dresser mirror, amidst the deafening sound of the blow dryer. Her raven hair sways in the gusts of hot air, and she delicately applies her makeup, accentuating her bright eyes and rosy cheeks. She reaches into the accessories drawer, feeling the smooth texture of the pearl necklace and earrings, and the velvety fabric of the white headband adorned with pink polka dots. She ties the headband and savors the sensation of the soft fabric against her skin, feeling a surge of contentment and confidence. With a flutter of her thick, luscious eyelashes, she completes her look, adding a hint of mystique and allure. The sweet scent of her perfume lingers in the air, complementing her captivating appearance.

Alice takes a step forward, admiring her reflection in the full-length mirror, and feels the softness of the plush carpet beneath her toes. She slips into her pink undies and pulls on the baby doll dress, admiring the dark red and blue floral patterns. The skin tone cashmere ballet flats feel like a warm hug for her feet as she slips them on. She studies her reflection in the mirror, feeling content with the simple outfit she chose for the day.

Alice stands on the ball of her foot and spins gracefully in front of the full-length mirror, her flowy dress twirling in perfect unison. She smiles at herself, admiring her temporary new look, and tests it out on her husband. The door to James' home office is ajar, and she pokes her head through the gap. The room is dimly lit, and the only sound is the soft clicking of James' computer keyboard. He knits his brow as he concentrates on his work. Alice greets him with a voice full of energy and excitement, breaking the silence. "Good morning, James," she says, her voice echoing in the quiet room.

With a start, James gazes up at his wife. Annoyance flickers across his face, but her beaming smile quickly melts his irritation away. "Good morning, sleepyhead," he says with a smile, eyeing Alice up and down. "Look at you, all dressed up. Are you headed back to school?" he asks teasingly. Alice's face lights up with joy as she hears the expected reaction, causing her to twirl in her dress, and it flutters like a butterfly's wings. James notices her cheerful demeanor and becomes curious. "You seem chirpy," he remarks. "Please, tell me all about your evening with your mystery date. I'm eager to hear every detail."

Alice gazes at James with a dreamy expression, her eyes fixed on him as if he were a celebrity she had always admired. Her eyes seem to be lost in a far-off world, and a contented smile plays on her lips. Suddenly, she shakes her head, as if to clear away the dreamy haze, and her husband's kind words linger in her mind.

"No, I'm not going back to school," she chuckles. "I'm meeting my therapist. I had a crazy night, lots of fun, and I even got a lift home in a flashy limo, with champagne. I think I met Thor in person," she says with excitement. "I'll tell you everything over dinner." She says, with a rising inflection that makes it sound like a question. As if a lightbulb goes off in her head, her face suddenly lights up with a smile. "Look at this," she rummages through her clutch bag and takes out her phone, eager to show James the pictures of Sam's backside adorned by her artwork.

James' jaw drops in awe as he stares at the phone screen. "Whoa, you got him good. All hands and lips. Nice butt, by the way. Hmm, yummy." The sound of his voice is low and husky, filled with admiration for the impressive artwork on display. Alice can smell the faint scent of his aftershave, along with the aroma of freshly brewed coffee and toasted rye wafting from the kitchen.

She lets out a hearty laugh at James' pun. Her eyes glint with curiosity as she asks, "How's Robert doing?"

With a wide smile spreading across his face, James leans back in his chair. "Quill's doing great, thank you. We had an early night and enjoyed scrumptious food paired with the most delectable South African wine. To top it off, we binge-watched Schitt's Creek from the very beginning, again and again. Sparky was in expert hands."

Sparky's ears perk up as soon as he hears his name, and he jumps up, barking excitedly with his tail wagging. Alice can't help but smile at the adorable pup. "Who's Quill?" she asks, her voice filled with curiosity.

Her question brings a smile to James' face, and his eyes twinkle with happiness. "Quillen is Robert's last name, and that's where the nickname comes from," he explains.

A pang of envy shoots through Alice's heart, but she puts on a gracious smile. "Sounds lovely. Do you need more wine?"

Alice's offer takes James by surprise. His eyes widen in disbelief. "Yes, please!" he exclaims. "Quill and I love the wine. Would you like to watch a movie with us sometime? I'll make the popcorn," he adds. A mischievous grin spreads across Jame's face as they both remember a recent mishap when Alice forgot to set the timer on the popcorn in the microwave. Thick, acrid smoke filled the kitchen, setting off the fire alarm and triggering the sprinklers. Deafening sirens blared throughout the house, and Sparky darted out through the pet door, straight into the arms of a good-hearted firefighter.

Alice's cheeks flush with embarrassment as she recalls the incident. "Okay, it's a deal," she says, trying to move on. "I'll get the wine from my web developer in South Africa and we can catch up later. I have a busy day ahead."

With a playful grin, James calls out to her as she walks away, "Good luck, Spid! See ya later!" He adds a silent "t" at the end and watches his wife disappear around the corner.

The delicious aroma of sizzling fried eggs, toasted bread, and steamy coffee waft through the air, guiding Alice towards the kitchen. Following her to the breakfast nook, Sparky settles down and rests his head on her feet.

Alice takes a big bite of her egg sandwich, savoring the rich taste of the runny yolk and crispy bacon. She relishes the peaceful silence of the morning, broken only by the soft murmur of the TV in the background. The warm glow of the screen bathes the kitchen in a cozy light, casting long shadows on the walls. A young blonde news anchor appears on the screen, her perfectly coiffed hair and bright smile contrasting with the serious tone of the news. As Alice watches, Samuel Granger's face suddenly pops up in a small thumbnail on the right-hand side of the screen. Her heart skips a beat, and she frantically looks around the kitchen for the remote. Finally, Alice spots the remote hiding under a banana in the fruit bowl and turns up the volume, eager to hear the latest news about Samuel.

The anchor's melodic voice fills the room, and a breaking news headline appears on the news ticker, featuring white text on a blue background: 'Samuel Granger survives a near-fatal assassination attempt.' Alice's thumb reaches for the volume button, cranking it up until the anchor's voice fills the entire kitchen with urgency. "Samuel Granger, a debonair who was asleep after a late-night social event, survived a fatal assassination attempt in the early hours of the morning. A contract killer, disguised as a cleaner, snuck into his hotel room and tried to shoot him with a silenced pistol. Fortunately, one of his bodyguards checked on him at that exact time and spotted the cleaner, which led to a chase. The killer showed exceptional skills and escaped through the hotel window, disappearing like a ghost. Joining us in the studio is Dr. Mortimer Vanthorn, a world-renowned assassination expert. We welcome your calls and comments, so please dial the number on your screen." The anchor directs her attention towards her studio guest, "Dr. Vanthorn, it's a pleasure to have you here with us today. As an expert in your field, could you please share your opinion on how—"

Alice slams her finger on the mute button and tosses the remote into a corner. She whispers to herself, "The killer is Artemis. The Moon's Shadow."

With a loud thud, she slams her hand down on the table, causing the plates and cutlery to clatter and dance. The loud thud startles Sparky, who sprints out of the kitchen, his feet slipping on the slick floor. "Sorry, Sparks," Alice apologizes to her furry companion in an innocuous tone. Her breakfast turns cold as she sits lost in thought, a million questions swirling through her mind.

Alice's heart thunders in her chest as she struggles to process the shocking news. Her trembling hands reach for the coffee cup, and she takes a sip, desperate for the warmth to soothe her frazzled nerves. But the acrid smell of the coffee only intensifies the churning in her stomach, and a tight knot forms in her throat. She cannot believe that Artemis, her former mentor and friend, is involved in the attempt on Samuel Granger's life. Anger, sadness, and confusion swirl together, creating a jumbled mess of emotions inside her chest. She wonders what could have driven Artemis to take such a drastic step and whether there is anything she can do to stop her. Her mind races with possibilities, but she knows she needs more information before she can make any moves. Alice takes a deep breath, focusing on the sounds of her own breathing, and tries to calm herself down. She knows she must remain level-headed if she wants to sort this out.

Alice steals a quick glance at her watch and notices it is already eleven-fifteen. She quickly gulps down her lukewarm coffee and finishes her cold sandwich. As she heads out, she unexpectedly collides with Natalie, who assesses her appearance with folded arms.

As she heads out, she unexpectedly collides with Natalie, who assesses her appearance with folded arms. "Well, well, sugar, you're looking mighty improved," Natalie drawls with a grin. "You off to them fairgrounds again? You roam this city like a stray cat, darlin'," she teases playfully.

Alice chuckles softly, flipping through the pages of her diary. "Nat, thank you for the delicious brunch," she says. "I noticed that I have a late afternoon appointment with a Mr. And Mrs. Holms. Do you know if they're new clients?"

Natalie thinks, scratches her chin and murmurs, "Hmm hmm hmm." Suddenly, she exclaims, "I've got it, as new as a rainy day!" She then points at a window splattered with raindrops and warns, "You'd better gear up, hon. It's raining cats and dogs out there."

Alice follows Natalie's finger and sees the rain pouring down in sheets, the sound of it a constant drone in the background. She unclasps an umbrella and raincoat from the coat rack, and steps outside, quickly taking cover under the awning. She holds the umbrella tightly as the wind picks up, and the raincoat offers little protection from the driving rain.

Alice breathes in the sweet scent of rain and listens to the sound of cars swishing through puddles as she orders a ride through a ride-sharing app. She watches people scurrying for cover as she waits for her ride. Suddenly, her phone chimes, and she quickly descends the stairs to find a sleek black sedan waiting for her. She feels the cool water droplets touching her skin and hears the rhythmic tapping of rain against her umbrella.

Alice closes the umbrella, feeling the satisfying snap of it folding neatly into itself. She opens the car door and sinks into the plush back seat, enveloped in its softness. Leather and freshly cleaned upholstery permeate the air. The car pulls out into the streets, and the cacophony of honking horns and revving engines assaults her ears. The young driver's fingers grip the steering wheel tightly, his knuckles turning white as he navigates through the labyrinth of city streets. His phone's moving map illuminates his face, casting an eerie blue glow on the dim interior of the car.

He pulls up to 193 West Street, and Alice steps out onto the busy city sidewalk. The sign at the top of the entrance displays the name of the building: City Practice, incised in black letters on a bronze plaque, listing the initials and last names of several mental health practitioners. She shivers as the dampness from the puddles seeps into her socks and chills her feet.

Alice inhales deeply, steadying her nerves before she pushes open the door to the pristine clinic. A soft chime announces her arrival, and the people in the waiting area briefly glance up from their phones and magazines before returning to their distractions. A calming blend of chamomile and lavender infuses the air, while soothing classical music plays in the background.

Alice takes off her raincoat and shakes off the droplets before hanging it up on the coat rack. She straightens her shoulders, puts on a brave face, and approaches the reception desk—carved from gleaming black marble. On one corner of the desk, a delicate vase holds a vibrant bouquet. A red-headed receptionist with perfectly manicured nails holds up a finger, motioning for quiet as she speaks into the phone. Alice's eyes wander around the room, taking in the cool blue hue of the walls and the polished wooden floors that shine beneath her feet. Alice surveys the waiting room, and a poster of the Grand Canyon catches her attention. The setting sun casts a warm, golden light over the rocky landscape depicted in the image. The poster features white motivational text that reads, *When you look into an abyss, the abyss also looks at you.* Alice's lips curl into a sly grin as she arches an eyebrow. She shifts her gaze back to the receptionist and waits patiently, tapping her foot softly on the floor.

The receptionist hangs up and greets Alice with a warm and melodic tone, but her eyes remain fixed on the computer screen, avoiding any eye contact. "Sorry about that," she apologizes. "Good morning. How may I help you?"

Alice responds in a hushed tone, "Good morning, I'm scheduled to meet with Dr. Ross at twelve-thirty."

The fiery redheaded lady nods, her long earrings swaying, and quickly types on the computer keyboard to check the appointment. After a moment, she confirms, "Ah, yes, Doctor Loo-Rear. Please take a seat in the waiting area. Doctor Ross will be with you shortly." She gestures towards the waiting area.

Alice grins, emphasizing the pronunciation of her name. "It's Doctor Laurier, Law-ree-ay, but my friends call me Alice." She finds an empty seat, the cushions firm but comfortable, and picks up a lifestyle magazine. The glossy, thick paper is cool to the touch, and the faint smell of ink wafts up from the pages. Alice sinks into the chair and takes a deep breath, ready to wait.

The waiting area is eerily quiet, with only the sound of magazine pages being flipped and the occasional sniffle breaking the stillness. Alice looks around the room and notices curious glances from her fellow patients. She distracts herself by reading an article about an art museum in Beacon. Suddenly, she hears a heavy door creak open, and a woman exits the therapist's office, tears streaming down her face. Alice can't help but feel a pang of pity with the poor woman and wonder what struggles she is facing. After a brief wait, the receptionist calls out, "Alice Laurier!" With a deep breath, Alice stands, tosses the magazine onto the chair, and heads towards the door labeled Krystin T. Ross, PhD, Clinical Psychologist. She knocks gently and hears a warm, inviting voice say, "Come in, Alice. The door is open."

The consultation room smells sweet, and Alice breathes in the scent of perfume as she enters. She kicks off her shoes and settles into a comfortable chaise lounge. Dr. Ross, a middle-aged woman, presents herself with a sharp face and large, observant eyes. Her form-fitting attire hugs her slender frame, emphasizing her professional demeanor. She grabs her notes, takes a seat across from Alice, and greets her with a warm smile. "It's good to see you again, Alice. How has your day been treating you so far?" Her sultry, hypnotic voice draws attention to her glossy pink lips, causing people to stare.

The question prods Alice's memory back to the incident with Samuel Granger, and she shudders at the thought but quickly puts it out of her mind. In a calm tone, she replies, "It's good to hear you say that. I'm doing well too, thanks, Krystin."

Krystin's warm grin shows off her perfectly straight teeth. "You look lovely, Alice. I'm happy with your progress and appreciate your openness. Can I get you something to drink?"

Alice breathes a sigh of relief, and a faint smile plays on her lips. "Thank you, Krystin. Yes, I would love a coffee." She feels the soft fabric of the chaise lounge against her skin, and the gentle breeze from the air conditioning brushes against her face.

Krystin winks mischievously, her eyes crinkling with amusement. "I can do with coffee myself." She picks up the phone on her desk and calls the reception, her voice clear and crisp. She requests two cups of coffee and sets the phone down. The pages of Krystin's notepad rustle as she flicks through her notes, the sound like leaves rustling in the wind. Alice watches as Krystin concentrates, her pen moving quickly across the page.

Soon, the door opens, and a young woman enters the consultation room, holding a tray with two steaming cups of coffee. Alice savors the rich, smoky aroma of the hot brew, which fills the surrounding air. She takes a sip, and the smooth, rich flavor floods her senses, making her feel content.

Dr. Ross tosses her notes on the coffee table with a soft thud, and the sound echoes in the quiet room. She pours the coffee into her cup, the liquid dark and velvety. "I am pleased with what I have learned from your experiences as an adult. Please tell me more about young Alice." Her voice is low and soothing, and her eyes are piercing and inquisitive.

The question catches Alice off guard, and she feels a lump form in her throat. She knows she must be honest, and there is no one other than her therapist who she would tell her story to. The gut-wrenching memories of her past are hard to bear, and she struggles to find the right words. Despite her best efforts, tears well up in her eyes, and she blinks them back, not wanting to show any weakness. She takes another sip of the coffee, hoping that the warmth will soothe her frayed nerves.

Her voice quivers slightly as she speaks, revealing the intensity of her emotions. "When I was seven years old, my father passed away. A year later, my mother remarried, and we moved in with my stepdad immediately. A foreign embassy employed him and he owned a big, spacious house, which was a stark contrast to the small apartment we used to live in." As she breathes in, she can smell the familiar scent of her childhood home. "At first, everything seemed perfect. I had my bedroom, and a driver would drop me off at school every morning. The newfound luxuries distracted me from my father's passing much faster than I thought they would." She stalls, her body tense with the memories of her past.

Her therapist leans forward and rewards Alice's honesty with an approving smile, the corners of her lips curling upwards. She picks up her notepad and jots down a few lines, the sound of her pen scratching against the paper filling the room. "What was your mother's line of work?" She asks, her voice laced with compassion.

Alice's face betrays a wistful expression as she anticipates the moment. "My mother was a country singer," she says, her voice soft. "She sang in smoky pubs, bustling casinos, and diners. She was a small-time country gal." Alice scans Krystin's face for any sign that she had uncovered the truth about her mother and stepfather's affair prior to her father's death.

Krystin keeps her discoveries to herself and follows up with the next sensible question. "Are you the only child?" she asks, her voice a soothing balm. The coffee relaxes Alice, and she reclines on the lounger, draping her long legs over the armrest.

She glares at the ceiling, the bright lights making her squint. "When I was growing up, I always looked up to my brother Michael, who is much older than me," Alice says, her voice heavy with emotion. "He left home when I was nine, joined the army, and went missing in action in Afghanistan two years later. His whereabouts have been unknown since then. I'm convinced he used the opportunity to fade away. He and my daddy were close, but he and my mom never saw eye-to-eye, and he loathed my stepfather..." Alice's voice trails off, and she absentmindedly taps her fingers on the backrest. "I don't really miss him, but I think about him sometimes. Before he left, he said he will return someday to k—" Alice bites her tongue just in time, disarmed by how easily her therapist distracts safeguarded information from her. She squints up at the ceiling with a fierce glare, her mind racing. *Krystin, you're quite clever*, she thinks to herself, impressed with the tactics.

Krystin sits calmly in her plush armchair, her pen scrawling across the pages of her notepad as she steals a glance at her luxurious wristwatch. "How would you define the relationship between you and your mother?" she asks in a measured tone. "Don't say good or bad. Tell me everything."

Alice furrows her brow, her eyes darting back and forth as she takes a deep breath and recalls her experiences. Her voice is soft and sad, filling the room with a melancholic melody. "At first, I was angry," she says, her words punctuated by a deep sigh. "I thought she didn't miss my father. To me, it seemed like she never mourned his passing, or so I thought." Alice's voice carries over the faint scent of lavender, wafting through the air from the vase of flowers on the desk. Deep furrows show on her forehead as she continues to speak, her eyes distant as she remembers. "In her own strange way, she was happy. I was told that my dad was a drinker, and he sometimes abused my mom. However, I can't say if it's true because I was too young to remember."

As Alice fidgets with the edge of her dress, she feels the soft fabric brushing against her skin. "My stepfather was the object of her affection, or perhaps she even worshipped him. They bonded over their shared love of music, and he showered her with everything she ever desired, including a Steinway Grand Piano. I can't recall seeing my mom that happy with my dad."

Through the window, a faint sound of traffic drifts in, the distant hum of cars and trucks filtering through the curtains. Alice continues speaking, her voice growing softer. "My mom and I got along well enough. She taught me how to read music and play the piano, and sometimes she even helped me with my homework." Alice pauses for a moment before adding, "Yet, she wasn't your typical mother figure. She was passively present, if you know what I mean."

An unsettling quiet fills the room, broken only by the ticking of a wall clock.. Alice feels her anxiety mounting as she notices her therapist's expression shift from thoughtful to neutral. Suddenly, Krystin throws a question at her, and Alice winces in response, swinging her legs to the side and sitting bolt upright. "Your stepfather," Krystin says. "You never talk about him. How would you describe the relationship between you two?"

Alice is struggling to catch her breath, and her heart is racing. Her voice quivers as she reveals, "His name is Alistair Taylor." The sadness in her tone is palpable. "I hate him with every fiber of my being. It hurts so much when I think about him." Alice's eyes well up with tears, but she holds them back. "We didn't have a father-daughter relationship. I was his toy, his random pleasure."

Krystin notices Alice's discomfort mounting, "Alice, would you like to take a break and stretch your legs?" She fixes her gaze on Alice, waiting for an answer.

Alice's mind goes blank, and she can't remember what she was about to say. Biting her lip, she tries to remember and suddenly the memory hits her like a ton of bricks. "No, I am okay. I must face it, and I have never spoken about it to anyone." With a reassuring smile, she continues on. "My mom was out most nights, singing. My stepfather would seize the opportunity to come into my bedroom and demand certain... pleasures from me." she inhales sharply, her eyes widening as she tries to hold back her tears.

"He used to call the petty pleasures favors, and I felt like I had no choice. He threatened me and said he would banish us from his home if I told anyone about our little..." she emphasizes her point by making air quotes with her long, slender fingers, "secret, or that was what he used to called it." She takes a deep breath, inhaling the scent of the room as she gazes at her therapist to see if she is listening. Krystin watches her with a bemused expression, her gaze intense.

"I felt cheap and violated, but I surrendered to his demands, because it felt like I had no choice. He scared me, and I thought he would hurt my mother if he did not get his way with me. I just had to be brave. No one ever suspected anything." Alice exhales, the sound of her sorrow echoing around her as she wipes away her tears with the back of her hand.

Dr. Ross reaches across the coffee table and hands over a box of tissues, but Alice gives a nonchalant wave of her hand.

"How long did it last for?" Krystin assuages Alice's sorrow with gentle words.

A wave of emotion washes over Alice. Her face crumples into a heartbreaking expression, and her tears flow. Her voice quivers, and each word punctuates with a guttural rasp from the lump in her throat. "Until I was seventeen, before I went to college. When I reached my teens, the nighttime visits became more frequent, and the favors more demanding, or rather, more adventurous. I had to take birth control pills. I became his pleasure doll, and he asked me to perform different poses, like bend over and touch my toes, or ask me to touch myself, while he watched," overwhelmed with sorrow, she stops and dabs her eyes with a tissue.

Alice takes a moment to throw a tear-streaked glance at her therapist. "His charm made things worse. Heck, he could charm the pants off a priest. He had a funny way of making me feel like everything we did was fine. I sometimes even laughed at his silly jokes. Whenever I think about the things he did to me, my stomach twists and turns, and I feel like throwing up." She takes a deep breath. Alice is a forlorn sight, with her dark makeup smears and smudges streaming down her face, and her sobs echoing in the air.

She closes her eyes tightly to prevent the tears from spilling over. "The worst part was hearing his and my mother's intimate sounds on the same nights he came to my room. He left their bedroom door ajar while they were in the throes of passion. One night, I couldn't resist the urge to peek through the opening, eager to see what was happening inside. As soon as he saw me, his face twisted into an evil grin, like he had been waiting for me. The pleasure emanating from his evil smirk made me shiver with fear." Alice's hands shake with rage as she desperately tries to forget the cruel events.

Krystin's eyes are wide and unblinking, her mouth slightly agape in surprise. "Is he still in your life?" she asks, as if it's the only thing that matters.

Alice takes a deep breath and swallows hard, her throat tight with emotion. Her therapist's reassuring presence is a comfort, but she knows she needs to push through before her courage gives out. "I tried to forgive him," she says, her voice trembling. "I really did. After I graduated, I called him to share my achievement, hoping for some kind of validation. But he only told me he'd remarried and to leave him alone."

Her foot taps incessantly on the ground as she continues. "He came to my mother's funeral, but he didn't stay long. When I tried to approach him, he walked away and got in his car, driving off. He never answers my calls or emails. He fled to England to start a new life, taking everything with him—even our family photos." Alice's eyes narrow with anger, and she tightens her grip on her fists. "Among the things he took was the vintage photo locket that my mother gave me for my sixteenth birthday, which had a picture of my brother in his army uniform."

Alice throws Krystin a sad glare, her eyes red and puffy from crying. As she remembers her cherished locket, her tears flow like a never-ending waterfall, leaving a salty taste on her lips.

The memories hit her like a tidal wave, catching her off guard. In an instant, the creaking of the old wooden floors and the murmur of patrons replaces the sterile silence of the consultation room. The familiar sounds of her mother's soulful singing, mixed with the clinking of glasses and the laughter of patrons fill her ears. Her mother's fingers trace the smooth surface of the vintage locket around her neck, the cool metal a tangible reminder of times gone by. She steals furtive glances at the faded photograph of her son, a bittersweet reminder of the love she held for him. With closed eyes, she says a silent prayer for his safety, and for the memories that will always hold a special place in her heart.

Alice's chest heaves, and her body trembles as she tries to stifle the sobs. The ache in her chest is physical, as if someone has ripped away a part of her. "I'll do whatever it takes to get it back," she murmurs. "I have nothing left from my childhood memories."

Krystin's eyes widen as Alice tells her the heartbreaking details of her story. She chucks the notepad on the coffee table, looks hard at Alice, and cries, "You are so brave, Alice, and I am glad you came to see me." she says, peering at Alice with a raised eyebrow over the rim of her glasses. "We will work through this together. I appreciate your openness and honesty in sharing your experiences with me." She keeps a firm gaze on Alice. "I have homework for you," she says, nodding her head, hoping they're on the same page.

Alice fights hard to hold back her tears, her sobs fading as she nods her head in agreement. "Okay," she says, her voice barely above a whisper, as she nods in resignation.

Krystin flings her stationery onto her large oak desk, then opens her diary to rifle through the pages. She speaks softly, never taking her eyes off the diary. "There's a book called 'Perception Detox' that I'd like you to read before our next appointment. You can purchase it at a discount from my office, or we can add the cost to your next bill. Please be sure to read it, as I will ask you questions about it during our next session in three months' time." Alice gathers her belongings to leave, while Krystin scribbles a quick note in her diary. "My receptionist can give you a copy of the book on your way out and schedule your next appointment," she says with a smile, holding the door open for Alice. "See you then."

Alice steps through the door, tucking her clutch bag under her arm. Turning back towards Krystin, she says, "Thanks for your time and support today." The sudden silence is jarring as the door shuts behind her, leaving her alone with her thoughts.

Alice approaches the bathroom mirror and winces at the harsh lighting that exposes every detail of her face. Her eyes glisten with unshed tears, the skin around them red and puffy from crying earlier. Alice's hands tremble slightly as she reaches for a tissue to wipe away the stray tear that escapes. Despite her efforts to hold back her emotions, it's clear that the conversation with Dr. Ross has taken a toll on her. At the reception desk, she schedules her next appointment and purchases a copy of 'Perception Detox.' Despite the weight of her session, she manages a genuine smile for the receptionist, who excitedly shares her plans for an upcoming date. Alice pays for her session and the book, tucking them into a paper bag before leaving the building.

Amidst the media frenzy about an assassination attempt, Alice finds sanctuary in a local café. Her interest piqued by the news of a secret assassin, she becomes captivated by the server's intriguing appearance and his unexpected connection to Samuel Granger.

The cook's cry interrupts their interaction abruptly. Alice orders a cappuccino and pastrami sandwich, and settles down with a self-help book her therapist recommended. The server returns, bringing her order and sparking a playful exchange about reading and self-help books.

Alice quickly loses interest in her book, scribbling a dismissive message inside before setting it aside. The server's curiosity leads him to read her note. Alice hands him the book, telling him he can keep it. In response, he surprises her with a complimentary coffee and reveals his name, Fabian.

The atmosphere thickens as Fabian hints at wanting to get to know Alice better. She gently rebuffs him, revealing her marital status, but leaves the door open for friendship by exchanging business cards. They share a light-hearted moment, joking about their professions.

Alice snatches the bill and hurries out of the café, leaving Fabian with a handful of cash. She steps back into the world outside, leaving behind the warmth of the café and an intrigued Fabian.

Impatiently, Alice taps her foot on the hot, grimy sidewalk, stealing anxious glances at her watch. The blaring honking of cars and the indistinct chatter of pedestrians fill the thick, humid air, mingling with the unpleasant odor of exhaust fumes and the acrid scent of burnt rubber. Suddenly, a screeching noise beside her makes her jump, and she glowers at the driver of a sleek black unmarked van, his face obscured behind tinted windows. He gestures towards something behind Alice, and she turns to look, her heart racing with unease. Before her mind has time to register the danger, two burly men jump her from behind, their rough, calloused hands gripping her tightly as they force a hood over her head, stifling her screams. The smell of gasoline and rubber intensifies as the van doors slide open, and they shove her inside, the metal walls cold and unforgiving against her skin. The tires screech as the van jolts off, leaving Alice disoriented and frightened, her body trembling with fear and confusion.

She shuts her eyes tightly and counts silently in her mind. The hum of the van's engine lulls her into a trance-like state as she focuses on the task at hand. With every sharp turn the van makes, she feels the gentle sway of her body, and restarts her count from scratch. The faint smell of gasoline and exhaust fumes tickles her nose, but she ignores it and continues counting. As the van turns left, she pictures the scenery outside shifting to the side, and adds a one to her count. When the van turns right, she imagines the view outside moving in a different direction, and adds a two to her tally. Despite the monotonous nature of the task, she remains steadfast in her counting, determined to keep her mind occupied until they reach their destination.

As the van gradually decelerates, her ears prick up, and she tunes in to the array of sounds around her, taking mental notes. The clacking of hooves to her left, the incessant pounding of a jackhammer to her right, and the melodious chirping of birds in a nearby tree all register in her mind. Meanwhile, the pungent scent of diesel fumes permeates the air, and the vibrations from the vehicle's engine reverberate through her body. Just before the van halts, she takes one last sensory snapshot of the bustling scene outside, etching it into her memory forever.

The van's doors screech open, blinding Alice with the piercing sunlight that penetrates the hood covering her head. The handlers yank her out of the van, gripping her arms tightly as they lead her forward. Alice's ears pick up the sound of her footsteps echoing off the cold, hard ground. The musty smell of damp concrete fills her nostrils, and she shivers as a chill runs down her spine. She clutches her bag tightly under her arm, feeling the weight of it pressing against her side. Suddenly, a slight crack emanates from within the bag, and Alice can't help but grin deviously beneath her hood.

The frigid metal seat sends a shock of cold through Alice's body, causing her to shiver uncontrollably. The silence in the room is deafening, and Alice can hear her own heartbeat drumming in her ears. She feels a warm sensation on her face despite the hood covering her head. Abruptly, someone pulls off the hood, causing her to flinch at the sudden brightness of the interrogation light shining directly at her. The light is so blinding that she cannot see clearly, but she can discern the vague outline of a man sitting across from her.

Her adrenaline is pumping, heightening her senses, and she can smell the man's aroma. It is a warm and rich scent, with hints of tobacco, vanilla, and spices. As the door creaks open, a dim light illuminates the room, revealing another man who enters and sits beside the first. He emanates an earthy and woody fragrance, with a hint of citrus, that fills the air around Alice, causing her to feel a sense of unease.

The two men converse in a foreign language that Alice cannot comprehend. They speak quickly in a foreign language that Alice cannot understand, with clipped words that sound similar to Dutch. Alice's body reacts to the man's accent, causing recognition to surge through her. She recognizes the man's voice and peculiar accent. She shuts her eyes and her mind swirls as she tries to recollect something from the previous night with Samuel Granger in the hotel room. Suddenly, a memory sparks in her mind. *The bodyguard*! As if an icy hand grips her heart, fear sets in, tightening and sending an icy shiver down her spine. The air around her feels heavy and the room feels smaller.

The man to her right exclaims, "Alice!" in a voice that booms through the room, causing her to startle in her seat. She can feel the bass trembling in his voice. His words cut through the air like a knife. "What was the motive behind your attempt to kill Mr. Granger?" Alice's heart races as she realizes this man is one of Mr. Granger's bodyguards. She quickly thinks to herself, *That's it! I need to call Samuel.* To calm herself down, she takes a deep breath. She knows answering their questions directly will only lead to more interrogations.

Alice needs to be careful, and speaks softly, trying to mask her fear. "Mind if I smoke, please?"

The man's voice rumbles like thunder. "Go ahead." Alice's clammy hands fumble around in her clutch bag, her fingers trembling as she searches for her vape. Finally, she finds it and slips her hand inside to pull it out. The metallic smell of the vape fills her nostrils as she brings it to her lips. She counts to three, takes a quick puff, followed by a long one, and finishes with two quick puffs. She doesn't inhale the vapor, just releases it in a long stream of white smoke, while she waits.

The blue light on the vape flashes three times, stops, and then flashes two more times. Alice tosses the vape into a corner and leans back, placing her feet against the side of the table. With all her might, she kicks the table, and the two men in front of her drop back. She sinks to her knees, the metal table providing a shield from the surrounding chaos. She braces herself for the loud blast by sticking her fingers in her ears and opening her mouth.

The vape suddenly transforms into a stun grenade, emitting a sharp metallic scent as it detonates with a deafening bang. Alice's heart races in her chest, as a blinding light, brighter than the sun, floods the room. The intense heat from the explosion causes her skin to prickle with sweat, and a sharp ringing in her ears drowns out all other sounds. Terror grips the two men as they scream out in fear, but their cries are futile. The acrid stench of burning metal and gunpowder permeates the air, assaulting Alice's nose with its pungent odor. The sound of glass shattering echoes through the room, sending razor-sharp shards flying in every direction. Alice can feel the shockwaves from the explosion reverberating through her body, leaving her trembling with fear. The interrogation light shattered into pieces after the explosion, leaving the room in complete darkness.

Alice jumps up from her seat and grabs her phone, frantically turning on the flashlight. The harsh smoke fills her nostrils with its pungent odor, making her eyes water. The beam of the flashlight reveals the shattered glass and twisted metal scattered on the floor, reflecting off its surface. Her knees quiver as she takes a step forward, and her heart races with adrenaline. She moves cautiously towards the two incapacitated men, her ears filled with the sound of her uneven breaths. Her stomach churns at the intensity of the scene before her. The men lie motionless, their chests rising and falling with each labored breath. As she approaches them, she notices one man groaning and stirring.

Alice's heart pounds so hard in her chest that she can feel it in her fingertips. Her eyes dart around the room, searching for any sign of escape. She notices a rectangular opening in the wall, where the glass used to be. Perhaps it was a mirror. She drags the metal chair over to the wall, climbs up on it, and removes her headband to wipe away any remaining shards of glass. As she makes her way through the opening, a firm hand seizes her leg and yanks her backwards. She kicks with her other foot, making solid contact, and hears a man howl in pain. As she wriggles free, the man clutches her shoe and wrenches it off. She relinquishes herself to the fall and plunges downward. Her dress snags on a sharp edge of glass, ripping it open on the side. She lands on the floor with a loud thud that knocks the wind out of her.

Alice stands, her head spinning from the fall. She quickly removes her remaining shoe and starts running down the poorly lit corridor. Her bare feet slap against the cold, damp floor, sending shivers down her spine. Suddenly, a loud commotion catches her attention, and she sprints towards it, her heart pounding in her chest. As she reaches a staircase leading down, she listens. A woman's voice echoes from below, urging her to hurry. Alice hears a man screaming in terror, followed by a sickening thud and then an eerie silence. The same female voice speaks again, urging her to follow. Suddenly, a man's voice booms, "Stop right there!" and Alice hears another thud, followed by a cry of agony. Then, she hears a familiar voice call out, "Hera!" Relief washes over her like a tidal wave, and she feels goosebumps rise on her skin. Without hesitation, she races down the stairs towards the voice.

Alice descends the final stair, and catches sight of three women waiting for her on the bottom landing. Their black gear fit them like a glove, emphasizing every curve and muscle. Suddenly, the tallest one tears off her ski mask, revealing a wild mane of wavy brown hair that cascades down her back. The adrenaline in Alice's veins subsides, and the sight of the woman plays out in slow motion in her mind. Her jaw drops open as she stares at the dark-headed goddess in disbelief, taking in the flawless, snow-white complexion of her skin.

"Artemis!" Alice gasps, barely able to believe her eyes. A sly grin spreads across the dark-haired woman's face as she reaches out to take Alice's hand. The touch of her skin sends shivers down Alice's spine, and she follows the deity as she leads her to a door with a bright red exit sign overhead. Alice's heart pounds in her chest as she surveys the scene of motionless bodies lying on the ground, each with a tranquilizer dart protruding from their necks. Soon enough, they emerge into the great outdoors, greeted by the gentle warmth of the sun and a pleasant breeze that playfully tousles their hair. A sleek black sedan pulls up beside them, its brakes screeching to a halt. The earthy scent that emanates from Artemis as she opens the door is invigorating. Alice sinks into the backseat, luxuriating in the feel of the supple leather. The pungent smell of air freshener stings her nostrils as she settles in, her heart racing to the beat of the excitement. Just before disappearing into the city's thrumming pulse, Alice turns her head one last time, meeting Artemis' eyes and offering her a mysterious smile that seems to hold a world of secrets.

The driver expertly navigates the city's veins, while Alice watches the scenery outside the window change into a kaleidoscope of lights and colors. She meets the driver's gaze through the rearview mirror and notices a subtle grin playing on his lips. She follows his gaze and looks over her shoulder, and her eyes light up at the sight of three goddesses on roaring motorcycles following closely behind. They sport shiny black helmets, and the sound of their engines is deafening, yet exhilarating. The leader of the pack revs the engine, pulls up beside the moving car, and darts off ahead, leaving a trail of dust behind. Alice breathes in deeply and feels a sense of calm wash over her as the motorcycles guide them through the bustling city. Overwhelmed with joy, Alice's eyes well up with tears, and a soft sob escapes her lips. The driver gives her an assuring look in the rearview mirror, and she feels the weight of the moment lift. The city rushes past her in a blur of color and light, a fast-forward montage of life. Inside the car, time seems to slow down, stretching each moment into an eternity, and Alice takes it all in, feeling every sensation, grateful for the experience.

Alice confidently strides through the threshold of her home, and the sweet scent of freshly baked cookies wafts through the air, filling her nostrils with a warm and comforting aroma. Her baby doll dress, with a small tear, displays a tantalizing slit, revealing her toned leg and a glimpse of her pink panties. Her tousled hair looks like a bird's nest, and as she runs her fingers through it. She is barefoot, showing off two dirty feet that feel cool against the polished wooden floor. In one hand, she clasps her clutch bag tightly, while the other hand clasps a spare ballet shoe. The sound of her footsteps echoes through the hall, each step echoing with a satisfying thud. As she strides confidently towards the staircase, the sound of her breaths add to the symphony of sounds.

Natalie hurries over and suddenly catches sight of her boss, causing her to gasp in surprise and quickly covers her mouth. "Cher!" she exclaims. "You look like a bomb has hit you!"

Alice rushes up the staircase, a thin smile on her lips as she taunts, "Stun grenade."

With surprise, Natalie's eyes widen as she glances at her watch. She calls after her boss, urging her to hurry. "Only ten minutes until the Holmes couple arrives, cher!"

The sound of the ticking wall clock seems to get louder and louder, making Alice's heart race as she quickly changes into a suitable outfit. She examines herself in the full-length mirror, noting the drastic transformation from a lethal operative to a composed therapist. Now, staring back at her is a polished, urban professional in knee-high socks, a plaid skirt, and a silk blouse. She revels in the luxurious feeling of the soft silk against her skin and the elegant embrace of the socks. She ties her hair back into a sleek, high ponytail and nods approvingly at her reflection in the mirror.

Alice sinks into the plush armchair in her office, feeling its softness envelop her. The doorbell rings and echoes throughout the house. She glances at the clock and sees that there are only three minutes left until the hour. The sweet scent of flowers from the nearby vase fills the air, making her feel calm as she hears Natalie's cheerful voice welcoming the newcomers.

Time seems to slow down as Alice's anticipation builds with each passing second. Finally, the door creaks open, and in walks her new clients. Alice stands and approaches the strangers with a friendly smile. "Hi, guys, my name is Alice. Please take a seat," she gestures towards the couch.

The plump brunette, in her twenties, steps protectively in front of her man, her eyes scanning for any sign of a threat. Her heavy, cloying perfume quickly overpowers the light, sweet smell of lavender that had been lingering in the room. Her cautious approach is obvious in her tense facial expression as she gives Alice's hand a firm shake. "Hello Doctor Alice, my name is Mary," she swiftly jerks her head towards her partner. "And this is Danny. Sit, Danny!"

The tall, skeletal figure with bulging cheekbones and huge, unblinking eyes plops himself down on the old leather couch, the springs creaking loudly with the pressure. Mary's face lights up with a triumphant smile. She takes her place beside her man, and their hands meet in her lap, fingers intertwined.

Alice opens her notepad, the crisp pages rustling under her fingers as she creates two neat columns on the front-page. She glances up at her clients over the top of her glasses, taking in the sight of Mary's fidgeting fingers and Danny's unwavering gaze, his eyes never blinking.

"Welcome to my home," Alice says, her voice warm and inviting. "It's wonderful to have you here with me today. Please tell me a little about yourselves. Something...interesting."

"Like what?" Mary asks, her voice tinged with a slight edge. Her size belies her voice, which sounds more like a little girl's than a grown woman's.

"Like... a story that you would rather not tell someone you've just met," Alice says with conviction.

"Oh, I know!" Mary exclaims, slapping her knee with excitement. The sound echoes in the quiet room. "Me and Danny are children of Jesus." She clenches Danny's hand tightly, and he bobs his head eagerly in acknowledgment, his cheeks glowing a bright pink.

Alice feels her face flush with amusement at the unexpected response. She turns her gaze on Danny, taking in his nervous energy. "And how about you, young man?" she asks, her voice gentle and careful.

Danny's eyes dart nervously to Mary, hoping for some sign of encouragement. His wife nonchalantly shakes her head and shrugs her shoulders.

With his shoulders hunched up to his ears, he admits, "I don't know." His voice is deep and lisping as he explains, "Mary asked me to come and see you."

Alice can sense his discomfort and writes 'henpecked' under his name, and 'domineering' under Mary's name. She looks up at Danny with an expression full of compassion and understanding. "Did Mary ask you to come here, or did you choose to come here on your own?" Her voice is gentle and peaceful.

Danny shoots his wife a glance full of anxiety. She leans in close to him, her arm around his shoulder, and her low, comforting voice a soft murmur. The scent of her blooming aromatics perfume wafts through the air. "Danny, can you explain to the kind lady doctor why you need to talk to her? I've got your back."

"No!" Danny barks and looks at his feet. The word hits Alice like a sharp dart, piercing her ears.

A rhythmic tap on the door interrupts the tense silence, and in comes Natalie with a tray of steaming beverages. As she walks, the sound of the tray clattering echoes through the room. With a start, the couple shifts their gaze toward the intruder, distrust clear in their eyes. The tension in their faces disappears when they realize Natalie is harmless. Mary grins and gives Natalie a friendly nod. Danny leaps up, takes the tray from Natalie and holds it in front of Alice.

"Danny, these treats are meant for you and Mary," Alice says, declining the tray he offers. "Can you place it on the coffee table, please?" She can feel the warmth of the tray as Danny puts it on the low coffee table.

Natalie looks at the young couple with a heartwarming smile. "Good morning, folks, my name is Natalie, and I am Alice's assistant," she points at the selection of items on the tray. The smell of freshly brewed coffee fills the room. "Decaf, filtered coffee, apple juice, orange juice, warm milk, cold milk, and—chocolate chip cookies—they be the death of me." She chuckles, her positive vibes fill the room, diffusing the tension.

Disappointment clouds Danny's face as he lifts his gaze to Natalie, droopy eyed. "Morning, Miss Natalie, may I have—"

"Danny! She is not a miss, she is a missus," Mary interrupts, jabbing him with her elbow.

"Sorry, Missus Natalie, may I please have a Coca-Cola?" Danny asks, owl eyed. The sound of his voice is soft and timid.

An endearing smile crosses Natalie's face, and she bobs her head. "Of course, Danny. Be right back with your soda." The sound of her footsteps as she walks out of the room is almost imperceptible.

Alice scribbles a few lines of personal notes while she waits for Mary to pour her coffee, the teaspoon clinking against the cup. The aroma of freshly brewed coffee fills the air, sending a ripple of excitement throughout the room.

The door flies open and Natalie strides in, whistling a merry tune, and places Danny's Coca-Cola on the tray, cold dewdrops trickling down the sides.

Danny's face lights up. "Thank you, Missus Natalie," he cries out, pouring his cola into a glass, his saucer eyes never leaving Alice. The foam billows and bubbles, overflowing the glass and pooling on the tray.

"Look what you're doing Danny boy!" Marcy exclaims, quickly snatching the cola can from his hand and giving him a sharp slap on the wrist. Danny shakes his head, trying to clear his salacious thoughts. His face contorting into a sad expression, he stares bug-eyed at his wife, tears streaming from the corners of his eyes before he lets out a heart-wrenching sob.

Danny wipes his nose with the back of his hand. "I am so sorry, Mary!" he says, his voice choked with emotion, and hastily rubs the moisture from his hand onto his blazer.

Alice feels guilt wrapping around her conscience. She reaches for a box of tissues on her desk and places it gently on Danny's lap. "It's okay, Danny," she reassures him. "everyone makes mistakes."

Danny takes a deep, shaky sniff and stares at Alice, his eyes glistening with tears. Mary challenges Alice with a how-do-you-dare look, her eyes ice-cold.

Alice flinches at Mary's expression, her eyes darting to her watch before she can steel herself and face the skeletal figure with the glossy eyes. "Danny, why did you want to come and see me?"

Danny takes a long swig of the cola, releasing a pleasant fizz as he exhales. He traces the patterns in the carpet with his eyes, his gaze never leaving them. "Mary says I must come and ask you to help us fix our marriage, because Mary says I broke our relation—"

"Actually, Danny," Mary interjects, "I want to clarify something. I never accused you of breaking our relationship. What I said is that you broke your vows."

"Sorry, Mary," Danny says in a dull monotone voice, tracing the patterns on the carpet.

"You can call it anything you like, Danny. What did you do to break your relationship with Mary?" Alice asks, her voice like a gentle breeze.

Danny's face lights up with a rosy flush, and he casts a worried look at his wife. She pays him no mind, not even a glance.

"It's okay Danny. If you had the chance to reset your life to any moment before this one, when would you choose?" Alice asks kindly, her words dripping with sweetness.

Relief spreads across Danny's face, and he lifts his head to meet his therapist's gaze with newfound confidence. "To the Friday before I hurt Mary."

"So, let me get this straight. You hurt Mary on a Saturday?" Alice asks. "Something terrible must have happened that day," she says in a tranquil voice, like a lullaby.

"Yes!" Danny exclaims, his voice loud and excited as he jumps up from his seat. The sound of his feet hitting the floor echoes through the room. "It was only me and Elise-Marie working on the floor that day," he continues, his eyes sparkling with mischief. "I could smell her perfume. It was sweet and floral, like roses and honey," closing his eyes as he remembers the sweet memory of her perfume, and smiles. "She always flashes me her boobies!" He grins widely, his teeth gleaming in the light. "She grabs my hand and leads me to the bathroom. I can hear the lock click as she closes the door behind us. Then she kisses me everywhere," he says, his hands moving animatedly to emphasize his words. He points to his crotch. "Not even Mary kisses me there. It tickles. Brr," he shivers, his body convulsing subtly, as if seized by an invisible cold. His lisp becomes more pronounced as he speaks with enthusiasm. It's like he's conducting an orchestra with his tongue.

Alice leaps up and storms out, her laughter reverberating through the room in a loud guffaw, before covering her mouth to muffle the sound. Natalie glances up from her desk, her finger pressed against her lips in a signal to Alice to be quiet.

With a deep breath, Alice steps into her office, where the sound of her clients' lively conversation fills the room. She snuggles into her chair, feeling the warmth of the fabric against her skin, and puts on a straight face, trying her best to bluff like a poker pro. "Apologies for the interruption, Danny," she says smoothly, seamlessly transitioning back into the conversation. "What happened next?"

Danny stands, mouth agape, with his arms outstretched as though he were a gunslinger about to draw his pistols. "I pull up my pants and run home to tell Mary everything." He gazes off into the distance, his brow furrowed in thought, and then suddenly a smile brightens his face. "The next day Mr. Oliver asked me why I left the factory, so I told him I was very sick, I had the runs. He docks a day's pay. Mary was furious."

Alice's lips twitch into a faint smile as she scribbles down a few notes on her notepad. "Thank you, Danny. You are doing well. What happened to—"

A clamor coming from the entrance hallway startles Alice, and she wrinkles her brow and tilts her head to make out the conversation. Natalie protests vehemently, her objections rising louder and louder as the woman screeches. Alice furrows her brow, trying to place the familiar sound of the voice.

The office door flies open, and in storms Madison Granger, her eyes blazing with rage. "You call yourself a marriage counselor, but you are married to a gay man!" she lets out a piercing shriek and slams a brown envelope onto the cocobolo desk with a reverberating thud. Mary and Danny gape at the furious woman, who looks like she could rip them apart. Danny quickly hides behind his chubby spouse, hoping she can shield him from the wrath.

Madison's eyes bore into Alice, the intensity of her gaze radiating anger and venom. "My husband told me you no longer wish to see us, and frankly, I have no desire to know how or where he got that information from you!" Madison's voice reverberates through the room, causing Alice's ears to sting. "You can expect a call from my attorney this afternoon. Answer it and follow his instructions, or I will air your dirty laundry out for the world to see."

With a single, accusatory finger, she points towards the brown envelope resting on the desk, her nail catching the glimmer of the fluorescent light. A wicked smile spreads across her face as she notices the two young individuals seated on the couch, Danny hiding timidly behind his plump wife. Her finger moves slowly from the envelope to the couple, and her face twists into a menacing expression. "You must run for your lives!" she exclaims. "This woman can tear apart your marriage!" Her shrill cry echoes as her finger shifts its focus towards Alice. In a flurry of movement, she whirls around and storms out. She leaves behind a lingering trail of sickly sweet perfume that fills the room.

Alice hears Sparky's paws pounding against the steps as he rushes down to bark ferociously at Madison Granger. "Oh, be quiet, you flea-infested pest!" Madison screeches. The dog retreats, yelping meekly, and scurries up the stairs, his toenails tapping a hasty melody on the wooden floor. Alice strains to hear James and Natalie's conversation as they speak softly behind the closed door. His voice, soft and reassuring, offers comfort in the storm's wake. Their conversation ends, and Natalie shuffles into the room, her lips pursed in a solemn frown. Alice raises her hand, a stern signal for no entry. Natalie nods her head in agreement, walks out, the door closing with a soft click behind her.

With his eyes fixed on Alice, Danny slowly emerges from behind his wife, exclaiming in his signature lisp, "Holy cow, that woman is crazy!" His voice trembles slightly as he asks, "Doctor Alice, why is she angry with you?"

Even with an immense struggle, Alice pulls up a plastic smile and tries to focus on the moment. "I may not talk about it with you, Danny, but if I could, I certainly would."

Mary takes a deep breath and raises her eyebrows in curiosity. "I bet her husband hates her," she says. "It seems like he wants to leave her, and from what I can tell, he's quite wealthy. I can almost smell it."

Alice's eyes widen with surprise. "Good guess, Mary!" She smiles warmly at Mary. "How did Danny's actions affect you, and how does it make you feel?"

Mary squints and shrinks away as the spotlight moves to her. "I was furious. I telephoned my mama, and she offered to cover our expenses for coming to see you. She said the Internet search showed you're the top head doctor." She gazes lovingly at her husband and intertwines her fingers with his. "Please help us. I want to forgive my husband, but my heart—"

"I want to have a sexy time with my wife again!" Danny exclaims, interrupting their conversation and letting out a joyous howl. He then embraces his wife tightly, burying his head into her chest.

Alice feels a peaceful warmth in her chest as the couple's honest words ring like a gentle harp. Glancing at her watch, she realizes with a start that the session has run over its allotted time. "Please give me a moment." She strides purposefully towards her desk, her heels clicking ominously against the cold floor. She flips open her laptop, the blue light washing over her face, casting deep, foreboding shadows. Her fingers fly over the keyboard, seeking the elusive document she needs. She hit the print button with a determined jab, but the printer stayed silent, mocking her efforts. Alice grits her teeth and gives the printer a hostile look.

Danny's eyes widen in surprise as he takes in the sight of Alice's obvious distress. "What's wrong, Doctor Alice?" he stammers, his voice barely more than a whisper.

With a heavy sigh, Alice buries her face in her hands. Her muffled words barely reach Danny's ears. "The damned printer won't print."

"I can check it for you," Danny offers quickly, eager to help. "At work, Mr. Oliver always calls me when his computer acts up."

Alice makes way for him, and he settles into her chair. His fingers move rapidly over the mouse, the pointer darting across the screen like a trapped bird. With a triumphant grin, he flicks a switch. The printer whirs to life, spitting out a stack of pages as steam rises from the machine. The metallic scent of the toner mingles with the faint essence of warmth and singed paper, infusing the air with an industrial aroma.

Alice throws her hands in the air, her face lighting up. "You're a lifesaver, Danny!" she exclaims, pulling him into a grateful hug. Her heart races as she meets Mary's gaze and sees the jealousy burning in her eyes. Danny's cheeks flush ruby red, and he settles into the soft leather couch beside his wife, basking in the glow of Alice's gratitude.

Alice separates the printed stack into two neat piles, slides them into crisp envelopes, and carefully writes 'Danny' on one and 'Mary' on the other. She can see the excitement in their eyes as she hands them their envelopes. "Inside the envelopes, you will find a couple's exercise," she says. "It's a fun and exciting activity that can be very rewarding if you complete all the activities together as a couple."

With tears in his eyes, Danny eagerly raises his hand like a school kid and asks, "But won't we have the chance to see you again?"

Alice reassures Danny with a warm smile, "Don't worry, Danny, I was getting to that. Just make sure you answer all the questions on the questionnaire. Then when you come back to see me, we will go through it together. Alright?"

"When?" Danny asks, his voice rising with anticipation.

Alice's gentle and reassuring voice flows like a whisper of a summer breeze as she says, "Natalie can assist you with that." However, she suggests waiting for at least a month before meeting again.

Danny jumps with joy and wraps his arms around Alice, his broad smile radiating warmth. "Thank you, Doctor Alice!"

Natalie watches as Alice leads the couple to her desk, their animated conversation filling the air with excitement. With a smile, Alice greets her assistant. "Hi Nat, could you lend a hand to Danny and Mary by scheduling an appointment for them next month? I'm doing this pro bono."

Mary and Danny stare at Alice with wide eyes, their brows furrowed in confusion. "Who is bro boner?" Danny asks, his voice cracks with shyness.

With a kind smile spreading across her face, Natalie stifles her laughter, and her cheeks redden. She explains to Danny, "Pro bono means Doctor Laurier will not charge you for her time. It means it's free."

Danny's and Mary's faces fill with palpable excitement as they stare at each other in disbelief. "Thank you, Doctor Alice," they say in unison. Overcome with joy, Mary lets out an excited squeal as she wraps Alice in a tight hug. "We'll spread your kindness to those who need it," Mary adds with gratitude.

Alice smiles as the hug comes to an end. "It is my pleasure," she says, and then bids them farewell. "Bye guys, and remember to do your homework." With each step, her heels echo off the hard flooring as she makes her way to her office, her departure reluctant.

The sight of the large brown envelope lying on her desk fills Alice with a sense of foreboding. Slowly, she slides her finger under the flap, ripping it open and spilling the contents onto her desk. She gapes at the folded letter and quickly scoops it up, ripping it open to read, her hands shaking. Her heart races with anticipation, and she listens as Natalie greets and sees the clients out. After they exchange repeated "hallelujah", "amen sister" and "God bless you", the front door slams shut with a loud thud.

"Natalie strolls into the office, humming a merry tune that fills the air. She turns off the diffuser, and the scent of lavender gradually fades. After feeding the fish and tidying up, she bids her farewell. 'Goodnight ma darling, see ya in the mornin.'"

"Goodnight, Nat, and thanks for all your help today. Can you give the IT expert a call tomorrow and ask him to come and check out my laptop and printer?" Alice murmurs, her gaze never wavering from the letter.

"Sure boss, see you in the mornin', cher." As she walks out, her steps resound heavily on the creaky wooden flooring, and the heavy front door slams shut behind her.

With a frown, Alice reads the menacing letter. Her eyes widen as she reads the signature at the bottom of the letter, Robert Quillen. The ground beneath her feet seems to whirl around her as her world spins out of control. She can hear her heart pounding in her ears, the sound reverberating through her chest.

With an expression of intense concentration, she reads the letter once more. It details James' involvement with a man, one of Madison's goons. The man confesses to a gay relationship with James, their times together, and that he is aware of the fact James is married to a woman called Alice Laurier, a respected marriage counseling therapist.

Alice hears a faint buzzing coming from her phone, vibrating against the wooden flooring upstairs. Her steps gallop and echo through the quiet house as she bounds up the stairs, skipping every other step. On the top landing, she darts left and rushes into her bedroom, throwing herself onto the soft bed to answer the phone. Sparky chases after Alice, barking happily in anticipation of a game, and as he humps onto the bed, his tail wags in delight.

With a swift movement, Alice hits the answer button and lifts the phone to her ear. Her voice is calm and collected as she greets the caller. "Hello, Alice speaking."

"Good afternoon, Dr. Loo-Rear. My name is Riley Pierce, and Madison Granger informed me you were expecting my call," the caller utters, his words flowing out of his mouth with a sense of self-assurance and confidence, as smooth as butter.

Alice sharply corrects the cocky man on the other end of the line, her eyes closed as she pictures his face. "It's Laurier. What do you want?" she retorts. The sound of his strained breathing reverberates through the phone speaker, making her shiver with a sudden chill.

"Now, now, no need for hostility, doctor. We have a proposition for you." There's a pause, then the distinct sound of him biting into something, the crunch echoing eerily through the phone line. Sparky's fur bristles along his back as he fixes his gaze on the phone. His head sways slowly from side to side in a silent rhythm, punctuated by the low, rumbling growl vibrating deep within his throat.

"Madison said so." Alice enunciates Madison's name with a hint of encouragement as she says, "Carry on." She puts the phone on speakerphone, slides her feet out of her shoes, and massages her aching soles.

"I assume you have read the letter?" The sound of his chewing punctuates his words, and he breathes in.

"Yes, what a startling revelation." She says, her voice dripping with sarcasm.

"I am glad to hear you get the idea," he says, biting and chewing. "The court clerk tells me you have not submitted your psychological evaluation report on the Granger's yet?" He takes a sharp breath.

Alice confirms with a steady and unyielding voice, "Correct."

Riley Pierce responds with a deep, mischievous chuckle. "Music to my ears. Assuming my plan succeeds, this is how the pieces will fall into place. We will schedule three to four more appointments with the Granger's, but we'll keep your report confidential." Taking a pause, he inhales deeply. Alice's silence speaks volumes, daring him to follow through on his words. "Doctor, do you have a pen and paper on your person?" His approach is to suggest, not to ask.

Alice's tone is brusque and to the point. "I need a moment to get a pen and paper." Running downstairs, she hurriedly opens a drawer to extract a notepad and grabs a pen before dashing back upstairs to her bedroom. Sparky sits on the bed, glaring at the phone with a look of pure disdain. She plops down on the bed, causing the mattress to bounce slightly. "Go ahead," she says, her voice echoing into the empty room.

Riley Pierce clears his throat, signaling that he is about to speak. The phone falls silent, waiting for him to begin. "Write this down on your newly gained paper," he instructs. "Madison Granger may have a moral reason for divorcing her husband. This could be because of her husband's infidelity, abuse, or dishonesty in their marriage. Alternatively, it could be because of a fundamental difference in values or beliefs that they cannot reconcile. If her husband's actions are causing harm to herself, she may feel morally obligated to end the marriage. Did you get that, doctor?"

Alice responds with a simple "Yes," and shifts her attention to her nails instead of writing what he says.

"Before submitting your final report to the court, make sure to choose a persuasive rationale." Riley's advice flows effortlessly, with the eloquence of a seasoned attorney. "The goal is to sway the jury in favor of Mrs. Granger, but I'm confident you've already deduced that."

Alice closes her eyes and recalls the recent evening she spent with Samuel Granger. Tears threaten to spill over as she asks the attorney, "And what benefits do I reap from this intentional and illegal act of treachery?" Uncertain, she bites her lip while speaking.

With a tone dripping with sarcasm, the attorney scoffs and reminds Alice, "You saw the incriminating letter from your husband's dearest friend with your own eyes." He then reassures her, "I promise you, we will eradicate the evidence." Alice remains silent, her lips pressed tightly together.

Her lack of response prompts him to keep talking. "Doctor," he says, "Are you still awake and alert, or have you had a heart attack and collapsed to the ground?"

"I'm here," Alice says, her voice tinged with irritation.

"Good," he responds, before hanging up. "Now set the gears into motion."

Alice curiously gazes at the phone. Sparky wags his tail, his excited yaps echoing through the silent room. Gently tapping him on the nose, she leans in and whispers, "Mommy is in big trouble." Realizing the urgency of the situation, she continues, "We need to talk to your daddy about this right away. Let's go find him."

Alice walks down the dimly lit corridor, her footsteps echoing off the walls. Sparky follows closely behind, his nails clicking against the wooden floor. She reaches her husband's office and peeks inside but finds it empty. Her eyes scan the room, taking in the sight of the neatly arranged desk and shelves filled with books. The scent of his aftershave fills her senses, causing her heart to flutter with excitement.

With a sense of dread, Alice slowly opens her husband's bedroom door, the sound of the creaking wood echoing through the silent room. It reveals an empty room bathed in the soft glow of the bedside lamp. The neatly made bed and the smell of freshly laundered sheets strike her immediately. Her voice cuts through the silence as she calls out her husband's name. There is no answer, only the soft hum of the ceiling fan spinning above, its blades slicing through the stillness like a phantom dancer.

Alice ascends the steep staircase to the landing, her hand trailing along the smooth wooden banister. Her voice echoes through the house as she calls out to her husband. The sound of her own voice reverberates in her ears, and the eerie silence sends a chill down her spine. At the top of the stairs, she gazes down the empty hallway, the only sound accompanying her being the rhythmic panting of her dog at her side.

Alice trudges back to her bedroom, her shoulders slumped with disappointment. She sinks down onto the edge of the bed, feeling the soft cotton sheets rustling beneath her. Sparky jumps onto the bed, and she feels his warm breath on her skin as he rests his head on her lap. She runs her fingers through his soft fur, feeling the velvety texture beneath her fingertips. Her fingers tap against the smooth screen of her phone as she dials her husband's number. The sound of the ring tone echoes in her ear until she hears the distinctive beep of the voicemail. With a deep sigh, she leaves a message. "Hey honey, please call me when you get this. Miss you."

Alice tosses her phone on the bed, and it rings immediately, the loud tune reverberating through the once quiet room. The screen flickers to life, and Karen's face emerges from the darkness. Her doe eyes, wide and luminous, catch the light in a way that feels almost ethereal. The platinum blonde of her hair, vibrant and radiant, shines like a vast field of sunflowers under the golden afternoon sun. But beneath her striking features, there's an undeniable hint of mystery—a secret hidden just out of sight, adding a layer of intrigue to her captivating beauty. Alice's face lights up with relief, and tears well up in her eyes. She taps the answer button and presses the speakerphone button with caution, careful not to wake Sparky, who is sound asleep on her lap. "Hey bestie," Alice says, her voice trembling with emotion, "It's fantastic to hear your voice." A feeling of warmth spreads through her chest.

"Hey Spid, is everything okay?" Karen asks, her voice laced with concern. "I am on my way to the gym. Want to hook up for a bouldering session?" The sound of her voice is soft and soothing, like the gentle rustle of leaves in the wind. The simple act of kindness unlocks the floodgates of pent-up emotions. Tears well up in Alice's eyes, a complex mix of relief, gratitude, and overwhelming sentiment. "Spid, are you there?" Karen asks, noticing her best friend's silence.

Alice finds it difficult to speak with the lump in her throat, and her voice quivers as she tries. "Yes," she says, "a workout is exactly what I need right now." Her voice trembles with the weight of sadness.

Karen's response is immediate. "Pack your swimsuit. See you at the gym in thirty." And with that, she hangs up.

Alice tilts her head, puzzled, wondering why she needs to pack her swimsuit. She tosses her phone on the bed, stands up, and disturbs Sparky, who was sleeping soundly on her lap. He stretches his legs and jumps to the floor, his paws sinking into the plush carpet, and lets out a soft yawn. Alice freshens up and dons her gym outfit; a blue tank-top, snug graphic color black leggings, and a turquoise fleece jacket. The soft fabric of her clothes feels comfortable against her skin.

With a sense of urgency, Alice quickly stuffs her one-piece swimsuit, towel, and cosmetics into her sports bag before rushing down the stairs. She takes a pen and a paper from her office, and scribbles a note for James to call her.

"Bye Sparky!" She calls out and walks out, glides down the stairs, and follows the sidewalk while she hails a cab. A passerby raises his eyebrows at the sight of her in a snug gym outfit. The sound of cars honking and people chatting fills the air. Brakes squeaking, a cab pulls up beside her. She gets in and listens to the wolf whistles fading as she closes the door.

With a glance in the rearview mirror, the cab driver raises an eyebrow at Alice. "So, where can I take you this fine evening?" The cab smells of air freshener, with a hint of cigarette smoke. Alice sinks into the seat, feeling grateful for the relief of the cool air conditioning.

"Skyline Athletics Club, Madison Avenue," she says with a plastic smile as she meets his sultry gaze in the rearview mirror. The cabbie revs the engine, aiming the nose at a gap in the traffic, and hits the gas, jolting into the far right-hand lane. The sound of the engine fills the cab, drowning out the noise of the city.

He navigates the city's veins with ease, honking and passing hand signals at other drivers. In fewer than ten minutes, the cab stops in front of the gym, brakes squeaking.

Alice fumbles for her wallet and hands the cash to the driver before bounding up the stairs. The scent of sweat and chlorine permeates the air as she enters the gym. She presents her gym membership card. The reader beeps, and she proceeds through the turnstile, the metal gears clicking and locking behind her.

Alice's sneakers squeak on the polished floor as she walks towards the locker rooms, the sound echoing through the space. Suddenly, a piercing scream shatters the stillness, causing her heart to race. She stops dead in her tracks, her pulse pounding in her ears. Karen runs towards her, panting and her cheeks flushed, like she had just run a marathon. Alice can smell the faint scent of perfume wafting off Karen as she gasps for breath.

"Spid, hey! Spid!" Karen exclaims, her voice full of excitement. Her eyes wander over Alice's form, taking in the snug fit of her gym clothes. "Just look at you! Snug as a bug", she exclaims, and leans in close, "give me a kiss," she teases, her lips puckered and her breath hot against Alice's mouth.

Alice's eyes frantically scan her surroundings in embarrassment as she steps back, taking in Karen's appearance. "Not bad for a giraffe who tries to get into a camel-only club," she counters, her voice echoing off the tiled walls.

Karen gasps, moves her shiny sports glasses to her head, and poses in a boxing stance with her fists clenched. "You wanna fight me?" she retorts with a smirk on her face, "get over here and take it, you biatch," she chuckles, playfully punching Alice's shoulder.

Alice puts on a show of fear, gasping theatrically and widening her eyes in shock. With a loud smack, she playfully hits Karen on her rear, making a dull thud. Her heart pounding, she rushes towards the changing room, seeking solace from Karen's teasing. Karen gives chase, her footsteps pounding against the tiled floor, trailing a short distance behind. Alice shrieks as she looks over her shoulder, spotting Karen short on her heels. She swerves and runs around the set of lockers lining the center of the changing room. She skillfully weaves her way through the crowds until Karen loses sight of her.

Alice's heart races as she frantically scans the changing room, her eyes darting back and forth until she finally spots her friend sprinting through a crowd of women in fluffy towels. As Karen walks ahead, she fails to notice her friend sneaking up behind her. With a mischievous grin, Alice tiptoes up and jabs her fingers into Karen's ribcage. "Boo-ya!" she exclaims playfully. Karen's ear-piercing screech echoes through the room, causing the onlookers to jump in surprise.

Impersonating an angry teacher, Karen wags a finger at the onlookers. "Ha! You think you can take me on?" She exclaims with a playful challenge in her eyes, resting her hands on her sides. One woman's eyes twinkle with mischief as she peels off her towel, revealing a toned and athletic gym body. Her grin widens as she twists the towel in her hand, forming a tight coil.

With a swift, calculated flick of her wrist, she sends it hurtling towards Karen. The towel connects with Karen's side, releasing an ear-splitting snap that echoes around them. Karen winces and lets out a sharp cry of pain as a stinging sensation spreads through her side. A chorus of "Ouch" erupts from the group of bystanders, their voices in perfect harmony.

With a firm grip on the towel's end, Karen reels the girl in, planting a wet kiss on her lips. The resounding clapping of the onlookers reverberates off the changing room walls as they cheer for Karen's courageous act. Karen beams with excitement as she revels in the thunderous applause of the crowd. She gracefully bows, blowing kisses to her adoring fans.

Alice's eyes widen in amazement as she watches her friend's antics, and she quickly turns to leave. Karen blows her new friends a kiss goodbye and trails Alice to her locker room. "You're amazing, I swear," says Alice, opening her locker and tossing her sports bag inside. The air thickens with the sweet, heady aroma of hairspray and perfume as more women filter into the changing room, their voices blending into a chaotic symphony of chatter and giggles.

Jealous stares bore into Alice and Karen as they approach the daunting climbing wall at the back of the gym. The towering edifice looms over them, its surface rough and challenging. A shiver of anticipation runs down Alice's spine, her heart pounding like a drum in her chest. She stacks their crash pads at the fall zone near the bottom of the vertical rock-face and faces her friend. Suddenly, Karen turns to her, her eyes gleaming with a mischievous spark. "Race you to the top," she teases, a playful grin tugging at the corners of her mouth. Before Alice can respond, Karen starts her ascent, her lithe form moving with grace and agility.

Alice watches Karen for a moment, her breath hitching in her throat. Then, spurred on by Karen's challenge, she plugs in her earphones, and starts her own climb. The rough texture of the rock beneath her fingers sends tingles up her arm.. Her focus is entirely on Karen, who is now several feet above her, her limbs stretching to find purchase on the rough surface of the rock face. The spirit of competition wound its fingers around Alice's determination, spurring her into action. She pumps her arms and legs with willpower, eager to match and even surpass her friend's pace.

The music's upbeat tempo resonates through Alice, encouraging her to keep pace with Karen's synchronized movements. Just as she is about to reach her friend, Karen slips. Her scream pierces the air, causing a hush to fall over the gym. Before anyone can react, Karen regains her balance and lets out a chuckle, brushing off the incident with a cheeky wink. The crowd erupts into applause, and Alice can't help but smile at her friend's audacity.

Their playful competition continues, their rivalry fueling their determination. As the first one to reach the top, Alice slams a palm against the rough surface and calls out, "Off belay!" The sound echoes across the gym, bouncing off the surrounding walls. The thunderous applause from the onlookers reverberates through her body, easing the pain in her muscles. She looks down and spots Karen scanning the rock face for a route to the summit. A defeated expression crosses Karen's face, and she calls out to Alice. "Beta?"

Alice has a clear view of the holds, she scans the surface, and spots a route. "Jug, One-o'clock high, pocket, ten-o'clock low. Send it!" Her voice is firm and clear, cutting through the noise of the spectators gathered at the bottom of the climb. Their synchronized clapping echoes through the gym, urging Karen upwards as they chant, "go, go, go" in perfect unison.

The crowd's chanting sparks her determination, and Karen's eyes light up as she looks towards the holds. Her eyes squint, and she clenches her jaw, bracing herself for the jump. Taking a deep breath, she leaps forward, her eyes filled with unwavering determination. Her fingers barely graze the hold, and she loses her grip, plummeting towards the crash pads below. As her body hits the crash pads, the sound echoes throughout the gym. With a collective gasp, the bystanders hurry to her side.

Alice's piercing scream echoes through the air as her friend falls to the ground. She feels the adrenaline rush through her body as she watches her best friend's misfortune unfold before her eyes. With each step down the rock face, she feels the weight of her body against the rough surface. Just before she reaches the ground, she releases her grip and lands flat on her back, next to her friend. The sensation of the soft pad beneath her back is a welcome relief after the rough texture of the rock.

With a swift motion, she jumps up and kneels beside Karen. "What a whipper!" she exclaims. "Are you okay?" The scent of sweat mixed with sweet perfume fills her nostrils as she leans in closer to her friend.

"I'm fine,." Karen says, taking deep breaths to recover. Alice reaches out and helps her up, pulling her into a warm embrace. The sensation of her friend's body against hers is comforting, and she feels a sense of relief wash over her. The bystanders cheer and applaud loudly, creating a boisterous chorus. Karen turns to face them, gracefully bows, and blows them kisses.

Alice wraps her arm around her friend's shoulder and steers her to the changing room amidst rowdy cheers and applause. "That is exactly why I love you, my bestie," she says with a smile. "You nearly kicked the bucket, but you turn it into a joke."

"And I love you too, Spid," Karen says, her voice overflowing with affection.

Alice unzips her sports bag and takes out a fluffy towel and cosmetics bag. With a reassuring presence, Karen places her hand on Alice's shoulder and whispers, "Hold on, I have a plan." She grins impishly and suggests, "Get your swimsuit on." Alice scowls quizzically at her friend before rummaging through her bag for her swimsuit.

They step out of the changing room, their towels draped over their shoulders. Alice wears a sleek black one-piece that hugs her curves, while Karen rocks a fiery red swimsuit that accentuates her figure. They make their way to the pool amidst a ripple of playful cheers. The scent of chlorine lingers in the air, mixing with the warm gym air. A lifeguard, perched high above, takes notice of their captivating appearances and nearly tumbles from his post. The rough, textured concrete of the pool deck is a stark contrast to the cool, refreshing water that beckons them closer.

Karen smiles warmly as she takes Alice's hand, leading her towards the diving boards at the edge of the pool. They reach the bottom of the winding staircase that leads up to the diving platforms. A stark safety sign, with the words 'Dive At Own Risk', incised in red letters on a white background, covers the small metal gate, signaling a potential hazard. Their determination blinds them to the warning sign at the bottom of the plaque that reads 'Members Only' and the additional caution 'No Unauthorized Access to Diving Platforms'. Despite this, they forge ahead.

Karen drapes their towels over the railing. She tries the gate; it is open. They look up and spot a young female athlete with a toned and athletic body executing a tricky synchronized diving routine from the five-meter platform.

The young diver's body twists and turns, making a loud slapping sound as she hits the water face first, causing Alice and Karen to wince. Emerging from the water, the diver's teammates and coach's cheers fill the air, but she winces in pain, her smile not reaching her eyes. With a round of applause for the young diver, Karen leads the way up the stairs. Alice's stomach twists in knots, and she hesitates before following her friend up the metal staircase.

Alice's eyes draw level with her friend's peachy bottom, snug in the fiery red swimsuit. Each step accentuates the graceful curvature of Karen's backside, adding a touch of allure to her movements. They pass the sign of the five-meter board, heading for the top. Alice's breaths come in quick gasps as her heart races with every step she takes. They finally make it to the ten-meter platform, and Alice feels a chill run down her spine as she's hit by a gust of cold air, setting off a trail of goosebumps that cover her skin. Her eyes never leave the surface as she takes her friend's hand and shuffles to the edge of the platform, her knees weak with fear. Alice peeks over the edge, her eyes fixed on the people frolicking in the blue pool below.

An unexpected wave of dizziness sweeps over her, and her heart hammers in her chest, its rhythm erratic and wild. She gasps, her voice trembling with fear, and asks. "What are we doing?" She stands there, transfixed on the pool below, not daring to look away.

With an endearing smile, Karen reassures her friend, giving her the strength she needs to confront the challenge ahead. "I heard you were feeling off when I called," she says in a gentle tone. "But don't worry, this will help you face your fears." She gives Alice's hand a reassuring squeeze and softly asks, "Are you ready?" Alice nods silently, her eyes fixed on the pool below as she shuffles to the edge of the diving board, toes curling over the edge.

Karen's grip on her best friend's hand tightens as they prepare to take the plunge. "Don't worry, you can do it," she says with a reassuring smile. "I am going to count to three. One...Two..." Alice squeezes her eyes tightly shut and takes a deep breath.

"Three!" Karen's voice echoes through the silence, bouncing off the walls. Alice's scream echoes through the air as they leap, a blend of both terror and excitement. The butterflies in her stomach flutter wildly with the rush of adrenaline. The air against her skin is a thrilling contrast to the impending splash. They hit the water, creating an eruption of waves that ripple across the pool's surface. Slicing through the refreshingly cool liquid, they descend towards the pool's bottom, embraced by an eerie silence. Alice kicks off, her strength sending her rocketing back to the surface. Gasping for air, she breaks free from the water, frantically scanning the area for Karen. She spots her friend surfacing nearby, a triumphant cheer escaping her lips. The crowd's deafening roar washes over them, bringing a victorious smile to Alice's face. They raise their arms in gratitude, feeling the cool water splash against their skin as they paddle towards the pool's edge, basking in the deafening cheers of the crowd.

The spectators cheer them on as they climb out of the pool, dripping wet and grinning from ear to ear. Alice's face lit up with a big smile as she basked in the warm compliments and praises. She relishes the feel of the soft, fluffy towel as she dries herself off. Karen speaks passionately to the group of worshipers, gesturing wildly with her arms to emphasize her words.

The piercing sound of a security guard's whistle jolts Alice and Karen into alertness. Alice's heart races as she whirls around, searching for the source of the sudden noise. Alice and Karen's footsteps falter as they catch sight of a group of security guards approaching. The guards' whistles blare and their voices shout, "Hey you!" while gesturing towards them. Alice's eyes widen in surprise as she realizes they are the ones being called out.

She looks at her friend with a questioning expression, silently asking for an explanation. Karen's mischievous grin widens as she shrugs, and suddenly she twirls around and bolts for the exit. Alice races after her, her breath coming in gasps as she tries to keep up.

Alice and her companion are running through the crowded gym, the sounds of the guards' footsteps echoing behind them. One guard sprints towards them and reaches out, his fingers closing around the fabric of Karen's towel. Karen lets out a high-pitched scream and darts off in a different direction, leaving her towel behind.

Alice follows her friend into the changing rooms, abruptly halting just inside the entrance. Karen whirls around to face the guards, hands on her hips, and breaks into a victory dance, singing "U Can't Touch This" by M.C. Hammer. Alice joins in, their voices harmonizing perfectly as they dance to the beat. A group of onlookers forms a tight cluster around them, clapping their hands in perfect unison with the singing. The sound of their exuberant cheering and clapping reverberates off the walls, fueling the anger of the already incensed guards.

A plump guard finally arrives, panting and sweating, and joins his colleagues, who are already on the scene. He blows his whistle frantically, and the sharp, ear-piercing sound echoes through the area. The guards ogle the beautiful woman before them, their faces red with excitement. One guard, his face flushed with anger, regains his composure and addresses Karen. "Ma'am, you did not have the authority to use the diving boards."

Karen turns around and sways her hips, daring the guards with the curve of her backside. "Catch me if you can!" she exclaims, her voice echoing off the walls. The onlookers burst into laughter, teasing the guards. The sound of whistles, laughter, and cheering fills the air, creating a chaotic and exciting atmosphere.

In response to the taunting, a guard becomes visibly angry and pulls out his taser, pointing it menacingly at the crowd. The onlookers jump back in fear, hands raised in surrender. A tense silence hangs in the air as everyone stands still, waiting anxiously for the guard's next move. Suddenly, he fires a warning shot, shattering the silence. The taser crackles as its prongs deploy with a swift and serpentine motion. A metallic tang of electricity fills the air as the prongs strike an onlooker's back. With a piercing scream, the man throws his arm up dramatically before collapsing to his knees. The crowd scrambles in disarray, scattering in all directions.

Alice's eyes widen like saucers as she grabs Karen's hand and dashes towards the lockers, pulling her along. They find themselves hidden from the guards, and their hysterical laughter echoes behind the row of lockers.

"Ladies!" shouts a guard. "There's only one way out, and we'll be waiting for you." Alice cracks up and plops down on her butt, muffling her laughter.

Suddenly, Alice and Karen freeze, startled by the sight of a bodybuilder. Her muscles rippled under her dark skin, her stature formidable. She towers over them, a look of curiosity on her face. "What y'all gigglin' at?" she drawls. The duo stand up slowly, unable to say a word under the imposing woman's shadow. Arms folded, the bodybuilder gives them a stern stare.

Karen approaches the imposing figure with hesitant steps. "We're screwed. We messed with the wrong people and now they won't let us go," she says, jabbing her thumb towards the entry.

The bodybuilder's forehead creases with concern. She stalks forward, her gait powerful and assured, and peeks around the corner. "Mm-hmm, now looky here, this here ain't no good," she drawls.

She returns and walks past the wide-eyed twosome, who scramble to catch up with her as she sets off. With a swift motion, the bodybuilder pulls open a locker door, revealing a collage of photographs neatly arranged on the inside. Karen's gaze locks onto the glossy images of bikini-clad women, their bodies glistening with oil as they strike powerful poses. The clanging of metal echoes through the room as the bodybuilder searches through the locker, her face set in determination. Finally, she grabs a lace-front wig and a red headscarf, tossing them into Alice's hands.

She gives Karen a quick once over. "Aight, you miss light 'n bright, you rock the headscarf," she commands in a resonant voice. Then, swiveling her attention and pointing a long finger at Alice, she adds, "Mm-hmm, you there, you're straight fire, you go 'head with the wig." She mirrors the rhythm of her words with the confident sway of her hips.

Alice and Karen exchange a frown before heading to their lockers to change into their workout clothes, covering their swimsuits. The bodybuilder joins them, her eyes fixed on them as they get dressed. With the help of the mirrors on the inside of her locker doors, Alice effortlessly slips on the lace-front wig, which transforms her into a rebellious rockstar. Karen nods appreciatively as Alice helps her tie the red headscarf around her head, making her look like she's about to set sail on a pirate ship. They hold back giggles, their eyes sparkling with shared amusement at their impromptu transformation.

The powerful bodybuilder sweeps her gaze over them, taking in their appearance. After a moment, she gives an approving nod, her satisfaction clear. "Aight, ya'll lookin' good. Now, stick with me," she declares, her voice booming with authority as she strides confidently towards the entrance. The dressing room is a cacophony of sounds as swimmers scramble to get ready for their exercise. With determined expressions on their faces, Alice and Karen prepares for the great escape. In the cramped dressing room, the sounds of zippers and rustling fabric are all around them as they move.

The muscle sculptress strides ahead, her determination evident in the way she walks. Alice and Karen follow short on her heels. With their eyes locked on the entrance, they share a mutual feeling of sheer determination and support between them. The muscle-bound figure confidently strides towards the group of security guards, forcefully making her way through the men. The guards flinch and step back, giving her a wide berth as she advances towards them. Her eyes are like icy daggers, her muscles tense and ready for action. With a feral growl, she lunges forward, ready to take on the entire group. Alice could almost taste the fear in the air, and it only makes her more determined. Each step they take sends her heart pounding against her chest as she keeps her gaze fixed on the ground ahead of her.

The muscular dame abruptly stops in her tracks as she approaches the exit, her perfectly chiseled body glistening with sweat under the harsh overhead lights. "Go!" she shouts, her voice reverberating off the walls. Alice and Karen frantically sprint towards the exit, their breaths ragged and the sound of their pounding footsteps echoing through the turnstiles. The pungent smell of sweat and rubber lingers in the air as they burst out onto Madison Avenue, the blaring horns of taxis and the clamor of pedestrians filling their ears. The adrenaline rush of their escape courses through their veins as they leave the gym and the piercing whistles of the security guards behind.

"I need a drink," Karen says, wiping the sweat from her forehead. They walk down the street, feeling the press of bodies as the crowds of locals and tourists jostle them, all in a hurry. The surrounding sights are a cacophony of the old and new, with grand, historic buildings standing alongside sleek, modern storefronts. Everywhere they look, there are colorful signs advertising fresh foods, each smell more tantalizing than the last.

"Look!" Alice exclaims, pointing to a cocktail lounge. The neon sign with flashing orange letters on a white background hums and buzzes above them, advertising 'The Gilded Lily'. They dash across the noisy street and hurry inside. Alice feels her heart race as she takes in the wondrous sight, her eyes wide and her cheeks flushed with excitement. The dark interior glitters with the muted shimmer of golden lamps, and the sound of clinking glasses and laughter fills the air. Intricate tapestries and colorful paintings adorn the vibrant walls, and the scent of exotic spices and roasted meats wafts through the air. Alice hears the soft strumming of a lute and the melodic hum of a singer's voice, the words of the song unknown to her but still stirring something within her soul. The room is alive with energy, with people chatting and laughing, clapping along to the music, and raising their glasses in celebration. Alice embraces the present moment, forgetting her worries and fears, and allowing herself to be caught up in the joyous atmosphere.

In a sea of people, Karen's eyes dart around, and she spots a peaceful nook in the far corner. They snuggle into their cozy chairs, feeling the soft fabric against their skin. A young server with bright red hair, dressed in a tight miniskirt and a purple blouse, gracefully approaches their table. With every step, her bright red hair bounces, making her stand out in the vibrant, electric atmosphere. Her warm smile and sparkling green eyes give her a radiant glow. She places two colorful menus on the table and greets Karen and Alice with a drawl, "Well, howdy there! Welcome to The Gilded Lily. What can I fetch for ya this fine evening?"

Karen inhales deeply, savoring the refreshing floral fragrance that envelops the server. Overwhelmed by the server's elegance, Karen asks in disbelief, "Are you actually real or is this all just a dream?" Her gaze sweeps over the server, admiring her grace from head to toe. She deftly pulls out a crisp bill and slides it into the server's black stocking. Her fingertips graze the smooth skin above the stocking's edge as she says with a suggestive smile, "Take special care of us, and there is much more where that comes from."

Without batting an eye, the fiery redhead points to their heads. Her finger traces an arc from Karen to Alice. "What in tarnation is goin' on with them get-ups? Y'all tryin' to be the next Joan Jett and Anne Bonny or somethin'?" she asks, squinting in disbelief. Alice's heart races as she meets Karen's eyes, and they both rip off their disguises with a sense of relief.

Karen offers a sheepish smile and admits, "We had a bit of a situation."

The redhead's green eyes linger on the wig before she snatches it from the table and places it on her head. With her hands resting on her hips, she strikes a confident pose. "Well, whaddya reckon? Could I pass for one of them movie stars?" Settling her eyes on Karen, she finishes her elegant pirouette. Karen sweeps her gaze over the server's form, and a wave of heat washes over her.

"Tiffany!" a man's voice suddenly calls out from behind her. "Quit fooling around and take care of your waiting customers."

With a start, the redhead jumps and rips off the wig. "You jackass!" she exclaims, glaring at the mam's back. "I'll be back quicker 'n a hiccup," she reassures them, and spins around, her red hair swirling like a fan.

"Can you get use two lychee martinis please?" Alice calls out to the retreating figure.

"Sure thing!" Tiffany hollers over her shoulder. "Be there in two shakes of a lamb's tail."

"Wow, what do you make of her?" Karen asks, her eyes sparkling with delight.

Alice grins at her friend, her smile as warm as a Southern evening. "Well, bestie, you know me. I'm more of a cowboy gal."

With a dreamy expression, Karen scans the lounge, gazing off into the distance. She fixes Alice with a stern gaze. "Did facing your fears on the high dive help you find a solution to your problems?"

Alice's brow furrows as the abrupt question surprises her. "Yes, you know, it made me forget about it, but it solved nothing."

Karen keeps probing Alice about it. Eventually, Alice opens up, recounting the afternoon's confrontation with Madison Granger in her office, leaving out no detail.

"Does James know?" Karen asks, her voice heavy with concern.

"No, I think he's away on a business trip. I tried calling him, but his voicemail picked up."

Emerging from the hushed shadows, Tiffany balances a tray of martini cocktails with an ease that betrays her experience. The ambient lighting casts a soft glow on her silhouette, lending her an air of enticing mystery. "Apologies for the hold-up, darlings," she purrs, her voice a provocative whisper against the hum of quiet conversations. "Might I tempt you with somethin' delectable from our menu?"

Her emerald eyes, deep wells of unspoken longing, find Karen's gaze across the table. A silent exchange, an electric charge, passes between them, a conversation understood only by the two of them. Karen's eyebrow arches subtly in response, a silent question directed at Alice.

Alice feels momentarily taken aback by the whirlwind of their silent communication. She clears her throat, her voice coming out steadier than she feels. "Could we have a charcuterie board, please?" she asks, her request punctuated by a pause as she gathers her thoughts. "And two wild mushroom risottos for mains," she adds, her voice betraying a hint of distraction.

Tiffany's lips curl up at the corners, forming a small smile. "Sure thing, be back in a jiffy," she says, moseying off.

Karen takes a swig of her martini, and her eyes sparkle with mischief. She raises her glass to Alice. "Cheers."

Alice raises her own glass and smiles. "Cheers. Here's to a night of fun!"

"That damn Madison Granger should see a psychiatrist, not a shrink." Karen says, her gaze wandering off into the distance.

With a furrowed brow, Alice concentrates deeply, and suddenly her face lights up. "That's it, that's just it!"

Alice's sudden shriek startles Karen. Her heart pounds in her chest. "That's what?" she asks in a dreamy whisper. Absentmindedly, she swirls her martini. The ice cubes clink against the glass, creating a soothing rhythm amidst the chaos. The liquid spins into a tiny whirlpool, mirroring the storm of emotions within her.

Alice's eyes shine with a newfound sense of hope as she lets out a deep sigh of relief. "I will not sit back and allow them to bully me," she declares, taking a long sip of her drink. Her brow furrows in concentration as she continues. "I'll write to her attorney and inform him that Madison is dealing with a medical condition that requires medication."

"I don't understand," Karen says, tilting her head in confusion. "How will that help?"

The question seems to ignite a fire in Alice, who readily offers her expert opinion, each word dripping with years of experience. "The court has scheduled the divorce hearing in three weeks. However, if I disclose this information in my psychological evaluation report, it may cause a delay in the proceedings," she warns, her voice steady as a drumbeat. "Revealing her medical condition during the court session could potentially influence the jury's perception of her. They may question her intentions—"

Tiffany interrupts, her voice slicing through the tense air like a sharpened blade. "If she needs to testify, her mental condition could potentially impact the reliability of her testimony, particularly if it affects her memory or perception." Her deft hands arrange the meats and cheeses into an artful display, the tantalizing aroma of cured meats permeating the air.

Alice and Karen gawk at her, and Tiffany, with a sly grin, drawls. "Well now, don't look so surprised. I'm in my fourth year studyin' forensic psychology over at CU." She jabs her thumb in a random direction, hoping it's the right way, and giggles to herself.

Alice's laughter gives way to a contented sigh. The mouthwatering scents of cured meats, cheeses, and vegetables fill the space. A fire crackles gently in the hearth, and the warm glow of the flickering flames creates a homey atmosphere, casting dancing firelights on their faces. The sound of laughter and the clinking of wine glasses fill the lounge. Alice and Karen savor every bite of their food, enjoying the burst of flavors that accompany each morsel. The burden of her secret has weighed Alice down, but now she can finally relax and enjoy the moment.

With a generous smile, Karen picks up the check and leaves an eye-widening tip for Tiffany. At the bottom of the bill, she hurriedly scribbles a heartfelt thank you note. Alice gives her bestie's hand a tight squeeze and says, "I had a wonderful time tonight, thanks to you."

Karen's lips curl mischievously into a smile and she says, "Hold on, Spid, we're not finished yet. The night is still young."

Alice cocks her head to the side and gives Karen a quizzical look, asking, "What's the plan?"

Karen replies with excitement, "It's a surprise. Let's swing by my place first."

Alice nods in agreement and quickly gathers her belongings before following her friend to the entrance. Karen's eyes dart around, searching frantically for Tiffany, but she can't seem to find her anywhere. Her face falls with disappointment as she hands the bill holder to the manager.

Alice and her closest confidant, Karen, stride down the lively street, the night alive with the city's pulsating heartbeat. Alice stands tall and composed as she signals for a taxi to stop. With a loud screech, the vehicle comes to a stop, its headlights illuminating the dense evening fog. Karen holds the door open gallantly, allowing Alice to slide into the back seat.

"Karen! Hold up, darlin'!" A familiar voice cuts through the clamor, halting Karen mid-action. Tiffany, bundled up against the chill, pushes through the throng, her face lit up by the neon signs. The cabbie, growing impatient, revs the engine, the exhaust pipe spewing out steam like a dragon's breath.

Karen's face splits into a wide grin at the sight of Tiffany. "Quick, get in," she urges, motioning for Tiffany to join them. Tiffany scrambles into the backseat, sliding next to Alice as Karen shuts the door behind her. The sweet scent of Tiffany's petal-scented perfume fills the cab, transporting Alice to a garden filled with butterflies.

"Where to?" asks the cabbie, ogling the trio in the rearview mirror, his round face red with excitement. Karen gives him the address. He revs the engine and pulls away, narrowly dodging a bus as he weaves through the nighttime traffic. His eyes twinkle with excitement as he navigates through the bustling city's veins.

The sound of Alice's ringtone echoes through the air. She eagerly digs through her sports bag, finding her phone and answering it with a beaming smile on her face. "Hey darling," she greets him, her voice affectionate. "Yes, I'm out with Karen and her friend Tiffany. Can't wait to see you then. Oh, and I miss you too." Suddenly, Alice's tone changes and she asks, "Are you with Robert!?" Her sudden outburst causes everyone around her to turn and stare in surprise. The sound of her husband saying the traitor's name sends an icy chill down her back.

Karen looks icy daggers at the phone in Alice's hand and crosses a finger over her lips. With a sound like a banshee's wail, the cabbie slams on the brakes to avoid hitting a group of young pedestrians crossing the road. The sudden stop causes the three passengers to jolt forward and slam into the backs of the front seats.

The cabbie yells, "Hey! Watch where you're going!" as he leans out of the window and wags his finger. The youngsters pay no attention to the warning and hurl a barrage of insults at the driver. They continue on their way, laughing and joking without a care in the world.

Alice speaks into her phone. "Yes, I'm still here." After a brief pause, she continues, "Yeah, yeah... no, I fed him before I left." She says goodbye with a cheerful "Love ya, cheers," and ends the call.

The cab pulls up beside a towering apartment building, its exterior swathed in shimmering glass. Alice pays the fare and follows her friends through the entrance.

The concierge stands tall and professional behind the reception desk, welcoming Karen and her company with a warm greeting as they enter the building. With a tap of his top hat and a warm smile, he greets them, "Good evening, Miss Delaney, and co."

Karen gathers her friends before the elevator and introduces them to the concierge. "Good evening Mr. Roberts, these are my friends, Alice, and Tiffany," she says, gesturing to Alice and Tiffany. The elevator doors slide open, and the sound of high-pitched laughter and excited chatter fills the air as a group of ladies emerge. Karen leads the way; the calming notes of a classical composition enchant them as they ascend to the twenty-third floor.

Tiffany's eyes widen in amazement at the sight of Karen's luxurious apartment. Her footsteps echo through the spacious interior as she wanders, admiring the enormous paintings on the walls. She pauses in front of a particular piece that catches her eye. The painting depicts two women in profile, their faces almost touching, creating an intimate and shared space. Their slicked-back hair accentuates their broad foreheads and strong, Romanesque noses, which testifies to their bold individuality. Both women are looking to the right, drawing the viewer's gaze in the same direction.

Their serene and introspective expressions hint at a deep emotional bond, and the simple background emphasizes their faces, making the viewer feel like they're intruding on a private moment. The painting's muted tones add to its timeless elegance, while the stark contrast between the subjects' pale complexions and dark attire adds dramatic intensity. The pale strokes on the canvas create a visual masterpiece that captures Tiffany's attention. Her eyes light up with excitement as she points at the portrait. "I sure do like this one," she exclaims. "It's a masterpiece, with beautiful brush strokes and intricate details," she adds while hovering her hand over its rough texture to emphasize her admiration. Then she asks, "Who are they supposed to be?"

Tiffany's insight surprises Karen, causing her eyebrows to shoot up. "That painting is called the Medallion," Karen explains. "It's a notable painting by Hannah Gluckstein, also known as Gluck. The painting is a double portrait that depicts Gluck and her lover Nesta Obermer. She painted it in 1936." Karen then adds, "I ordered the prints while I was in London."

Tiffany gazes at Karen's mouth, her eyes fixated on every subtle shift and curve of her lips as if they hold the secrets of the universe. The tension between them crackles like a live wire, and the air is thick with unspoken promises and hushed expectations. They stand in silence, their eyes locked, waiting for someone to break the tension.

Suddenly, Alice emerges from the steam-filled sanctuary, her figure swathed in a fluffy towel, shattering the spell like a stone through glass. A cloud of steam billows out of the bathroom, filling the room with a comforting, clean scent. The steam settles on their skin, leaving them feeling invigorated and revitalized.

The threesome convenes in Karen's lavish bedroom, a fashion enthusiast's dream lined with racks upon racks of designer clothes and accessories. Karen, with an artist's eye for detail, meticulously selects outfits for each person. She takes great care to match the colors and styles to their individual tastes, a thoughtful gesture that underscores the depth of their friendship. The room is alive with the sound of rustling clothes, hangers clacking against the metal rods, and the soft murmur of their voices as they discuss their preferences. The sight of Karen's bedroom is a feast for the eyes, with its bright colors, intricate patterns, and exquisite fabrics.

Alice pats herself dry, feeling the rough towel against her skin, and asks, "Where are we headed?"

Karen's eyes light up as she arranges three outfits on the top of the bed. "Dancing," she says, clearly excited about the prospect.

Tiffany throws her hands in the air. "Yup, I sure do love m'self some dancin.'"

Karen grins at Tiffany as she sheds her garments, revealing her dark designer lingerie. "It makes me happy to hear that," she says before stepping out of her lingerie. Her porcelain skin and toned body are on full display as she heads towards the bathroom. Tiffany's eyes widen as she watches Karen move, her body swaying with a grace that is almost hypnotic. Karen's alluring figure beckons her forward, and a smile spreads across her face as she moves towards her.

The sound of ice clinking against glass fills the room as Alice steps inside. Lost in her lustful thoughts, the sudden noise distracts Tiffany and she whirls around. She quickly grabs a glass and takes a sip, flashing Alice a sheepish grin. "How'd y'all know I take a fancy to vodka soda?" Tiffany asks, raising her glass.

With a wet cough, Alice asks, "What else do people drink around here?"

Karen emerges from the bathroom, draped in a towel, and motions for Tiffany to go. Tiffany places her glass on the nightstand and sheds her garments, revealing her porcelain skin clad in striking red lace lingerie. Karen watches intently as Tiffany undresses, her eyes filled with envy and desire. Tiffany feels a surge of confidence as she sees the look of longing in Karen's eyes. She stands a little taller and tosses her hair back, reveling in the power of her own sensuality. The air between them crackles with tension as they stand there, both acutely aware of the other's presence.

Alice can feel the heat emanating from them, her own body responding with a flush of warmth as she watches. The room feels charged, as if a single spark could set it ablaze. Alice feels the heat of their desire growing stronger. She coughs nervously, hoping to divert their attention. A sly grin appears on Tiffany's face as she saunters into the bathroom. Karen sits down on the side of the bed and can't help but flash Alice a guilty smile.

Soft moonlight filters through the window, casting a warm glow on the walls and furniture. Tiffany emerges from the bathroom, and the soft moonlight casts a delicate glow over her exposed skin. Her hair, falling gracefully down her back, catches the moonlight and shimmers as she moves towards the bed. A look of sadness clouds her face as she speaks up. "Would any of you happen to have a towel I could borrow?" she asks.

Karen gasps and jumps up, frantically searching through a drawer until she pulls out a soft towel. She drapes it around Tiffany's shoulders and offers a soothing rub on her back as an apology. "Sorry, darling, that was downright inhospitable of me."

With a warm smile, Karen quickly pulls on her dress and high heels, eager to hit the bustling city streets. She calls over her shoulder to the other ladies, a hint of laughter in her voice, "I hope you don't mind if I light a few candles. It is Friday night, after all."

Alice and Tiffany are all too caught up admiring their dresses to notice. The room fills with a soft, warm light as Karen carefully lights each candle. The girls exchange glances, their smiles reflecting the flickering glow. They don't need to ask why; they simply enjoy the serene moment before the night of revelry ahead.

As if time has rewound to the roaring 1920s, three stunning ladies appear, their dresses adorned with sparkles and fringes, echoing the iconic flapper style of the Gatsby era. Their dresses swish and sway as they move, the sound of fabric brushing against skin creating a soothing rhythm. They style their hair in elegant finger waves, their makeup bold and daring. The rich, alluring scent of vintage perfume permeates the air. With its complex bouquet, the scent of jasmine, rose, vanilla, and sandalwood intertwines, creating a lingering aroma that evokes memories of long ago.

The sound of their laughter and playful banter fills the air as they take turns posing for photos, sipping their drinks. In the mirrored walls of the elevator, they admire their reflections. Alice, who is taller than Karen, showcases her long legs in a shorter dress, and the fabric feels silky against her skin. A rush of cool air from outside hits the ladies as the elevator doors on the ground floor open, and Mr. Roberts gasps at the sight of them.

Karen's slender fingers slide the phone over to Mr. Roberts, and she can't resist a sly grin. "This way, you can cherish the moment, Mr. Roberts," she suggests in a honeyed voice. The concierge's face lights up, and his cheeks turn a rosy shade as he takes the phone. The vintage trio can't stop giggling as they shuffle around the foyer, striking poses for the camera. Mr. Roberts can't contain his excitement as he snaps photos of the threesome in different poses, looking like he's won the lottery. With a tight grip on the phone, he becomes lost in the moment, his eyes shining with excitement. His body writhes with ecstasy, his knees trembling, his attention glued to the phone screen. Karen and Tiffany break up their poses, their eyes meeting briefly, before flicking over to the concierge with curiosity.

"Thank you, Mr. Roberts. That will be all for now," Karen says, snatching her phone from his grasp. He releases it reluctantly, as if parting with a treasured possession. "Could you send those to me, please, Ms. Delaney?" he asks, his voice trembling slightly, and drool escaping the corners of his mouth.

"Goodnight, Mr. Roberts. Take care now," Karen replies, her voice conveying concern as she senses the intensity of his gaze.

The sound of their heels echoes loudly in the empty foyer, emphasizing their hurried exit.

The vintage goddesses turn heads as they sashay down the sidewalk, eliciting wolf whistles and honking horns from passersby. With a flick of her wrist, Alice signals for a cab. It is only a matter of seconds before a yellow cab pulls up beside them. The familiar scent of nostalgia wafts through the air as they cram into the backseat.

The cabbie turns his attention to his passengers, admiring their beauty in the rearview mirror. "Where to?" he asks, his eyes sparkling with curiosity. Karen slowly spells out the address of the infamous suburb, her voice tinged with caution. Excitement fills the cabbie's eyes as he slams on the gas pedal, and the car lurches forward with a sudden jolt.

Sometime later, the cab leaves the grandeur of uptown behind and winds through the notorious suburb, passing by crumbling buildings and graffiti-covered walls. As they drive down the road, the haunting sight of the abandoned vehicle wrecks lining the roadside strikes Alice, making her feel like she's in a world without people. The air is thick with the pungent scent of garbage and exhaust fumes, occasionally punctuated by the wail of sirens in the distance.

The cab shudders to a stop, and the warehouse walls loom before them, a mishmash of vibrant colors, yet the peeling paint gives them a dreary appearance. Alice and Tiffany exchange apprehensive glances as they step out of the cab, the atmosphere heavy with uncertainty. Karen pays the cabbie, who gives them a concerned look before speeding away, leaving them alone in the desolate neighborhood.

Karen takes a deep breath, trying to steady her nerves. "Alright, girls. We're here. Trust me, this place may not look like much, but it's going to be an unforgettable experience."

Alice glances around warily, her eyes scanning the surroundings. "Karen, are you sure about this? It doesn't seem safe."

Tiffany, her voice trembling slightly, adds, "This place gives me the willies."

Karen's face softens, understanding their concerns. She places a reassuring hand on each of their shoulders. "I promise you both, this is going to be an adventure of a lifetime. Just trust me, okay?"

Alice and Tiffany exchange another glance, their initial trepidation slowly giving way to a flicker of curiosity. After a moment of contemplation, Alice nods. "Alright, Karen. We trust you. Lead the way."

With a resolute stride, Karen approaches the towering metal doors of the warehouse, her companions trailing closely behind. Three forceful knocks echo through the stale air. A small, rectangular section at eye-level slides open with a loud creak, revealing a pair of eyes that glitter like diamonds in the dim light. Inside the frame stands a man, his colossal head towering atop wide shoulders. A black outfit hugs his frame, and thick golden chains weigh his neck down. Despite the shadows that obscure his chiseled features, his air of authority is palpable. "Password!" he demands in a deep bass voice that reverberates off the walls. He was the gatekeeper, the bouncer, the one who decided who got to see what lay beyond the metal doors

Karen murmurs, "Please don't tell," as she pulls out a handful of crumpled bills and shoves them into his open hand. The towering metals doors creak open with a loud groan, revealing a dimly lit world. Karen signals Alice and Tiffany to follow her with a quick snap of her wrist. Alice's pulse quickens with excitement, and she listens intently to the echoing shuffles of their footsteps through the ca. The cool air inside sends a chill down her spine, but she presses on, eager to uncover the secrets within.

A stunning transformation has turned the warehouse's interior into a lively and electric jazz club. The dimly lit atmosphere is heavy with the distinct aroma of cigars, which mingle with the sweet scent of aged whiskey and the rich fragrance of leather upholstery. On stage, a saxophone player steals the spotlight. His soulful melody fills the air, weaving its way through the throngs of patrons. Each note holds them spellbound, their attention riveted on the mesmerizing performance. The warm, amber glow of the radiant crystal chandeliers illuminates the polished mahogany bar and glistens off the gleaming brass instruments on stage.

As the trio nestle into their leather seats, the clinking of glasses and the hum of conversations fill the air. Throngs of jivers, beboppers, and swing dancers crowd the dance floor, their bodies swaying and twisting to the rhythm of the music. The atmosphere pulses with electricity, the energy as infectious as the jazz notes filling the air.

Suddenly, the band switches gears, and the distinctive tempo of the Charleston fills the warehouse. A murmur of excitement sweeps through the crowd. Alice looks up just in time to see Karen glide onto the dance floor, her body moving with grace and precision, her steps quick and lively. The crowd cheers as Karen spins and dips, her feet a flurry of movement, her arms swaying and twirling. She moves with a passion and energy that ignites the floor, her body alive with the rhythm of the music. The crowd parts to form a circle around her, their applause and cheers blending with the music.

Her lithe and graceful movements cast a spell on the audience, who can't take their eyes off her. Couples and singles alike crowd the dance floor, eager to show off their moves and compete for the title of the night's best dancer. Tiffany confidently makes her way to the dance floor to join Karen, driven by the infectious beat of the music. The spectators erupt into cheers and applause, their excitement palpable.

A medley of sweat, perfume, booming drums, and vibrating bass guitar permeates the atmosphere. Tiffany loses herself in the music, jumping, twirling, and moving her body to the rhythm. The vibrations from the drums shake the ground beneath her feet while the bass guitar reverberates through her chest. The lead singer's powerful voice soars above the crowd.

Alice watches from the sidelines, her eyes wide with wonder. Glamorous women fill the club, each dressed in their finest roaring twenties attire, harking back to the age of jazz and prohibition. Feathers, sequins, and sparkling headbands adorn their outfits, capturing the spirit of the era. They move with grace and confidence; the atmosphere charged with their laughter and animated conversations.

Alice scans the bustling crowd until her gaze settles on a captivating sight. Adorned in a stunning flapper-style gown that shimmers under the dim light, a mysterious blonde woman sits at a distance, her eyes fixed on the crowd. She sits with her back straight, her icy-blue eyes glinting in the low light, and a faint hint of a smile dancing on her lips. The atmosphere of the room is electric, and the girl's presence is almost tangible. She holds a slender cigarette holder between her fingers, from which she takes delicate puffs, creating long streams of smoke that swirl in the air. The scent of tobacco and sweet perfume wafts towards Alice, tantalizing her senses.

There's an unmistakable air of mystery that surrounds the blonde woman, a magnetic allure that draws Alice's attention. Her presence is so captivating that Alice can hardly look away, and when their eyes meet, she feels a jolt of electricity. Her gaze holds a hint of intrigue, like the flicker of a candle flame in a dark room, as if she knows a secret that Alice longs to unravel. Alice can feel her heart racing in her chest as she nervously twirls a strand of her raven hair, her blue eyes wide with apprehension. She silently gasps, the sound barely audible, as her porcelain cheeks flush a delicate pink in a show of restrained emotion, and she feels her lips parting slightly.

The moment passes, but Alice can't shake off the curiosity that lingers. Her eyes follow Karen as she collapses onto the plush leather couch, her chest heaving with exhaustion. The strobe lights continue to flash, casting sporadic beams of light that illuminate the room in a kaleidoscope of colors. Karen rests her head on Tiffany's lap, and Tiffany tenderly strokes her hair, the strands of hair slipping through her fingers like silk.

Karen's eyes glisten with excitement, and her cheeks turn a vivid rosy hue, brightening her features. Alice can feel the electric energy emanating from her friend, a comforting warmth that seems to fill the room. She watches as Karen's lips part in a satisfied sigh, her body visibly relaxing into the embrace of her friends. The energy between Karen and Tiffany is palpable, and their bodies hum with an intense sensation. Karen's chest rises and falls with each breath, her body quivering slightly with the strength of the emotions. Tiffany's slender fingers move in a gentle, circular motion through Karen's silky hair. Their eyes lock, and Karen's lips curl into a smile of pure contentment.

Karen raises her arm, and her silver wristwatch catches the light. "Ready when you are?" she says, her voice soft and musical.

They rise from their seats, their movements fluid and graceful, and weave their way through the thinning crowd towards the exit. Alice huddles with her friends, her fingers tracing the smooth surface of her phone as she opens the ride-sharing app. The moon hangs low in the sky, casting a soft light through the windows of the club. Together, they step outside, the cool night air hitting their flushed faces as they follow the blue car icon on the screen, watching as it makes its way towards them. The trio take a deep breath, the scent of fresh air and the distant aroma of street food filling their nostrils.

Their bodies are weary, but their spirits are alive, their laughter spilling out into the quiet streets, blending with the sounds of the sleeping city. Hand in hand, they make their way to the waiting car, their feet sinking into the cool sidewalk, the gentle breeze rustling through their hair.

They ride in silence, their eyes glued to the windows, taking in the mesmerizing neon city lights. Karen and Tiffany say goodbye to Alice as the driver drops them off at Karen's towering apartment building. Alice, Karen, and Tiffany hug each other tightly, feeling the warmth of their friendship, and promise to meet again soon, holding onto the magic of the night.

"Oh, no, not again!" Alice whines under her breath, frantically searching through her handbag, trying to find her house keys. With desperation setting in, she pulls at the doorknob, but it remains steadfastly shut. Her heart sinks as she looks at her watch and sees that it is past the time when she can call Natalie.

She kicks off her shoes, feeling the rough texture of the concrete step beneath her feet, and sinks down onto the top step. Sparky leaps through the pet door, his tail wagging excitedly as he hurries to her side. As they watch the cars rushing by in the road below, she runs her finger through his soft fur.

The road is a constant stream of vehicles, each one in a hurry to reach its destination. Sparky wags his tail and barks excitedly at the cars in the road. "What is it, Sparks?" Alice asks, looking at the dog with a puzzled expression. The dog can hardly contain his excitement, yapping and wagging his tail. Her eyes wander down the road, and suddenly she spots a gleaming white limousine. The limo creeps by, its occupants hidden behind the tinted windows. A street cleaning truck slowly edges by, and the sound of rushing water and spinning brushes fills the air. The truck's emergency light is pulsating, casting a yellow glow on everything around it. The sound of its engine fills the air with a deafening growl.

Alice squints, her eyes struggling to adjust to the blinding yellow emergency light. She catches sight of a white limo creeping up behind the cleaning truck. Alice's eyes widen as she watches Samuel Granger emerge through the sunroof, and she quickly covers her mouth in shock. His tuxedo glimmers and sparkles in the light. His face is bright red, and his white collar stands out like a beacon of light against the dark sky.

With a sparkle in his eyes and a broad smile spreading across his face, Samuel fixates his gaze on Alice. "Pardon me, miss!" he exclaims with a slurred voice, swaying back and forth like bamboo in the wind. "You look lost. How may a chivalrous man be of service?" The sound of the cleaning truck's engine grows louder as it edges forward, and the limo driver hastily maneuvers into the parking spot that opens. Startled by the sudden movement, Sam jumps and glares at the driver. "Oi, watch where you're steerin', you wee numpty," he barks in annoyance.

With each step down the stairs, Alice's excitement grows, and her face lights up as she approaches the limo. Samuel steps out and fidgets with his hands behind his back, his eyes darting around nervously. The acrid scent of exhaust fumes mixing with Sam's cologne is so strong it makes Alice's nose twitch. Samuel's eyes rove over her figure, and he lets out a low whistle at the sight of Alice in the short, flapper-style Gatsby dress. He inhales deeply, taking in the intoxicating scent of her vintage perfume that has him under its spell.

Samuel drops to one knee, presenting Alice with the ballet flat she lost during the skirmish with his bodyguards. He tugs at her leg, and she feels his gentle touch as he slips the shoe onto her foot. "Shall I compare thee to a summer's day?" Sam recites, his voice carrying over the noise of the bustling street. Alice's eyes widen in surprise as she looks down at the ballet flat in Samuel's outstretched hand. Nosy bystanders crowd around them, their murmurs and whispers blending into a steady hum. Alice can feel her heart racing in her chest, and her palms growing clammy with nervousness. The memory of the confrontation with Samuel's guards flashes through her mind, and she can't help but feel a pang of guilt for causing such a scene.

But as she looks up at Samuel's face, she sees only kindness and understanding in his eyes. And in that moment, all of her anxiety and fear melt away. She feels a warm rush of gratitude and affection wash over her, and her eyes well up with tears. Her face turns from pink to a deep ruby red. "Sam, you're embarrassing me. Get up," she pleads, burying her face in her hands. The heat of embarrassment spreads through her body, and the sound of her own heartbeat fills her ears.

A nosy bystander captures the moment on his phone, the sound of the camera shutter breaking the silence. Two burly bodyguards emerge from the shadows and approach the man, their heavy footsteps echoing against the concrete sidewalk. The man senses danger and takes off, his feet pounding against the asphalt as he weaves through the traffic. The blare of horns and the screech of brakes fill the air as drivers curse and swerve to avoid him, the chaos of the city intensifying in the wake of his hasty escape.

Despite their size, the bodyguards struggle to keep up with the man's agility. The chase is short-lived as his unbroken determination to escape quickly becomes apparent. Samuel turns to the nearest bystanders and throws his arms in the air. "The better part of valor is discretion." As he recites, he adds emphasis to his words with graceful hand gestures, directing them towards Alice. "This lady doth protest too much, methinks," he declares, his voice rising above the city noise. The onlookers' loud cheers and applause erupt into a roaring cacophony, their clapping and stomping creating a rhythm that reverberates through the air.

Mattia, the chauffeur, joins them on the sidewalk, his face pleading as he squeezes himself between Sam and Alice. "I drive back from the theater, Signora Alice," he says, with a melancholic tone, fixing Alice with a sad gaze. "Signor Granger sees Shakespeare and eats plenty of oysters and drinks sparkling wine. I think he is a little dizzy from the wine. I take signor home now." Mattia raises his arms in the air and begs, "Please, get in the car, Signor Granger."

The mere thought of champagne sends Alice's mind reeling back to that fateful night when Mattia dropped her off. The sound of her heels clicking against the stairs reverberates in her memory as she approaches her house. She can't help but grin as she recalls the secret hiding spot of Natalie's spare house keys. "I know where the keys are," she whispers to herself.

Samuel's eyes wander over Alice's figure, a grin spreading sheepishly across his face. The aroma of alcohol wafts from his breath as he tries to address her, but a sudden hiccup interrupts his speech. Two burly bodyguards guide him towards the open car door, their footsteps echoing on the sidewalk. Samuel's shoulders slump in submission as he reluctantly follows their lead.

Samuel settles into the comfortable leather seat, and Alice notices an alluring woman sitting inside. The intricate pattern on her silk stockings, elegantly swathed around her long legs, and her shiny evening dress glimmer in the dim starlights of the limo's ceiling. Alice notices a sweet fragrance emanating from the woman, enhanced with delicate notes of rose and sandalwood. The glint of the woman's shiny evening dress and the way the roof lights dance on her stockings catch Alice's attention, despite her profile being partially obscured by the open car door. A strange sense of familiarity tugs at Alice. She shakes her head, but the thought of where she has seen the woman before plagues her.

Alice strains her eyes to catch a glimpse of the woman, but Mattia cut her efforts short as he abruptly slams the door shut. He greets Alice with a "Ciao, signora," but quickly adds, "Please, Signora Alice, don't kiss my head this time. My wife is big, and she threatens me with a rifle when she sees your lipstick stains on my head." He pleads with Alice and points towards Samuel with his thumb, teasing her by saying, "Your pretty face is his weakness."

Alice winces when she hears what Mattia says about Samuel. "Oh no," she exclaims, her mind suddenly flashing back to the night Mattia dropped her off. "I'm sorry, Mattia, I was tipsy that night," she confesses, her hands clasped over her mouth. "Cross my heart. I won't kiss your head again."

Mattia grins and scampers to the front of the limo. "I hope we meet again, Signora Alice." With a knowing smile, he quickly shuts the door and starts the engine, sending a cloud of exhaust fumes into the air.

The limo pulls away, and Sam rises through the sunroof, his hand crossing over his heart in a last goodbye. "A horse," he proclaims, "a horse! My kingdom is a horse. All that glisters are not gold."

Alice bids farewell to Sam, feeling the weight of sadness in her heart. Yet, she blows him a kiss and calls out into the darkness, "Good night, good night!" Wistfully, she adds, "Parting is such sweet sorrow," her voice tinged with sadness.

Samuel catches her kiss with a smile and playfully blows one back before waving goodbye. The sound of his voice fades away as the limo disappears into the distance, leaving only the peaceful silence of the night. Alice's heart races as she notices a black sedan parked on the opposite side of the road, and its two male occupants gazing at her. She peers through the open window and sees a man in the passenger seat, his thick mustache moving up and down as he chews on a toothpick. Squinting her eyes, she notices the floral shirts the men are wearing, giving off a Hawaiian vibe. The sedan speeds away, leaving the passenger's hair whipping in the wind and a faint scent of exhaust lingering in the air.

Alice's fingers twitch with the urge to capture the moment, but her phone is in her purse on the steps. Her palms breathing becomes shallow as she tries to shake off the feeling of unease that settles in the pit of her stomach. Her heart continues to race as she tries to calm herself down, reminding herself that it was probably just a coincidence. But the image of the men in their Hawaiian shirts and the thick mustache of the passenger continue to haunt her, making her feel vulnerable and exposed.

Alice's face is a picture of worry as she climbs the stairs, her shoulders hunching against the biting wind, which sends chills down her spine. The spare key slides into the lock with a metallic click, and the sound of Sparky's excited paws fills the hallway, echoing off the walls. The door creaks open, and the stillness of the house engulfs her. She rushes to the kitchen and pours a heaping scoop of dog food into Sparky's bowl. She climbs the creaky stairs to her bedroom, the sound of Sparky's eager chomping echoing through the house.

The cool air of the bedroom soothes Alice's skin as she peels off her clothes, the fabric of her nighties whispering secrets against her body. She finds solace in the mundane act of pairing her once-lost shoe with its long-lost partner, an unexpected gift from Samuel's kindness. Her husband's voice echoes through the room, a robotic drone of voicemail messages filling the silence. He sounds exhausted, stressed—the weight of his world evident in every strained word.

Her heart pounds as she scrolls through her text messages, the glow of the screen illuminating her face in the dimly lit room. Two payment notifications catch her eye—a partial reimbursement from her agency despite aborting her mission, and a substantial tip from Samuel, who remains blissfully unaware of her true intentions. A spark of excitement ignites within her; it's a dangerous game they're playing, a dance on the razor's edge of truth and deception.

Reading the glowing five-star review Samuel has left her, a sense of pride swells within her. It's not for the mission she has walked away from, but for the role she has played so convincingly.

Alice crawls under the cool sheets, but the gnawing thought of an unfinished task lingers in her mind, like a heavy weight pressing against her skull. The candles flicker and create a mesmerizing dance of shadows on the ceiling. Lost in deep concentration, she gazes at the elegant ceiling above her. The intricate patterns etched into the plaster catch her eye, and she can't help but trace the lines with her gaze. Suddenly, a memory of James's call jolts her out of bed, and she hurries downstairs to her office. The tropical and spicy scent of her cocobolo desk fills her senses as she rifles through her diary's crisp pages to find today's date.

She scribbles in bold uppercase letters at the top of the page, the ink smudging slightly: 'Set up an appointment with the Granger's or email Riley Piece,' adding a dash, and then writing 'Madison Granger psychiatric referral'. The pen scratches against the paper, filling the silence as she jots down 'Confess the letter about Robert to James' below the line.

4

A thick and eerie fog shrouds Alice as she walks through the cemetery, making it difficult to see and breathe. The fog muffles the sound of her footsteps, but the old and cracked headstones amplify each step, creating an unsettling feeling in her chest. She turns right at the mausoleum entrance, and the path ahead is dimly lit by the moonlight, which casts eerie shadows on the engraved names of the memorials.

Alice's breath catches in her throat as she notices her name inscribed on her father's memorial next to her mother's. The departure date on the memorial shows a date yet to come, sending a chill down her spine, making the hairs on the back of her neck stand up.

Suddenly, Alice's blood-curdling scream tears through the silence of the cemetery, causing a murder of ravens to take flight. The sound bounces off the headstones, creating a haunting melody. A figure materializes from the fog, its silhouette vague. It extends a hand, silently inviting Alice to approach. "Alice," it whispers, the single word resonating in the stillness.

A woman's face comes into focus as Alice approaches, and she realizes they have the same sharp cheekbones. Alice feels a sense of peace as the woman reaches out, her cool hand against Alice's skin. She feels a chill run through her body, and she shivers. Then the woman vanishes, leaving only the faint scent of lavender behind, which lingers in the air.

Alice's body convulses violently as she sobs uncontrollably, her desperate screams piercing through the eerie silence of the misty graveyard. The damp air clings to her skin, making her shiver with cold and fear. The smell of freshly dug earth and damp grass fills her nostrils, adding to the overwhelming sense of dread that grips her. Suddenly, she awakens, her heart pounding in her chest and her body drenched in a cold sweat. Alice lies there, feeling the warmth of Natalie's breath on her cheek as she leans over her. Her voice is full of concern as she whispers, barely audible over the pounding of Alice's heart. "Alice, cher, wake up. It's getting late."

Natalie opens the curtains, flooding the room with bright sunlight. The rays cascade off the mirrors, casting a kaleidoscope of bright colors against the walls. Alice bolts upright in bed, squints at the bright light, and throws the duvet off her. Strands of hair clung to her brow like tendrils, and she let out a sharp exhale to blow them away. "What time is it?" She asks, her voice hoarse.

Natalie lets out a sigh as she fills a glass with water, then sets it on the nightstand next to two aspirins. "It's time to wake up and start the day. Come on down and join me for some black coffee and breakfast," she says. "Can you smell that aroma, darlin'? It will give you a boost."

Alice's senses awaken as she lifts her chin and breathes in the fragrant scent of coffee and baked bread. "Hmm, I can smell the coffee and the croissants," she says, savoring the delicious scents. But as her stomach growls loudly, it reminds her she has eaten nothing at all.

With a light chuckle, Natalie corrects her boss, saying, "It's a bagel. I picked them up from the bakery on my way in."

Alice looks embarrassed as she tries to stifle a yawn and stretch her arm discreetly. "Nat, would you mind ordering some fresh flowers?" she asks in a persuasive tone. "I'm visiting my parents' graves this afternoon at the cemetery." Her voice grows in intensity as she speaks, emphasizing the importance of her request.

Natalie's face twists in pain as she speaks. "Darlin', you should know better than to visit the dearly departed on a weekday. They need their rest, just like us living folks. It's best to pay your respects on a Sunday. Weekdays only bring bad luck, sweetie. So, heed my words," she says while wagging her finger at Alice.

With a beaming smile, Alice turns to Natalie. "Oh Nat, you are just unreal. Could you please order the flowers?"

Natalie's scowl deepens as she says, "Suit yourself, but I warned you."

"I'm not usually superstitious, Nat. It's been quite some time since I last visited their graves," Alice says, her voice faltering as her throat tightens. Tears well up in her eyes as she continues, "But last night, I had a nightmare about my mother. I woke up in a cold sweat with my heart racing."

"Do you see now? I always warned you, cher. They do not welcome weekday visits," Natalie cautions, her voice conveying a sense of both dread and concern.

Deciding to avoid a losing argument, Alice takes a deep breath and shifts gears. She asks, "What time is my first appointment?"

Natalie looks at her wristwatch, and her eyebrows shoot up in surprise. "Well, I'll be," she exclaims. "You've got a half hour, darlin'. So, you better get your sleepy ass movin'."

Alice's heart is pounding, and her feet hit the cold floor as she launches herself out of bed and sprints to the bathroom.

Dressed in a figure-hugging miniskirt that accentuates every curve, Alice descends the stairs. Her knee-high socks, adorned with playful stripes, imbue her ensemble with a youthful flair. The silky blouse she wears drapes elegantly, enhancing each fluid movement. With every step, the staccato rhythm of her high heels clicking against the polished hardwood floor fills the house with a resonant beat, embodying her palpable confidence.

Alice's high ponytail sways in perfect rhythm with her steps, brushing against her back like a gentle breeze. The sweet perfume she wears lingers in the air, leaving behind an alluring trail of elegance. It's a scent as enchanting as the wearer herself—a blend of exotic flowers and warm spices that is impossible to forget. The radiance of her beaming smile and the sparkle in her eyes possess an enchanting quality that can captivate anyone who catches a glimpse. Her presence is nothing short of irresistible.

The rich, earthy aroma of freshly brewed coffee wafts through the kitchen, enveloping Alice in a warm, comforting embrace. The sound of the liquid gold bubbling and gurgling in the pot adds to the cozy ambiance. She pours herself a steaming mug of the dark, bold liquid, feeling the warmth seeping through the ceramic and into her hands. The scents that linger in the kitchen are as familiar and soothing as an old friend.

The warmth of the toasted bagel spreads to her fingertips as she slathers the cream cheese on thick. Alice mentally prepares herself for the day ahead, knowing that the spirited discussions with the Holmes couple can be quite draining. With a deep breath, she takes a sip of the strong liquid energy and feels the caffeine instantly awaken her senses. The robust flavor of the steamy brew provides a much-needed jolt of energy, and Alice feels ready to face the day.

The Holmes', a lesbian couple, who are regular visitors to Alice's consultation room, sits facing her. Alice knows the couple well, having shared many laughs with them during their previous visits. Today, however, the tension is palpable, and their usual warmth is absent.

With her commanding presence, Evelyn Holmes often wears tailored suits and exudes a distinct, heady aroma of musk. She has a strong, square jawline that lends her an air of authority and dominance. Her partner, Lorelei, epitomizes grace and femininity. Often found in flowing dresses. She exudes a floral fragrance that seems to dance in the surrounding air. Together, they make an intriguing and perfectly balanced pair.

Alice, with her notepad and pen at the ready, peers over her glasses at the duo. "Good morning, ladies! Nice to see you again. What's occupying your thoughts?"

As Lorelei parts her lips, Evelyn cuts her off with an impatient gesture. "We're hoping to start a family. I think it's only right that we give a child in need a home. Lorelei wants to pop out a kid, but I don't see the point. Adopting would be the most responsible decision."

Lorelei rolls her eyes at the notion. "But don't you want to experience the joy of carrying our own baby?" she protests with great intensity and passion. "We can't put a price on that."

"Congratulations on deciding to start a family!" Alice cuts in, her eyes darting between the couple, sensing an impending confrontation. "This is such an exciting time."

She scribbles on her notepad, her eyes darting back and forth as she tries to capture every detail. "You are making a life-changing decision." She glances at Evelyn, searching her face for any sign of emotion. "Evelyn, what's your reason for opposing Lorelei's decision to carry a baby?"

Evelyn's hand envelops Lorelei's, their fingers interlocking, and she gives her hand a firm squeeze. "The thought of someone poking or even touching down there gives me the creeps. Lori is my baby doll."

Alice chuckles softly, her gaze shifting to Lorelei. "Your wife is totally into you, Lorelei. Do you think she has a good reason to adopt instead of fertilizing?"

Lorelei smiles, her lips pressed into a line. "I understand her concerns, Alice, but I think there's something special about carrying a baby. I think it's worth going through the discomfort of experiencing that connection."

Evelyn nods reluctantly, her expression softening. "I understand, and I'm happy to support whatever you decide. I just want to make sure we're making the safest and most responsible decision for any child who comes into our lives."

Alice smiles warmly at the duo. "It sounds like you both have valid points. I think it's important to explore all your options before deciding. Have you considered talking to a fertility specialist or adoption agency to get more information?"

Lorelei nods. "I think that's a great idea. We should do some research and see what our options are, and then decide from there."

Evelyn squeezes Lorelei's hand once more. "I think that's a grand plan. We can look at the pros and cons of both options and make sure we make the best decision for our family."

Alice turns to the couple, her eyes bright. "It's great that you two are discussing this and making sure you've considered all the options. All I have to say is that whatever you decide, make sure it's the right choice for you."

Evelyn and Lorelei both nod in agreement. Lorelei smiles at her wife reassuringly. "We'll explore all our options and come to the best decision for us and our future child."

Alice smiles in response. "That sounds like a splendid plan. I'm sure you'll come to the right decision." She stands up, gathering her notepad and pen. "Well, I think this is all the advice I can give you. Take care and good luck with your decision!" She gives them both one last smile, her eyes twinkling, knowing that they will be back to discuss their options with her.

Leading the way, Alice directs them to the entrance, where they unexpectedly encounter Natalie holding a tray filled with coffee and goodies. Natalie's eyes widen in astonishment as she places the tray down and swiftly makes her way to her desk. "Mornin', Evelyn, Lorelei," she says, her sparkling charm infectious. "Brought ya'll some coffee an' snacks."

Evelyn's eyes widen with joy, and she grins at Natalie: "You're a lifesaver, Natalie! That's very kind of you."

Alice diligently arranges her notes and transcriptions while they relish their coffee and engage in lively conversation. An unexpected loud knock on the door shatters the peaceful atmosphere of their coffee-infused conversation. Lorelei lets out a small shriek as she jumps in surprise, her eyes bugging out. "Jesus!" she exclaims, muffling her voice with her hand.

Natalie's eyes narrow, and she shoots Lorelei a withering glare. Cautiously, she opens the front door, only to find a man with a leather satchel, wearing thick glasses perpetually perched on the bridge of his nose. Clad in monochromatic attire, the man seamlessly blends into the background.

Natalie sizes up the stranger, a hint of disdain playing across her face. "Well now, sugar, what can I do ya for?" she asks with a hint of hesitation.

The man sets his briefcase down and runs his fingers through his disheveled hair with a tired sigh. In a flash, his hand shoots forward. "Leo's the name, and IT is the game. Where is the sick laptop?" he asks with a theatrical lisp and pushes his glasses up his nose.

Surprised, Natalie blinks at the stranger before her poised demeanor snaps back into place. "You must be the tech wizard I done called for Dr. Laurier's machine. Step on in now, sugar," she says with an inviting gesture, stepping aside to clear the path.

The nerdy stranger positions himself between the ladies, his eyes darting back and forth as he tries to take in everything at once. "This way Leo," Alice says, and leads him to her office.

His delight is obvious as he lays eyes on the MacBook and Printer. "My babies, daddy's here, fear no more," he says, sinking into the plush leather office chair. His fingers dance over the keyboard with a rhythmic precision, each keystroke a dedication to his wizardry.

"Don't you need my password?" Alice asks, her eyebrows furrowed in confusion.

He pauses, glares at the screen, and shoots an irritated glance towards Alice. "No, your baby is sick. I'll cheer her up, soon."

"Okay, suit yourself. Don't forget to update the antivirus and firewall." Alice twirls and heads back to the front door where the heated gay debate is ongoing. She cuts off the conversation when she rejoins the group. An uncomfortable silence fills the room, only punctuated by the incessant ticking of the wall clock. Evelyn checks her watch. "Just look at the time already. We'd better get going, Lorelei." Natalie opens the heavy front door, and the blaring of car horns and sirens invades the room. "It was great to catch up with both of you." Alice says in a reassuring tone. "I'm sure you'll make the right decision for your family," she adds, straining her voice over the cacophony of honking cars and chugging engines.

"Thank you for all your help, Alice. We'll be in touch," Evelyn says, wrapping a comforting arm around Lorelei's shoulders. They glide down the staircase. Just as Natalie shuts the door, Alice watches the tender moment with a smile, her heart full of warmth and admiration for the couple. The door is about to close when Alice spots a familiar black sedan parked on the other side of the street. Memories flood her mind, and she feels a mix of familiarity and apprehension. Her eyes stay fixed on the car, wondering if the people inside have spotted her too. She debates whether to run across the street and confront them or to just continue on her way. She hesitates, feeling the gravity of the decision before her. Natalie shuts the door loudly, and the sound of honking cars and chatter from the street fades away. Lost in thought, the abrupt silence startles Alice, snapping her back to reality and prompting her to shake her head to refocus.

Alice carries the tray to the kitchen, the clinking of dishes and silverware filling the air. She turns to Natalie and says, "I don't know about you, but I could use another cup." Without hesitation, she powers up the coffeepot, ready to brew another round. The relic hums with familiarity, its comforting melody evoking memories of friends gathered around the kitchen table. Natalie stands in the kitchen's doorway, her fingers drumming an uneven rhythm against the wooden frame. Her eyes dart around the room, avoiding Alice's direct gaze. She chews on her lower lip.

Alice, noticing these subtle cues, leans against the counter with folded arms, her eyebrows raised in expectation. 'Spit it out, Natalie,' she urges, her tone gentle yet firm. Natalie exhales deeply, her shoulders sagging with the weight of unspoken words, and finally meets Alice's gaze.

"Uh, Cher," Natalie speaks up, a hint of concern in her voice. "I couldn't help but notice your diary flapping in the breeze. My peepers took a little stroll, and I saw you were considering seeing the Granger's again. Are you serious?"

Natalie's voice shakes with a mix of curiosity and worry. "I thought you had your fill of that god-awful lady," she rushes out, hoping to dissuade Alice from making a decision she might regret.

Alice's eyes light up with recognition as the memory floods back. "Shit!" she remembers and curses under her breath. "Thanks for reminding me Nat, please setup an appointment with them ASAP."

Natalie's face scrunches into a scowl as she asks, "Cher, are you serious or just pulling my leg?"

Alice shakes her head to signal no, and the sound of the coffee pouring into the cups fills the room. Suddenly, Sparky's bark echoes through the room, and his toenails skid on the hardwood floor as he runs towards the front door. With a loud bang, the front door slams shut, and the sound reverberates through the empty hallway.

Alice hears male voices and heavy footsteps approaching from the hallway, their steps echoing off the walls. The distinct noise of a suitcase being dragged along fills the room, leaving a faint scratching sound in its wake.

Alice's heart flutters with anticipation as James' voice reverberates through the hallway. "Welcome back, honey!" she says, her eyes lighting up as he enters the kitchen. The bright overhead light casts a warm glow on his face, highlighting the adorable dimples on his cheeks.

James' embrace feels warm and familiar, and she breathes in the comforting scent of his aftershave. As she catches a whiff of his cologne, she can't help but smile, remembering their first date.

Her eyes dart to the tall man standing behind James, whose fiery blue eyes and dark curly hair immediately catch her attention. The light catches his hair, making it shine like a halo around his head. She stares in amazement at the man's ears, which are comically large and seem to defy gravity. He gives Alice a sly smile, causing her heart to race with anticipation.

James steps back a pace and gestures towards the man. "Alice, this is Robert." Robert steps closer, offering a hand. "Hey, nice to meet you at last! James has talked about you a ton, so it's like I already know you." His voice is like a low, rumbling thunder that sends a shiver down her spine. Natalie's scoff in the background momentarily diverts Alice's attention. Her frown deepens as she glares at Natalie, but she quickly puts on a fake smile and turns to face Robert.

"Hi Robert, pleased to meet you," Alice says, her voice barely above a whisper. She shakes his hand, feeling his large hand engulf hers, and notices the roughness of his calloused hands. Sparky emits a low growl from deep within his chest, and his fur bristles.

Alice's gaze falls upon Robert, and her stomach twists in anxiety. The tension between them is almost palpable. Her cheeks flush and her breath becomes ragged. Beads of sweat form on her palms as she stares into Robert's eyes. His gaze seems to penetrate her very soul. Her pulse quickens, her stomach flips, dread coiling within her. Suddenly, an unexplainable urge overwhelms her—she needs to warn James about him.

James senses the bad vibes and speaks up to ease the tension. "It was a long flight." He says, nodding at Robert. "Let's get settled in and relax." Robert's smile is barely there as he clutches the handle of his suitcase, heading towards the kitchen door.

James leads the way. "Come on, Sparks," he says, gesturing towards the dog. Sparky is motionless, like a statue. With a disapproving look, James turns his back on the dog and leaves. Robert trails behind him, shooting angry glances at Sparky.

Natalie raises her eyebrows and shoots Alice a questioning gaze. "Who the—"

Alice silences Natalie with a finger to her lips and speaks up. "Now where were we? Yeah, give Madison Granger a call and schedule a time that works for them. Just ditch any of my meetings to make room for them."

Natalie nods in agreement, scooping up the empty cups and causing a bit of a ruckus as she dumps them into the sink. She swivels around to face Alice, an inquiring glint in her eyes. "So, I can just go 'head and schedule a sit-down with 'em anytime, can't I?"

Alice strains her ears, her eyes darting back and forth, trying to catch any sign of the men's footsteps on the creaky wooden stairs, but the only sound that echoes through the still air is the gentle hum of the refrigerator. A frown creases her brow, and her voice takes on a sharp edge. "Absolutely," she says, her tone leaving no room for doubt. "They're free to select a time that fits their schedule." Her heart races as she tiptoes towards the kitchen doorway, peering around the corner, trying to glimpse what lies ahead. James stands motionless at the foot of the staircase, the blue light from his phone casting an eerie glow on his face.

With a fiery rage burning inside her, Alice charges towards Natalie, her footsteps echoing loudly against the floor. She hisses out her exclamation, "That dude's eavesdropping on us!" Flicking her finger towards the staircase, Alice directs Natalie's attention towards it.

Shock registers on Natalie's face, and she takes a step back, her hand instinctively reaching for her throat. "What?" she hisses in a whisper, "Somethin' 'bout that man gives me the heebie-jeebies." Alice can't help but laugh out loud, the sound bouncing off the walls and causing her to cover her mouth to quiet down.

Suddenly, the sound of footsteps approaching breaks through their conversation, causing both women to turn their heads towards the doorway. The footsteps are heavy and deliberate, and Alice can't help but feel a sense of foreboding wash over her.

Leo stands in the doorway, a smug expression playing across his face. "All set, your little ones are feeling much better now," he says in his signature lisp, adjusting his glasses and smirking at Alice. "Not even a single virus or malware could escape my scrutiny after updating the antivirus," he taunts with a wicked grin.

"Thanks Leo," Alice says, her voice echoing off the high ceilings of the kitchen. "Natalie will take care of your bill and show you the way out." Alice says, with a nod at Natalie.

"Guess I gotta make that dang phone call and be done with it," Natalie declares, the sound of her footsteps echoing softly on the polished wooden floor. She whistles a melancholic tune on her way to the office, the sound bouncing off the walls of the narrow hallway. Leo falls into step behind her, copying the way she walks. Alice shakes her head in disbelief, a grin playing at the corners of her mouth.

The excitement and energy of the moment fill the room, and Alice can feel it in the pit of her stomach. "It's time to confess to James about Robert's letter," she grumbles to herself, the weight of her guilt palpable in the heavy silence. Her footsteps echo through the empty house as she makes her way up the wooden stairs, their creaks and groans accompanying her every step. The hand of fear grips her heart tightly, its icy fingers sending shivers down her spine.

The gentle strains of a classical composition led her to James' office. She approaches the door, and the sound of a hushed voice from inside becomes more distinct with each step. Before stepping inside, she taps out a rhythmic pattern on the door.

James, wearing a headset, raises a finger to his lips, signaling for silence as he continues his conference call with his computer. "Sure thing! We'll update the software on those faulty units ASAP," he says, his voice tinged with annoyance. "Nah, just a little bug because of the time diff from the mainland to Oahu." He scribbles on his desk pad, lost in thought. "Cool, we'll update it at eight tomorrow morning, since they're six hours behind us." The sound of a gentle chime rings out, signaling the end of the call.

James peers over his glasses and greets Alice with a friendly smile. "Sorry Spid, this messed up thing needed my immediate attention. Sup?"

"Don't worry, you'll figure it out," Alice says, her voice slightly trembling. "Where is Robert?"

"Resting, he still feels groggy from the jetlag." James says with a grin, his blue eyes bright behind his glasses. "Oh, and by the way, can you recommend a restaurant that serves homemade meals in a cozy atmosphere?"

Alice's forehead furrows as she concentrates. "Hmm, let me think about it, and I'll hit you up later."

"Thanks," he says with a smile. "Why don't you join us?" he asks with a smile.

The unexpected question catches her off guard, but she quickly gathers her thoughts. "Sounds good." She says, feeling overwhelmed and cannot bring herself to tell him about the letter, knowing how much he is already dealing with. With a twirl, she bids farewell, saying, "We'll catch up later," and heads for her bedroom.

"Catch you later, Spid," James calls out as she walks away, the sound of his voice fading in the distance.

Alice approaches her bedroom, and the sound of her phone's soft melody fills the air. She quickens her pace and throws herself onto her bed, just in time to answer the call. "Alice speaking," she says, propping herself up on her elbow.

"Hey Doc Alice, love the sound of your voice over the phone." The man's voice is familiar, but she cannot quite place it—a client's, perhaps.

Alice kicks off her shoes and rolls onto her back, her eyes tracing the intricate designs on the ceiling. She hears the familiar sounds of a cash register and a coffee machine hissing in the distance, bringing back memories.

Her face lights up. "Fabian!" she exclaims, jolting upright. "What's up?" she asks, her voice full of surprise.

With a chuckle, he asks, You know I was the one who called, right?

Alice's cheeks flush with a rosy tint. "I'm busted." She says with a sheepish tone. "We've only chatted once, and I've never heard your voice over the phone.."

"Sure, no problem!" he responds enthusiastically. "By the way, did you know that yesterday when you left the shop, I ran after you to give you your change? But it was like you disappeared into thin air, like a ghost or something!"

The memory of the van stopping suddenly and Samuel's bodyguards overpowering her comes to Alice's mind. She's overwhelmed by the memory and her body is on high alert. She closes her eyes and takes a deep breath, trying to calm herself down and push the memory to the back of her mind.

Fabian notices Alice is quiet and suggests something to get her talking. "Hey, I was actually thinking of inviting you over for dinner tonight to make up for the change you left. I'm cooking up a storm! Would you like that?" Alice can hear him inhale deeply over the phone, the speaker amplifying the sound.

She can almost smell the delicious aromas of Fabian's cooking wafting through the phone. "Sounds good! Can my hubby and his business partner crash the party, too?" She asks, biting her tongue.

Fabian chuckles and says, "Yeah, bring whoever you want." His voice is electric with excitement as he adds, "I'm cooking enough for an entire football team."

Alice lets out a soft sigh of relief. "Thank you! When would be a good time for you? We'll bring the drinks. Do you have any preferences?"

"Come by at seven or whenever. I'm not picky about drinks. I'm a city guy." He says with a hearty laugh.

Alice giggles joyfully at his witty pun. "Wait a sec, is it okay if I check with my hubby first?"

"Take your time," he responds. "I'm currently on speakerphone and multitasking."

Alice sprints to her husband's office, her bare feet pounding against the polished wooden flooring. The sharp sound of her footsteps echoes through the hallway, adding a sense of urgency to her movements. She puts the phone on speakerphone and storms excitedly into his office, the warm glow of the afternoon sun filtering through the window.

James gives her a warm smile, his eyes filled with curiosity as he looks up from his desk. "Back so soon?" he asks, his voice low and inviting.

Alice can feel her cheeks flush with excitement as she steps closer to him, her eyes sparkling with anticipation. "Hey love, I found the perfect spot for us to have a home-cooked meal with Robert." She signals him to be quiet with a hush sign and walks in a full circle, her shoulders back, hips swaying from side to side, and adding a limp wrist for good measure.

James catches her drift and leaps up, exclaiming. "Beyonce!"

With a playful scowl, Alice speaks up so that Fabian can hear her. "Just a sec Fabian. Need to confirm with my hubby."

Fabian's voice booms through the phone speaker, his words echoing in the small office. "Take your time, doc," he says.

James's face lights up, and he mouths a playful "jazzy voice" to Alice from across the room.

Alice lets a thin smile cross her face. She knows what she has to do. Taking a deep breath, she starts to move. Her body language shifts, becoming more fluid, more graceful. She channels Mick Jagger, shimmying her hips and holding her arms aloft. Each movement is a word, a sentence, a paragraph in the unspoken language she shares with James.

James watches, his eyes wide with surprise and then dawning comprehension. The laughter that bursts from him shakes his office chair, but there's relief mixed with the mirth. Alice's message finally clicks with him, and he realizes the truth she's been trying to convey about Fabian.

"Thank you for inviting us," he says, giving Alice an encouraging thumbs-up. "We're in."

"Awesome, catch you later." Fabian says and hangs up, the sound of rustling and shuffling slowly fading away.

Alice's playful smile lights up her face, and her pearly white teeth dazzle. She gives James a small flirtatious bow.. "My Lord, I beg your pardon for interrupting your valuable time," she says in a flawless British accent. "I shall take my leave and catch up with you later." James's eyes widen in awe as he watches Alice back out of his office, the sound of her footsteps fading into the distance.

Alice retraces her steps to her bedroom, and an eerie silence settles in around her, making her feel uneasy. She spins around to find Robert standing in the dim-lit hallway, his imposing figure making her heart race. His eyes, like a predator's, remain fixated on her, causing a chill to run down her spine.

The mounting tension magnifies the silence of the house. Alice can hear the faint sound of her own breath, the only rhythm breaking the stillness. The air between them is heavy, laced with the faint musk of his cologne. Its scent is overpowering, like an unwelcome embrace that wraps around her. Alice feels trapped, like a prey caught in the predator's hold. The hallway seems to stretch into eternity as Robert steps into the shroud of shadows. Each step he takes is slow, deliberate, and echoes in the house's quietness. The soft click of the door shutting behind him punctuates the silence, and Alice's pulse quickens. Her heart beats like a staccato drum against her ribs.

She feels like the walls are closing in on her, and the room seems to shrink. The echo of her heartbeat fills the space, and she feels suffocated. She can't help but wonder what Robert wants and why he's here.

The tinkling notes of a melodious tune reverberate through the old house, filling the air with a sweet melody that seems to dance around the walls. Alice's heart races as she rushes to the front door, her bare feet pounding against the old, creaky wooden floorboards. Halfway down the stairs, her phone rings, its piercing tone slicing through the air. She hesitates, her mind racing as she imagines all the likely outcomes of her decision.

Alice hears the muffled sound of Natalie's conversation drifting up the stairwell and feels an urge to investigate. She dashes towards the front door, her breath coming in short, ragged gasps. When she sees the delivery man, her eyes widen with surprise and delight at the vibrant bouquet of wildflowers.

"Thanks, Natalie. I'll take those," she says, snatching the flowers from the man's hand. She brings them close to her nose, inhaling their sweet fragrance before placing them carefully on the dark console table in the lobby.

Natalie rolls her eyes and continues to flirt shamelessly with the delivery man, her laughter tinkling like glass as she tosses her hair back. Sparky is still cowering under the kitchen nook when Alice walks in, his face obscured by the shadows. She opens the fridge, the cool air washing over her skin like a refreshing wave, and grabs a bottle of water, the condensation slick against her fingers as she chugs it down.

Alice's face lights up with a smile as she sees Karen's missed call on her phone in her cozy bedroom. She eagerly dials her friend back, collapsing onto her soft bed, feeling the comforting vibrations of her phone in her hand.

"Thanks for calling me back, Spid," Karen says, her voice slightly muffled by the sound of a radio playing in the background.

"Where are you?" Alice asks, her curiosity piqued.

"On my way home from Grand Central," Karen replies. "Just got back from Beacon... hold on a sec." Alice can hear Karen's conversation with someone in the background.

"Sorry Spid," Karen continues. "But I wanted to let you know that I just signed an upcoming contemporary artist."

As Alice inspects her nails closely, searching for imperfections, she suddenly remembers something. "The other day, while waiting for my shrink, I read about Dia Beacon," she says. "It's a stunning art museum. By the way, what's he like, your new artist?"

In the background, Alice can hear the slam of a car door, the click of Karen's heels, and the sound of wheels scraping against the sidewalk. "It's a guy, and he seems pretty promising," Karen responds. "His name is Hans Von Sieberhagen, and he's from Germany."

Alice musters a smile despite feeling a twinge of envy in her heart. "Congratulations!" she exclaims with genuine excitement. "We should celebrate your accomplishment sometime."

"That is exactly why I called you, Spid," Karen says, her voice brimming with renewed excitement. The sound of her voice echoes in the empty room, bouncing off the walls. "I was hoping we could hang out tonight since Tiff is working."

"So, now I'm second best, is that it?" Alice teases. "Who's Tiff?" She asks, while she looks at herself in the mirror, examining her expression.

Karen reminds, "Remember Tiffany, the spicy redhead server? She's also a psychology student."

Alice tilts her head and studies the way her face changes with each expression in the mirror. "Oh yes, of course," she replies, acknowledging Karen's reminder. "By the way, I'm planning to visit the cemetery before we grab dinner with a new friend. It'll just be me, James, and Robert."

"Robert!" Karen exclaims, shocked. "What in the world, Spid? Have you lost your mind?"

Alice winces as the words sting her ears, feeling a twinge of embarrassment. "I didn't have the nerve to do it," she admits, "but I'll deal with it later, okay?"

"I'll take care of Robert," Karen says with conviction. "Would it be alright if I joined you tonight?" She asks, inhaling deeply, leaving her question hanging in the air.

"Give me a sec while I confirm with Fabian." Alice puts Karen on hold and dials Fabian's number. The phone's piercing ring breaks through the stillness of the room.

"Doctor Alice, please don't tell me you are canceling?" Fabian asks, his disappointment palpable.

"No way." Alice says. "Can my bestie come along?" she asks, biting her lip.

In the background, Fabian's rhythmic chopping fills the air. "Invite as many people as you want and don't forget to bring the drinks." He says and hangs up.

Alice activates the call she has placed on hold with Karen. "Hey, bestie, Fabian's good with it." She says with excitement. "We just gotta bring the booze." The sound of an elevator chime echoes in the background as Karen's voice resonates from inside the car.

"Great, thanks. What time do you plan to visit the cemetery?" Karen asks.

Alice attempts to say, "I'm gonna change into something black and bounce, but—" before being interrupted by Karen's firm declaration.

"I'll come with you," Karen asserts. "You're not going by yourself." And with that, she hangs up. Alice grins widely, and with a triumphant fist pump, she strides confidently towards the wardrobe.

Alice handpicks her outfit for her somber visit to the cemetery. She opts for a sophisticated look, wearing a fitted black turtleneck sweater and high-waisted, wide-legged pants that flow elegantly with each step. Her silver hoop earrings catch the glint of the sun as she steps outside, and she adjusts her delicate silver pendant necklace, feeling its weight against her skin. As she wraps herself in a long, tailored woolen coat, she catches a whiff of the sharp autumn air, filled with the scent of new beginnings. She clutches the bouquet of wildflowers tightly in her hand as she hails a cab and tosses her handbag over her shoulder.

Karen, a vibrant contrast against the cemetery's somber backdrop, waits on a bench next to its imposing black iron gates, clutching a bouquet ablaze with colors. Alice's sly grin deepens at the sight of her best friend's rebellious fashion statement—vibrant sunglasses that add a pop of color to their otherwise dull surroundings.

A chilling breeze sweeps over Alice as they step into the cemetery, causing goosebumps to rise on her arms. The air carries the scent of damp soil and decaying leaves, a haunting perfume that tugs at her heartstrings. She tightens her grip on her small black leather handbag; her knuckles turning white.

They weave their way through the labyrinth of tombstones, their journey punctuated by the eerie shadows cast by the sun, the rhythmic chorus of sprinklers, and the occasional chirping of birds overhead. A pair of magpies catches Karen's attention, their heads bobbing in sync as they peck at a marble headstone.

"Look, Spid!" Karen exclaims, pointing at the magpies. "Wonder whose grave they're scoping out."

Alice approaches the headstone, her heart pounding as she reads the name etched into the marble—'John Sterling'. A gasp escapes her lips, her eyes widening in disbelief. "I'm in awe," she confesses, her voice barely above a whisper.

Karen laughs, her eyes twinkling with mischief. "Gold diggers!"

The laughter fades as they approach Alice's parents' plots. Alice's heart clenches at the sight of the familiar headstones, her eyes welling up with tears. The stranger, dressed in a blazer and jeans, kneels beside the graves and touches the headstone tenderly. His head bowed in what appears to be prayer or contemplation.

Karen squints at the man. "Who's that?" she whispers, her voice laced with curiosity. Before Alice can reply, the man spots them. He leaps to his feet and races towards the trees, blending seamlessly into the shadows. Alice gives chase, her heart pounding as she tries to catch up to the man's rapidly fading figure. The man's shadow flickers ahead, taunting her. Alice grits her teeth and pushes harder, her determination overpowering the pain. He moves through the shadows with a practiced ease, disappearing into the shadows. Alice skids to a stop, scanning the area for any sign of him. Her breaths come in ragged gasps as she finally gives up the chase and turns back towards her parents' graves.

She stands before the two headstones, overcome by emotion, her eyes brimming with tears. The sun hangs high in the sky, casting long, ominous shadows as Karen takes Alice's hand. She feels a shiver down her spine, a stark contrast to the warmth emanating from Karen's hand. A sense of grief washes over her, yet it's tempered by the comfort of her friend's presence.

Alice sucks in a deep breath, savoring the earthy smell of damp soil and fresh flowers. She kneels, the coolness of the ground seeping through her pants, grounding her in the moment. With trembling hands, she places the bouquet on the graves, the vibrant colors a stark contrast against the dull gray of the tombstones. She swallows hard, fighting back tears as she takes a moment to compose herself. The cemetery is quiet, save for the gentle rustling of leaves dancing in the breeze, their whispers echoing amongst the gravestones.

Raising her gaze to the cerulean expanse above her, Alice feels a sense of peace envelop her. She kneels before the headstone, feeling the weight of her parents' absence as her heart swells with gratitude for all they did for her. Each beat of her heart seems to echo the distant toll of a bell, its somber melody tugging at the threads of her childhood memories.

With a comforting arm around her shoulders, Karen kneels beside Alice. Her embrace, soft and reassuring, offers solace amidst the sorrow. Alice's body trembles with grief as she clings to Karen's embrace. Tears stream down her face, leaving trails of mascara on her cheeks. Karen holds her tighter, knowing that sometimes there are no words that can ease the pain. She simply offers her presence, a shoulder to cry on, and a listening ear. Wordlessly, she guides Alice away from the graves, their figures growing smaller against the backdrop of towering ebony gates.

Alice's eyes mist over as she leaves the cemetery, feeling the weight of finality at her parents' resting place. Yet as she clings to Karen's hand, she's reminded that while grief may be a solitary journey, she isn't alone. With each step, she carries her parents' love and the promise of new beginnings, embodied in the enduring friendship with her best friend.

Alice and Karen's heels click rhythmically against the polished wooden floor as they step into Alice's home.

"Remember," Karen warns, her eyes narrowing into slits as she studies Alice. An air of unwavering conviction surrounds her as she declares, "I'll handle Robert." She leans in closer to Alice, her hushed whisper sending a tickle down Alice's ear. "Do you have the letter?"

A spark of excitement ignites in Alice's eyes. With a nod, she rushes to her office, Karen trailing closely behind. Alice's fingers deftly glide over the keypad of the safe, entering the combination. The satisfying click of the unlocking mechanism echoes in the quiet room. Alice's heart races with excitement as she hands Karen the damning letter from Robert.

Karen's eyes widen as she quickly scans the contents of the letter. The reality of the situation weighs heavily on Karen, and tears well up in her eyes. "Did you make copies?" she asks, her gaze darting nervously around the room.

Alice furrows her brow in bewilderment, her face contorting in confusion. "No, it completely slipped my mind. Thank you for reminding me," she says, the sound of rustling paper filling the room as she hastily makes copies. She locks the copies securely in the safe, the satisfying click of the lock echoing in the room. Finally, she hands the original document back to Karen, the smooth texture of the paper rubbing against her fingertips.

With a swift motion, Karen places the letter on the desk, snapping a few quick photos with her phone before tucking it safely into her purse. Just as she zips it closed, James saunters into the room, his confident swagger filling the space.

"What are you girls up to?" he asks, his eyes flicking between the two women with suspicion.

Alice instinctively hides her hands behind her back, a mischievous sparkle lighting up her eyes. "Nothing much," she replies nonchalantly, twirling a lock of her hair around her finger. "Just girlie stuff."

James's eyebrows furrow, suspicion creeping into his gaze. "I know that look, Spid," he remarks knowingly. "Once you're done here, join us in the kitchen."

Alice's smile broadens, a faint blush warming her cheeks as she nods in agreement. A flicker of suspicion remains in James's gaze, lingering between Alice and Karen. He turns on his heel and strides away, his footsteps gradually fading into the distance.

Karen exhales a sigh of relief. "That was close," she murmurs.

The closer they get to the kitchen, the more distinct the indistinct murmur of men's voices becomes, accompanied by the excited yapping of Sparky. The dog leaps into Karen's arms, lavishing her with enthusiastic licks as she steps into the kitchen. James and Robert pause their conversation, their glasses of wine momentarily forgotten, as they turn to greet the newcomers.

Karen flashes a bright smile, shaking Robert's hand with a firm grip. "Pleased to meet you, Robert."

Robert sinks back into his seat, returning her smile with a wry one of his own. "Likewise."

With a delighted twinkle in her eyes, Karen gently sets Sparky down before turning to James. "James, it's good to have you back!" she exclaims, wrapping him in a warm embrace.

An awkward silence descends upon the room, and Alice can't shake off the feeling that they've walked in on a private conversation. She gestures towards the half-filled wine glasses on the table. "Any left for us?" she ventures.

"Of course, my bad," James quickly apologizes, springing up to pour wine into their glasses. He hands them over with a smile and raises his own glass in a toast. "Cheers," he proposes.

Glasses clink in unison as everyone shouts, "Cheers!" Alice lifts her glass towards Karen, "Here's to your success with your new client!"

Alice takes a generous sip of the wine, feeling a comforting warmth spread through her body as the rich aroma fills the room. The room buzzes with lively chatter as the evening wears on, punctuated by bursts of laughter. James stands up from his seat as the clock chimes half-past the hour and he checks his watch. "Time to head out," he announces, gathering his basket of snacks and drinks.

Sparky trails behind them to the front door, his hopeful yap echoing in the cool evening air as they step outside. His drooping tail betrays his disappointment at their departure, adding a touch of melancholy to his lonely state.

5

The quartet steps out of the yellow cab in front of the Cozy Corner deli, the place where Alice first encountered Fabian. Alice reaches for the door, the rusted handle resisting her pull—it's locked. The creaking sound echoes loudly in the quiet evening. Straining her eyes, she tries to peer through the smoky window into the pitch-black interior. Her hand dives into her handbag, retrieving her phone to dial Fabian's number

"Hey Doctor Alice, I see ya," Fabian's voice comes through the speaker, muffled by a mouthful of food.

Alice's eyebrows furrow in confusion as she looks around, searching for any sign of him. "I tried the deli, but it's locked," she says, uncertainty creeping into her voice.

"Look up here," he guides her, "Behind you."

At the sound of his voice, Alice spins around to find Fabian leaning out of his apartment window above, waving down at them. "Blue door, I'll buzz you in," he directs, pointing towards the entrance.

Alice hangs up and follows his instructions, her friends trailing behind. As they approach the blue door, a loud buzzing sound fills the air, followed by the grating creak of the metal gate opening.

"I've got it," James offers, holding the door open for his companions.

"Look at you guys down there!" Fabian calls from above, leaning precariously over the railing.

Alice lifts her gaze to meet his calm expression. "Hey Fabian!" she calls back, her voice tinged with excitement. They navigate their way down the dimly lit hallway and up the creaky stairs, congregating outside Fabian's front door.

Fabian's smiling face greets them as they approach the doorway. "Welcome to my humble abode," he says, waving them in with an inviting gesture. James and Robert step aside in a chivalrous gesture, allowing the ladies to enter first.

Fabian scans Alice and Karen critically. "You two look like you're headed to a funeral," he comments, raising an eyebrow.

Karen smirks, "We just visited the cemetery to pay respects to Alice's parents."

A wave of embarrassment washes over Fabian, his cheeks flushing a deep red. "Ah, my apologies! That was thoughtless of me."

Alice offers him a consoling smile and steps into the apartment. "Fabian, meet my friends Karen, James, and Robert. Thanks for having us."

After introductions and handshakes, James presents the basket of wines and snacks with a glint of mischief in his eyes. Fabian chuckles, "I've got it," he assures, heading towards the kitchen. "It's great to meet you all! Please, make yourselves at home."

Stepping across the threshold, Alice's breath catches as she takes in the breathtaking elegance of Fabian's apartment. A world apart from the stark exterior, the interior radiates warmth and sophistication. Soft yellow light spills from strategically placed lamps, their glow bathing the room in a comforting aura.

Fabian's impeccable taste in decor is evident. Rustic furniture pieces, lovingly restored, dot the room, creating a harmonious blend of vintage charm and modern elegance. Vibrant artwork adorns the walls, each piece brimming with intricate detail that speaks volumes about the artist's passion. Framed photographs of Fabian's travels tell a silent story, instilling a sense of awe and wanderlust in the beholder.

The deep mahogany floors gleam under the warm light, their polished surface reflecting the cozy atmosphere. A tantalizing mix of scents—home-cooked meals, soothing incense, and flickering candles—wafts through the air, creating a heady, romantic perfume that stirs the senses.

The soft strains of a jazz tune fill the room as Alice sinks into a plush seat. The deep, pulsating rhythm of the bass, the playful trills of the piano, and the seductive drawl of the saxophone weave a melodic tapestry that tugs at her soul. Her body responds almost involuntarily, swaying subtly in time with the music, a shiver of delight running down her spine.

She allows herself to sink deeper into the cushions; the music enveloping her in its warm embrace. A slow smile curves across her lips as she succumbs to the enchantment of the moment. The cozy ambiance, the enticing aromas, and the soulful music mingle together, making her feel as if she's stepped into a dream.

Everyone takes their seats around the solid, dark oak table as Fabian appears with a tray of effervescent cocktails. The drinks, garnished with skewered olives and citrus twists, sparkle under the soft lighting, their vibrant hues casting a tantalizing glow. Whispers and gasps of excitement ripple through the room, making the air electric.

Alice, unable to resist the allure, reaches for one of the inviting glasses. "This looks wonderful, Fabian. What is it?" She takes a moment to savor the heady scent of tropical fruits and crisp orange wafting from the cocktail.

With a proud sparkle in his eyes and a broad grin on his face, Fabian exclaims, "In my homeland, this drink is called a Spritz Veneziano, but you may know it better as an Aperol Spritz. Salute!" He lifts his glass high, and his infectious cheer resonates in his voice.

A chorus of enthusiastic cheers echoes through the room, the sound sending a thrilling shiver down Alice's spine. Fabian leans back, his face glowing with satisfaction as he takes in the scene before him: friends engrossed in lively conversation, laughter ringing out, glasses clinking in a symphony of celebration.

The tantalizing aromas of homemade Italian cuisine fill the air—the tangy scent of ripe tomatoes mingling with the delicate aroma of marinated seafood—provides a briny counterpoint, enhanced by the bright notes of lemon and the robust earthiness of garlic.

Karen sways to the rhythm of the music filling the room. She closes her eyes, letting the pulsating rhythm carry her away, and a smile spreads across her face.

Fabian gathers the empty glasses, balancing them carefully on the tray before disappearing into the dazzling kitchen, donning his apron with a sense of purpose. Alice, drawn by the tantalizing aroma of simmering sauces, joins him amidst shiny stainless-steel appliances and a large marble countertop. Her face lights up with joy at the symphony of sizzling pans and clinking dishes. "What can I do to help, Fabian?"

The question takes Fabian by surprise, and his eyes widen in astonishment. "Wow, Doctor Alice, you're too kind. Anything works."

Alice smiles, her hands gracefully dancing between cutlery and dishes as she stacks the dishwasher. She lays out plates, cutlery, and napkins on the table with practiced ease, adding a feminine touch to the culinary concert. Together, they form an unexpected yet harmonious team in the kitchen.

"Drinks anyone?" Alice's voice carries from the warmth of the kitchen.

"Wine please!" James exclaims, and the others nod their heads in agreement.

Alice gracefully carries the silver tray, adorned with a vibrant red wine bottle and crystal glasses, to the lounge. She places it on the low table, and the clinking of the glasses echoes throughout the room. The sweet aroma of the wine fills the air, and the sound of the cork popping out of the bottle punctuates the silence. Suddenly, the bottle slips from Alice's hand, and the sound of sharp inhales fills the room as everyone gasps in unison. Before the bottle hits the ground, Robert's hand shoots out with lightning-fast reflexes, catching it inches from the floor. Alice's eyes widen in shock, and the lounge erupts in a cacophony of applauses for Robert's skill. Robert stands and motions for Alice to sit as he gracefully tops up the wineglasses. A strange silence blankets the lounge as everyone fixates their eyes on his impressive wine-glass-filling skills. Alice and Karen share a fleeting glance, their eyes conveying a silent understanding.

"Cheers!" James exclaims with a wide smile, lifting his glass and aiming it at Robert. The clinking of the glasses echoes in the room as everyone follows James' lead and point their glasses towards Robert. The fragrance of the wine tickles their noses, and the sight of the deep red liquid sloshing around in the glasses is enchanting. Robert's face turns crimson, matching the hue of the wine in his glass, and he bows his head in humility. Their animated conversations fill the air with a buzz, and a grin of satisfaction appears on Fabian's face as he relishes the lively atmosphere in the company of his new friends.

With great care, Fabian inspects Alice's table setting and adds a tablespoon to the arrangement at the head of the table.

"What did I miss?" Alice asks with a curious expression and a tilt of her head.

Fabian chuckles, charmed by the adorable expression on her face. "Nope, my dad's coming too. He's just gotta drop his boss off at the hotel first."

"Cool, can't wait to meet the man who raised you to be so charming." Alice says, and a genuine smile lights up her face.

Fabian's cheeks flush with a warm, rosy hue. "Nah, he doesn't know me." His lips curl into a sly grin. "My mom went to Italy to visit family and I can't let the old man starve."

"Wow, that's so nice of you. Get ready, I've got a ton of questions for your dad." Alice smiles and walks back to her seat, bouncing along to the upbeat rhythm.

The aroma of the food still lingers in the air as Fabian turns the stove plates off and joins his guests in the lounge. A surrealistic painting on the wall evokes a heated debate, electrifying the room. The painting is breathtaking, showing the profile of a young man, depicted from the waist up. He turns slightly to the left, yet his direct and serene gaze creates a sense of intimacy with the viewer.

His lavish attire, reminiscent of the Renaissance era, is a testament to his status and affluence. With elegance, he raises his left hand to his chest. Long, artistic fingers hold a fur coat draped over his left shoulder. The garment, an embodiment of luxury and opulence, seems to whisper tales of wealth and sophistication. Its exterior, a plush showcase of meticulously painted fur, contrasts starkly with the shiny, sleek lining visible on the inside.

The figure sits confidently, with a satisfied, somewhat arrogant smile playing on his lips and a black beret resting atop his head. It's perched at a jaunty angle towards the back. The beret, a timeless symbol of sophistication, adds an air of enigmatic charm to his persona. He styled his vibrant shade of ginger hair in a middle part, and it cascades down his shoulders in a riot of bouncy curls. The unruly waves add a wild contrast to the disciplined cut of the beret, creating a captivating interplay of order and chaos.

The painting's surrealism is so captivating that everyone burns their eyes on it. James takes a closer look at the art, examining the intricate brush strokes and vibrant colors. "Hmm, it's a Titian," he says, scratching his chin

Spurred on by the fiery debate, Karen's eyes light up with excitement. "Almost James, but not quite. Think nuanced when you look at the brushwork." Leaning forward in her chair, she is fully engaged in the discussion, her eyes sparkling with enthusiasm. Her cheeks flush with a rosy hue, reflecting the passion that burns within her. Sitting with perfect posture, she exudes confidence and enthusiasm, ready to unleash her creativity at any moment.

James's eyes narrow as he inspects the brush strokes. He inhales deeply and releases a cinematic sigh. "I tell you darling, it's a Titian, or..." suddenly his eyes light up. "Giorgione!" he exclaims with conviction.

Fabian's eyes light up, and he breaks into a wide grin, clapping his hands in delight.

"Yup, Italian, you're doing great, James. Need a hint?" asks Karen. "Despite not being old, the way the light dances off the surface is mesmerizing," she implies

Fabians raises an eyebrow in surprise at Karen and gives her a thumbs up.

"Hmm, light, not old, young..." James murmurs, while absentmindedly scratching the back of his head. Suddenly, he beams with excitement. "Portrait of a young man, Raphael!" His loud shout echoes through the room and causes everyone to jump.

The room is alive with the sound of rowdy cheers that echo off the walls. James' face flushes with embarrassment, and he sinks into his seat.

"Karen, your art knowledge is impressive," Fabian says, winking at her.

"I guess so," Karen says nonchalantly, giving a slight shrug. "Art blogging is a passion of mine, and I get excited to share my collection of unique pieces."

"That is an authentic copy of the original," Fabian declares with a smirk as he gestures to the mysterious canvas. But as he speaks, a nervous twitch betrays his bravado. His smirk wavers for a split second, before returning with even greater intensity, as if he is trying to convince himself more than anyone else. Despite his attempts to appear confident, it's clear that something about the painting has gotten under his skin.

At the sight before her, Karen's eyes bulge out of their sockets in disbelief. "No!" She lets out a high-pitched shriek, like a star-struck teen meeting her idol.

With a proud smile, Fabian confirms, "Yes, my dear. We have safely stored the original painting at our family estate in Calabria." He then stands up and approaches the painting.

Karen cries. "No, impossible." Her eyes widen in disbelief, and she jumps up, frantically searching for her handbag.

James asks, "How would you know?" He then explains, "Unfortunately, there are no photographs or reproductions of the original painting as it's been missing for over seventy years." He emphasizes the last two words, elongating them and letting them roll off his tongue with particular emphasis.

Karen rummages through her handbag and pulls out her phone. She unlocks it and taps on the screen with a sense of urgency. "This is the real thing," she insists, pointing to the phone in her hand. Her phone becomes the center of attention as everyone gathers around, fixating their eyes on the picture on the screen.

The picture shows a young man in a black hat and a gold chain, looking at the viewer with a confident and calm expression. His face is oval-shaped, with a straight nose, thin lips, and dark eyes. His hair is brown and straight, falling over his forehead and ears with an inward curve. He wears a dark coat over a white shirt, with a fur collar and cuffs. The background is plain and dark, creating a contrast with the light on his face and clothes. In his left hand, he holds a scroll that is partially rolled up and has some writing on it.

"Check it out. He's holding a scroll and not messing with his coat." Karen says, pointing at the letter in the man's left hand.

"Give me a sec." Fabian replies. He stands and collects his phone. As he kneels beside Karen, everyone crowds around him, gaping at his phone screen. He scrolls through a list of thumbnails, brings one up, and enlarges it. "Look, that's the original, safe and sound in our family estate where it belongs."

"Well, I never," Karen gasps, "I'll be damned," she says and gently strokes the phone screen. Excitement sends shivers down her spine, and she rubs her arms to get rid of the goosebumps.

"But it's on a list of missing paintings and nobody's found it!" James protests, throwing his hands up.

With a mischievous grin, Fabian locks his phone and slides it into his pocket. "You know what they say," he says, "some stories are best left unsaid."

Karen gracefully rises from her seat and strides across the dimly lit room to where Fabian is sitting. She kneels between his legs, and her hands clasp together in prayer, causing the room to fall silent as all eyes turn to her. She takes a deep breath, looks up at Fabian, and shyly asks, "Please marry me."

Her face contorts into a puppy dog expression, and her eyes grow wide and pleading.

The room suddenly falls into a hushed silence, punctuated only by the collective sighs and soft "ahh's" of admiration. The soft glow of the candlelight flickers, casting a warm and inviting glow on the faces of the guests. Karen's proposal surprises Alice, but she quickly warms up to the idea. Her eyes wander around the room, taking in the sight of the guests, until they land on Robert, whose distant gaze and solemn face catches her attention. She sees the sadness in his eyes and wonders what might have caused it, thinking if he has guessed that she knows something about him.

Karen turns to Alice and says, "We're good to go. You're a commissioner of oaths. Alice, would you mind doing the honors?" The sound of her name jolts Alice back to reality. She feels the cool surface of her Spritzer glass in her hand and crosses the air with her finger, uttering, "By the power of this Spritzer I declare..." she raises her glass aloft, and James follows suit. "You're officially hitched, Mr. and Mrs. Moneybags. This Spritzer in my hand states that Karen now owns a fair portion of Fabian's art collection."

"Hell yeah!" James exclaims, pumping his fist in the air as Alice joins in with a jubilant cheer. The sound of laughter and conversation fill the air as guests clink their glasses together in celebration. Karen leans in to give Fabian a playful, passionate kiss. The room erupts in laughter, and the mood becomes light and playful. Everyone basks in the warmth of the newlyweds' love, their eyes shining with joy.

The front door flings open and the whistling of a stubby, balding man follows as he skips into the room. He takes off his overcoat and gives the strangers a curious glance. Startled by his dad's sudden arrival, Fabian jumps up, accidentally knocking Karen off balance. Karen stumbles backwards, her arms flailing in the air. Fabian screams her name and lunges forward, grabbing her hand just in time. Their fingers intertwine as they stumble, and they end up in a tangle, with Fabian falling on top of her. Karen lies on her back, her short dress riding up and exposing her legs, making the old man at the doorway uneasy.

The stubby old man's eyes shoot daggers as he glares at the scene before him. He lets out a high-pitched squeal and yells in Italian, "*Basta così!*" Fabian's face turns beet red in embarrassment.

Meanwhile, Alice stands frozen, her hand clasped over her mouth. She murmurs under her breath, her heart racing with shock and disbelief. The air is thick with tension as the man continues to stare at them. The smell of his cologne, musky and strong, permeates the room.

Finally, Fabian stands up and greets his dad with a hug. He takes his overcoat and hangs it on the coat rack. "Hi dad, these are my friends." He gestures towards his guests. "Guys, meet my dad, Mattia Bertolli."

Mattia walks around the room, shaking hands with each person as he introduces himself. The moment Alice comes into view, he flinches with recognition. "You! *Donna birichina*," he exclaims in shock, his eyebrows furrowed. Alice feels her pulse quicken as she locks eyes with Mattia. The world around her seems to blur into a haze of noise and color. Mattia shakes his head in dismay and sinks into his comfy leather seat, the spring groaning beneath him.

Fabian's eyes flit back and forth between Alice and his dad, his gaze roving over their faces in rapid succession. The sound of his voice cuts through the tense silence, his tone brimming with curiosity. "Have you two met before?" he asks, his expression quizzical and uncertain.

Alice nervously clears her throat before speaking. "Yes," she stammers, "I actually met your father before. He gave me a lift home."

With a look of disbelief, Mattia shakes his head, his voice ringing out clearly in the hushed atmosphere. "Yes, I remember," he affirms, before turning to Fabian with a creased brow. Expressing concern, he warns, "Your friend is a troublemaker. She drank champagne in the limo and gave me a secret kiss on my head. Mama was very angry and now thinks I have a lover."

The sound of gasps fills the air as the lounge transforms into a symphony of shock and awe. Everyone watches Alice and Mattia's graceful dance of emotions. The air is thick with tension and anticipation as the guests watch their every move, their eyes darting back and forth between the two. The atmosphere is electric, charged with an energy that everyone in the room can feel.

Alice blushes deeply, her cheeks suffused with color as she looks down at her feet. Her eyes dart around the room, lingering on the rough patterns of the wooden floor. "I'm sorry, Mattia," she says quietly, "I never meant to cause any trouble."

Mattia's bright grin spread across his face, instantly lighting up the room and breaking the tension. "You were just tipsy from the sparkling wine," he reassures Alice, his voice warm and comforting. Turning to Fabian, he adds, "Keep an eye on her, my son. Signor Granger, my boss, thinks she is very beautiful." With a playful wag of his finger towards Alice, he emits a hearty chuckle that resonates throughout the room.

Fabian draws everyone's attention abruptly as he lets out a thunderous clap. "Lets eat." He announces and makes his way to the kitchen, strutting confidently.

A wave of excitement ripples through the lounge, creating a buzz of energy that is contagious. Alice jumps out of her seat and scurries after Fabian into the kitchen. "Hey, need a hand with anything?" She asks, her tummy churns with butterflies as she meets his ever-peaceful gaze.

He puts on a winsome smile that warms his face. "Thanks, look in that drawer," he gestures. "Grab some long spoons and forks, will ya?"

Alice grabs a tray and opens the cutlery drawer, sifting through the contents until she finds spoons and forks. Fabian's skilled hands move gracefully across the counter as he prepares the salad. The aroma of fresh basil fills the air, and Alice can feel her mouth water. With a tray in hand, she sets out napkins, salt, and pepper, and side plates before carrying it to the lounge. She wears a satisfied smile as she listens to James and Mattia's discussion about the intricate process of Parma ham production.

While the guests argue about the authenticity of Italian cuisine, Fabian moves around the kitchen with a flurry of activity as he prepares the classic dishes. Alice's ears perk up as James repeatedly mentions American pizza and carbonara, trying to convince Mattia. Despite James' attempts, Mattia remains defiant, his voice growing louder as he uses colorful Italian curses to express his displeasure.

Alice and James share a laugh as they continue their preparations, the tension from the debate melting away. The kitchen is a buzz with activity, the clanging of pots and pans and the sizzling of ingredients filling the air. The aroma of freshly baked bread mixes with the tangy scent of ripe tomatoes to create an irresistible fragrance of homemade Italian cuisine that fills the apartment. Alice deftly slices the lemons into wedges and snips fresh dill into sprigs, the sharp scent of citrus and the refreshing aroma of herbs filling the kitchen. The sound of the knife slicing through the lemon fills the room as she garnishes the plates, adding a zesty aroma that makes mouths water in anticipation of the meal to come.

In a matter of minutes, Fabian and Alice deftly fill the hurricane glasses with a rainbow of vibrant colors and flavors, each scent tantalizing the guests' nostrils. With skillful precision, Fabian adds a touch of elegance to each glass by garnishing it with a delicate sprig of dill.

The guest's anticipation builds as they catch a glimpse of the beautifully layered dishes, the vibrant colors of the ingredients popping against the clear glasses. With the first bite, an orchestra of flavors and textures emerges, as the briny taste of the sea pairs with the seafood's freshness, producing a melodious sensation on the tongue. It's a true celebration of the senses, a culinary experience that transports the guests to the heart of Italy.

Fabian beams as he watches the guests relishing his culinary masterpiece. "That, my friends, is a Caprese salad," he says, motioning towards the vibrant dish. "And over here, we have *insalata di mare*, a classic Italian seafood salad." He taps his nail against the hurricane glass, creating a musical sound like wind chimes on a breezy day. The contents of the glass intrigue the guests, their eyes dancing with anticipation. "Last but not least, we have *pane alle nocciole*, or hazelnut bread, as you guys call it," he adds, chuckling as he bites into a slice.

Mattia's eyes shine with delight as he raises his glass in a toast. "To Alice," he says with a warm smile, "the new sous-chef of the family."

Alice's face turns crimson as the sound of laughter and applause fills the room. With the food and drinks served, everyone settles in for a night of conversation and laughter, the scent of the seafood lingering in the air. The warmth of the fire crackles in the background, and the sound of clinking spoons fills the room as everyone savors the last bits of deliciousness from their glasses. Alice can't help but smile as she looks around the room, her heart filled with contentment.

This is what it feels like to be part of a family, she thinks, the sights, smells, and sounds of the evening etched into her memory.

The air in the lounge is thick with lethargy after dinner, and the quiet hum of conversation dwindles to a near silence. Fabian hurries to the kitchen and starts up the coffee machine. The machine hums and whirs, filling the room with the delicious aroma of freshly brewed espresso. Alice and Fabian prepare the coffee cups, scooping spoons of sugar, adding cream, and carefully pouring the dark liquid, creating a symphony of clinking spoons, steam, and murmurs.

The invigorating warmth of the coffee radiates from the cups as the guests gather around the table, indulging in a newfound energy. A wave of enthusiasm ripples through the room, igniting animated conversations.

A mischievous glint appears in Fabian's eye as he quickly heads to the kitchen. He emerges moments later, brandishing a bottle of Bailey's Irish cream, and generously adds a tot to everyone's cup. "To new family traditions," he says, raising his cup in a toast. Everyone nods in agreement and takes a sip of the heavenly concoction as they listen to the crackle of the fire, the sweet aroma of the Bailey's and coffee blending together. Alice grins, feeling the warmth of the room seeping into her bones.

She looks around the table, her eyes meeting Karen's. She winks at her, a silent understanding of the special bond they share. Karen smiles, her face lights up. "Let's play, never have I ever!" she exclaims, her voice filled with excitement. She fixes a firm gaze on everyone sitting around the table. "Who's game?"

Laughter and cheers erupt as everyone agrees to the suggestion. With excitement, Fabian rubs his hands together as he collects port glasses and snifters from the kitchen and neatly sets them on the table. He opens the liquor cabinet with a creak, and his eyes scan the shelves for the perfect drink. He selects a bottle of cognac and port and sets them on the table.

James expertly pours the drinks, and the sweet smell of port and brandy fills the room, evoking memories of a vineyard in autumn. Fabian waits patiently for James to finish, tapping his foot in anticipation before throwing his hands in the air and exclaiming. "It's showtime!" Everyone throws their hands up and gives a ten, feeling the warmth of the room, the taste of coffee, and the buzz of excitement.

Mattia lifts his glass high and makes a joyful exclamation. "*Dolce Italiano*," he sings the words with a high lilting tenor. The sound of cheers and laughter fills the room as everyone erupts at his unexpected pun.

Karen gestures towards Mattia and says, "You're up first since you volunteered."

A flush of crimson spreads across the old man's face. His eyes narrow in concentration, and his forehead creases before he breaks into a wide grin. "Okay, I know," he exclaims excitedly. "Never have I ever skinny dipped," he admits, throwing his hands up. One by one, everyone in the group puts a finger down, but he keeps all of his fingers up.

Alice and Karen simultaneously point at the glasses, shouting "Drink!" The sound of glasses thudding fills the air as everyone around the table chugs their drinks.

A look of bewilderment appears on Mattia's face. "But I win this round. Why must I drink?"

Fabian looks at his dad affectionately. "Dad, have you skinny dipped before?"

With laughter echoing through the room, he exclaims, "Yes!"

Shrugging and heaving a deep sigh, Fabian signals his resignation. "Drink," he says as he gestures towards the sherry. "Come up with something you think no one else has done in this game, okay?"

Mattia nods and chugs his drink. "Understood. Next round, you all drink," he says as he raises his empty glass.

Mattia and James last several rounds but eventually drop out one after the other. With bated breath, Alice and Karen watch Robert's hand intently, hoping to catch any movement that could give away his next move. Karen takes a stab at him. "Never have I ever ratted on my partner."

Everyone is still, not a finger moves, and the tension in the room becomes palpable. Alice watches closely, and she can almost feel the hesitation in the air as Robert's fingers twitch.

With only two fingers up, Fabian inhales a deep breath and tightly shuts his eyes. "Never have I ever been to Africa," he says, and slowly opens one eye and peers at Robert. Robert's finger inches downwards. Fabian's excitement mounts until he let out a triumphant yell and pumps his fist.

"Never have I ever made out with someone of the opposite sex," Robert says, his voice laced with mischievousness. James cheers Robert on, his claps echoing through the room. Fabian nervously glances at his dad, who slumps in his seat and emits soft snores. Alice lets out a sigh as she puts down her last finger, collapsing back into the chair with a heavy thud. Her eyes lock with Karen's, silently pleading for a glimmer of hope.

Karen has everyone's attention. Her chest rises as she inhales sharply. She puts on a show of concentration as she surveys the empty glasses on the table. "Hmm," she interjects, her tone betraying a hint of mischief. "Never have I ever sold my partner down the river," she admits and gives Robert a stern look.

The silence in the room is tangible, punctuated only by the occasional crackling of the fire. Robert's face turns pale, his fist tightens into a white-knuckled ball. All are motionless, gazing at each other's hands.

Finally, Fabian breaks the tension and speaks, his voice soft but firm. "Never have I ever danced in the rain," he utters, his eyes darting between Karen and Robert's hands.

Karen mutters "Bugger", her tone laced with faux frustration, as she puts down her solitary finger and slumps back into the chair.

Robert gives Fabian a cheeky grin. "Looks like it's just me and you, pal," he quips, sizing up his competition

"Last man standing," Fabian declares, his voice ringing with challenge.

Robert's chest expands as he takes a deep breath, before he puffs his cheeks and makes a popping sound as he exhales. He squints his eyes. "Never have I ever cooked spaghetti and meatballs for my family."

"No way, you sneaky bugger!" Fabian exclaims as he puts down his last finger.

Robert's face lights up as he throws his hands up in victory. "Yes!" he exclaims, collapsing into his seat.

"Well done, buddy," James says, patting him on the back.

Fabian stands up slowly, approaches Robert, and congratulates him with a firm handshake, his eyes brimming with pride.

Kare's eyes bore into Robert's, her stare unwavering and severe. "Cheater," she spits out the word with venom, her voice sharp and cold. The accusation hangs heavily in the silent room, the tension palpable. Alice fidgets in her seat, her fingers tracing the intricate design of the table, her eyes fixed on the polished wood.

"What did you call me?" Robert cries out in disbelief, his voice rising to a pitch.

"You are a cheater," Karen says, her voice laced with bitterness, her eyes never leaving Robert's face.

James sits up straight, his body tense with anticipation, his ears pricked, and his eyes never leaving Karen's face. "Is this a joke?" he asks, his voice barely above a whisper.

Karen meets their questioning gazes with a stern look of her own. "Decide for yourselves," she says, her voice firm, as she reaches into her handbag. The rustle of paper fills the room as she extracts the letter Robert wrote. With a flick of her wrist, she tosses it onto the low table.

Shocked, Robert gasps and snatches the letter, his fingers trembling as he reads the words. He crumples it into a ball before tossing it into the fire; the flames leaping and crackling as the paper burns.

James' eyes narrow as he glares at Robert. "Why did you do that?" he asks, his eyebrows raised in surprise.

Karen reassures, "Don't worry about him. I already made a backup." Her words spill out as she hastily retrieves her phone. The sound of her fingers tapping on the screen fills the room. She pulls up the document and slides the phone across the table, the smooth surface gliding against the wood. James moves quickly and grabs the phone before Robert can get his hands on it.

James's face goes tomato-red as he reads the letter. He sighs and looks at Robert with teary eyes.

Robert stares at the floor, his expression a mix of shame and defiance. He snatches the phone from James's hand and peers intently at the screen. "I'll be damned," he mutters. "I didn't sign it, that slimy snake!"

James furrows his brow and says, "I don't understand." He then asks, "Can you explain?"

Robert takes a deep breath, his chest rising and falling. "Madison Granger," he says slowly, his eyes fixed on James. "I can explain," he pleads, his voice cracking with emotion.

Karen leans back in her chair, waving her hand and urging, "Come on, spill the beans." The sound of her bracelets jingles softly. Alice playfully nudges her in the side to quiet her, the movement barely perceptible.

Robert starts with a deep sigh before explaining, "A while back, Madison Granger contacted me to install a security system in their large mansion." He looks around the room to make sure everyone is following along before continuing, "She told me she was being harassed by a stalker."

Once he checks everyone's faces, he continues speaking. "I've added motion sensors and cameras that she can access remotely from her phone," he explains. As his voice echoes in the room, the tension slowly dissipates.

Robert's voice resonates through the spacious room, enveloping every corner with its commanding presence. The silence that follows is almost tangible, as if it is a physical entity. The fire flickers and dances, casting shadows that seem to move and shift across his face. Robert's eyes dart around the room, as if searching for something. He jumps up suddenly, causing the poker to clang against the fireplace as he grabs it. Everyone leans in, captivated as his story unfolds.

Silence envelops the room until Mattia's snort pierces through it, echoing off the walls. Confused, Robert narrows his eyes at Mattia and uses the poker in his hand as a makeshift sword, pointing it towards the door. "To cut a long story short," he begins, "the stalker realized he was running out of time and took a chance. He then hid behind a bush and peered through the foliage to get a better look." Robert's eyes light up as he acts out the scene, swinging the poker through the air and making playful whooshing sounds like a pirate.

"Like a ghost, I moved around the house," he continues, his voice low and intense. The sound of his footsteps is barely audible, but the tension in the room is palpable. "My heart pounding in my chest as I approached the open balcony."

The wind outside howls, and the curtains in the room flutter and dance, causing everyone to gasp. Whirling around, Robert brandishes the poker menacingly at Alice and Karen sitting side by side on the leather couch. Alice lets out a dramatic gasp, pretending to be frightened, and then playfully collapses as if she has fainted. The sound of the poker hitting the floor echoes loudly in the quiet room as Robert drops it. Mattia wakes up to the noise and stretches his arms while observing Robert's playful behavior with tired eyes.

Robert lifts his arms as he describes his daring feat. "I approached the balustrade with a shuffle and carefully climbed onto it, feeling the wind rush past me," he says. He pretends to be perched on top of a high ledge. "And then," he continues, "with a leap from the balcony, I landed squarely on top of the stalker, rendering him unconscious." Robert drops back into his seat and closes his eyes, savoring the moment.

Alice's excitement is palpable as she asks, "So, what happened next?"

All around him, people hold their breath, eager for Robert to speak. He begins, "My bravery impressed Madison, and she asked how she could repay me." A hint of embarrassment creeps into his voice as he admits, "I was drowning in gambling debt, so I asked her if she could recommend me for other jobs or provide me with a good referral." But before he can finish, Robert's face turns rosy, and he shifts uncomfortably in his seat. "To my surprise, Madison offered to pay off my debts and even spoke to her husband about hooking me up with a job installing security units at his hotels."

Alice's eyes widen with surprise as she exclaims, "No way, not that snake!"

Robert nods and smiles with understanding as he recounts, "That's how I met James." The flickering light of the fire illuminates everyone's faces, casting a warm glow throughout the room.

"My mission was to find a skilled professional who could design and build the utility units required for the hotel rooms." Robert says. "As fate would have it, I stumbled upon James, and it forever changed our lives. Despite their usefulness, bugs still plague the units," he teases with a playful nudge to James's side. James's eyes light up with pride as he places his arm around Robert's shoulders.

Karen's sudden shriek pierces the silence, making everyone jump. Her stern gaze falls on Robert as she demands, "Why did you write the letter? You're not off the hook yet!"

With a heavy heart, Robert lets out a deep sigh, and then covers his face with his hands. "Madison forced me to write the letter," he says, "threatening me and saying that she'd get her husband to cancel our contract. She's aware of the unit's minor bugs and said she will force us to repay her husband. And—"

James interrupts and says, "Totally agree. I spent hours on it and can confirm we fixed the bugs." He then rests his hand on Robert's knee and continues, "During our meeting, I made a promise to the hotel managers that we would cover the expenses for the upgrades."

Alice's face turns a bright shade of crimson as she remembers the evening in the hotel room with Samuel Granger. Her heart races as she recalls the intense emotions of that night. Despite her attempts to calm down, memories of Samuel's touch and their intense connection overwhelm her.

Her face remains flushed and she can feel her cheeks burning, betraying the embarrassment and shame she feels.

Fabian places a tray of piping hot cocoa, topped with fluffy marshmallows, onto the coffee table. The scent of chocolate wafts through the air, causing everyone's taste buds to tingle with excitement.

James casts a pitiful look in Alice's direction. "Alice, I'm really sorry, but I knew about the letter. Robert told me earlier, and I was going to tell you," he confesses, silently begging for her mercy.

James' confession touches Alice deeply, and she feels tears prickling at the corners of her eyes. With a sniffle, Alice wipes away her tears and the dancing firelight shimmers in her glossy eyes. "I should have spoken to you about it, James. Thanks for being honest, Robert," she says, her eyes red and puffy. Karen moves closer and pulls Alice into a warm embrace.

The group sits huddled around the fire, the crackling of the wood and the warmth emanating from the flames filling the room. The sweet aroma of cocoa wafts through the air, mixing with the scent of smoke and pine. Alice can feel the rough texture of the carpet beneath her fingertips as she slowly relaxes her tense muscles and leans into Karen's embrace.

Alice takes a sip of the hot cocoa and feels a comforting warmth spread through her body. She takes a deep breath, savoring the taste of the chocolate and the feeling of warmth spreading through her body. The tension that has been building in her chest dissipates, and she releases a long sigh.

Robert's eyes dart around the room, searching for a reaction. He takes a deep breath before finally speaking. "I'm sorry, Karen. I made a mistake, and I regret it. You have my word that I won't do it again."

Karen watches him for a few moments before finally relenting. "Okay," she says. "I forgive you."

The tension in the room slowly dissipates as everyone lets out a sigh of relief. Fabian breaks the silence by taking a sip of his cocoa and grinning. "Well, I think that's enough excitement for one night," he says. "Let's call it a night, shall we?"

Mattia turns to Karen and gives her a warm hug as they make their way to the door. "You're a very brave woman, Karen," he says. "I'm proud of you."

Karen blushes. "Thanks, Mattia. I appreciate it." Alice smiles as she watches Mattia and Karen. She knows they will remember this night for years to come.

She swiftly pivots on her heel, her eyes meeting Fabian's intense gaze. "I have a plan to fix this. Fingers crossed it works. I won't forget this evening anytime soon," Alice says gratefully.

6

As young Alice slips beneath the water's surface, she's engulfed in a refreshing coolness that teases her senses. The world above fades into muffled echoes, replaced by the serene silence of the pool's depths. The buoyancy of the water cradles her, a comforting embrace that makes her feel weightless, free. All around her, laughter rings out like a cheerful melody, a stark contrast to the eerie tranquility beneath the surface.

A low, ominous rumble shatters the placid azure of tranquility, suddenly. It spreads through the water like a shockwave, transforming the calm pool into a frothy whirlpool. The once-clear water becomes murky, the laughter above now sounding distant and distorted, swallowed by the chaos below.

A sliver of light dances on the water's surface, an ethereal beacon amidst the dark underbelly of the bobbing boogie boards. Alice's heart pounds against her ribcage, a frantic rhythm that drowns out all other sounds. She kicks upwards, desperate to breach the surface, but a rogue board knocks her back into the depths.

Panic swells within her, a tidal wave threatening to consume her. Every beat of her heart feels like a drum echoing in the cavernous depths, a morbid soundtrack to her predicament. Precious air escapes her lungs in a rush, her scream drowned by the water. Her world turns monochrome, her body heavy as lead. She gasps for air as the icy water fills her lungs, and the darkness envelopes her, dragging her deeper into the abyss.

Just as she's about to surrender to the relentless pull, a strong grip latches onto her arm. A distant voice pierces the silence, calling her name with increasing urgency.

Alice jolts upright in her bed, gasping for breath. Natalie's worried face swims into focus, her trembling voice a stark contrast to the calm of the room. "Alice, wake up," she pleads, shaking Alice gently.

Blinking away the remnants of her nightmare, Alice stretches languidly and offers a weak smile. "Nat, you look like a cherub," she teases, her voice raspy from the residual terror.

"Did you have a bad dream again?" Natalie asks, her concern palpable. Alice doesn't answer, her gaze lost in the distance, haunted by the nightmare that felt all too real. She feels the warmth of the arm wrapped around her waist. Her fingers move along the arm and she spots Karen lying beside her, wearing a mischievous smile. She meets Natalie's scowl head-on, matching it with a fierce scowl of her own.

"Honeychild, what's goin' on in this here house? James got himself some fella sleepin' in his room, and Karen's all sprawled out in your bed." Natalie's finger wags as she chides Alice.

Karen stirs next to Alice, the rustling of the sheets breaking the silence. With a swift tug, Natalie opens the curtains, and the room is suddenly awash in bright sunlight. Alice groans in protest, her eyes squinting as the bright light filters through the windows. The soft morning breeze carries the scent of fresh flowers from the garden outside, filling the room with a sweet aroma. A shiver runs down Alice's spine as the cool morning air caresses her skin. Karen's eyes snap open, and she sits upright in bed. The sheet slides down, exposing Karen's waist and the smooth contours of her porcelain breasts.

Natalie's jaw just about hits the floor as she gets an eyeful of Karen's ample bosom. "Sweet Mercy! This here pale gal ain't never had no young'uns drainin' the life out o' her."

Without missing a beat, Karen gets up, stretches wide, and saunters off to the bathroom, her lithe body sparkling in the bright sunlight. In the morning glow, her blonde hair shimmers with a golden hue, casting a radiant halo around her head.

"Good Lord! I reckon I just seen me an angel!" Natalie exclaims, covering her mouth in surprise.

The sheet flies off as Alice springs out of bed, her body barely concealed by the scant nightie. The snug garment hugs her body, and the morning light accentuates every curve. Alice looks around, a bit embarrassed, and sheepishly quips. "Well, that's one way to make an entrance!"

Natalie shields her eyes and stumbles backwards into the door behind her. "Mercy! They oughta put a warning label on this room!"

The abrupt sound of the toilet flushing echoes through the room as Karen sashays into the bedroom, flaunting her curves. With a flick of her wrist, Alice tosses a robe towards Karen while slipping into a silky gown.

Alice grabs hold of Karen's hand and smiles warmly. She has a feeling that this day will be unforgettable, and excitement bubbles up inside her.

Natalie's eyes widen, her gaze flitting between Alice and Karen, the awe in her expression palpable. She stammers, "Well, I'll be... I reckon I should skedaddle outta here. Now y'all remember to break bread 'fore the Granger's come a-knockin'. They'll be here in the hour."

Sparky barks excitedly as he jumps up and down, his tail wagging furiously, as Alice and Karen gracefully descend the staircase. His joyful bark echoes through the house as he leads them into the warm, cozy kitchen, where the heavenly aroma of freshly brewed coffee and pancakes fills the air.

Natalie is standing over the stove, her spatula sizzling as she expertly flips pancakes, creating a golden-brown crust on each side. She piles them high on a plate, creating a tower of fluffy goodness.

Karen inhales deeply, her nostrils flaring as she takes in the tantalizing scents that fill the air. She playfully smacks Natalie's behind, her voice rising to a teasing pitch. "Looks like it's just you and me tonight," she jokes, her eyes sparkling with mischief.

Natalie blushes, her cheeks turning a warm shade of pink, and Alice can't help but giggle at Karen's pun. James and Robert stroll into the kitchen, their footsteps echoing off the tiled floor. Robert keeps his head down, trying to hide the signs of his hangover, while James beams at the ladies. The kitchen comes alive with the sound of "good morning" and "did you sleep well?" from all sides.

Alice's warm smile greets each person as she passes them a steaming cup of coffee, the fragrant aroma wafting up and enveloping them in its rich, earthy scent.

With a satisfied nod, Robert says, "That looks good," his eyes fixed on the towering stack of pancakes.

Karen's knife dances through the vibrant medley of bananas, blueberries, and strawberries, each slice releasing a tantalizing burst of freshness. Her fingers move with the finesse of a seasoned pianist, in harmony with the rhythm of her culinary symphony. She unveils the masterpiece—a vibrant mosaic of fruit—on the table, its allure heightened by a bowl of cream whipped to perfection and a pitcher of maple syrup, warm and fragrant, whispering sweet promises. The sight holds everyone captive, their mouths watering in unspoken anticipation, their eyes glued to the visual feast before them.

Natalie's soft cough shatters the silence, its echo reverberating around the room, ensnaring everyone's attention. The clatter of a plate being set on the table supplants the echo, its sound a precursor to the intoxicating aroma of freshly cooked pancakes that wafts through the air, teasing stomachs into a chorus of anticipatory grumbles. "Best get to eatin' before this here stack turns cold," she drawls her words in a cozy warmth. "Made 'em special, just for y'all."

As the group gathers for breakfast, the sound of forks and knives on plates fills the air. The kitchen comes alive with a harmonious chorus of satisfaction, as "mmm's" and "yum's" fill the air, a testament to Natalie's culinary prowess. The world outside the window blurs into insignificance as laughter and chatter fill the kitchen, weaving a tapestry of contentment under the ethereal glow of the sun's morning kiss.

Suddenly, Alice's voice slices through the serenity, soft but insistent. "Excuse me, please." Her gaze flits to the clock—time is a runaway train. The echo of her hurried footsteps on the wooden stairs is a stark contrast to the earlier tranquility.

James's curiosity piques. "Why the hurry?"

Karen's grin is all mischief. "She's off to meet your besties now," she quips, her wink a conspiratorial secret. "Slay, girl!" Her cheer echoes long after Alice has vanished from sight.

Alice's stomach performs a ballet of nerves as the doorbell chime fractures the house's silence. Muffled voices seep through the walls—familiar names uttered by Natalie. She is completely unaware that Robert is sitting in the waiting area, concealed behind a newspaper. His presence is like a time bomb ticking away at her carefully planned day.

Alice shifts uncomfortably in her seat, her fingers fidgeting with the notepad on her lap as she tries to quell the rising tide of anxiety. Her heart beats a frantic tattoo in her chest, and she feels a wave of heat wash over her. She takes a deep breath, trying to calm herself, and draws a line down the center of the page. On the left side, she writes Madison's name, and on the right, Samuel's name.

Suddenly, the office door bursts open, and Madison Granger strides in, the overpowering scent of her floral perfume trailing behind her like a wake. Samuel Granger walks in behind his wife, slamming the door shut. Madison's eyes glitter like embers, a dangerous warning of her fury, while her husband looks more confused than anything.

Alice's hands tremble as she takes a deep breath and forces herself to move forward. Her mouth is dry as she greets her clients. "Welcome back, Mr. And Mrs. Granger," she says, her voice sounding plastic and false. She motions towards the battered leather couch, inviting them to sit.

She observes them as they settle into their chairs, the aroma of freshly brewed coffee wafting in the air. The couch groans in protest as Madison plops down onto it, causing the springs to creak loudly. Samuel's eyes roam over Alice's figure, taking in the emerald green, form-fitting flared mini skirt, the sheer patterned stockings hugging her legs, and the ivory silk blouse she's wearing, the smooth fabric feeling cool against her skin. Alice can feel his gaze on her, and she can't help but feel a surge of pleasure as their eyes meet, the electric spark between them palpable.

Alice's high ponytail swings back and forth as she turns to glance at her seat before sitting down. She adjusts her glasses and peers at her clients with a scrutinizing gaze.

Madison stretches her sinister grin across her face as she speaks. "Doctor What's-her-name?" Her voice echoes in the room, sending shivers down Alice's spine. "I'm just happy you came around," Madison continues, her tone laced with a hint of malevolence.

"Thanks, Mrs. Granger, it's so good to have you here," Alice says, her tone dripping with sarcasm. Her fingers drum against the armrest of her chair, creating a faint tapping noise.

"Hold on," Samuel cuts in, his voice carrying a deep and authoritative tone. His voice resonates like a distant rumble of thunder, filling the room. "You said you were done with us the last time we spoke," he reminds her. "What persuaded you to reconsider?" he asks, eyeing Alice suspiciously

Alice taps her fingers on the armrest and says, "Well, several factors made me change my mind, but that is irrelevant." Samuel's piercing stare electrifies her body with a surge of energy. She takes a deep breath and continues, "There's some crucial information I need to tell—"

Karen bursts into the office, the scent of freshly brewed coffee and baked goods wafting behind her. Alice's heart skips a beat at the sight of her bestie, who's wearing a French maid uniform that hugs her curves perfectly. With her blonde hair artfully styled in a messy bun, Karen gives Alice a reassuring smile and a playful wink.

The click of Karen's heels against the hardwood floor reverberates through the room as she walks towards the Granger duo. Her uniform brushes against their knees as she moves with a graceful sway, shuffling between their legs and the low table.

With her back turned to Samuel, Karen places the tray on the low table, leaning forward with her legs straight. Her perfume, an intoxicating blend of sweet vanilla, sandalwood, and a hint of alluring jasmine, permeates the air, creating an irresistible aura around her. Leaning forward, her uniform stretches taut across her body, drawing Samuel's gaze to her curves.

Samuel's eyes widen in amazement as he takes in every detail of her love triangle, completely mesmerized. The peach-colored fabric juts out like a balloon, and the lace detailing adds a touch of elegance to the otherwise naughty lingerie. Samuel clears his throat and wets his lips, his gaze lingering on Karen's backside as she stands back up.

"Doctor What's-her-Name? I am glad to see you have upgraded your staff," Madison quips as she gives her husband a sharp nudge in his side. The sound of her voice pierces the air, sharp and aggressive. "I'm sorry, miss, but I can't stand the taste of that black cat piss. Bring me tea instead, pronto," she demands, waving Karen off.

A flick of the wrist and a pointed finger from Karen is all it takes for her to act out the role of a ditzy blonde. "If you want tea," she says, pointing a straight finger towards the kitchen, "it's that way." The sound of her voice is dripping with sarcasm, and her eyes glint mischievously. Samuel's laughter cuts through the air, deep and infectious. With a shrug and a wave of her hand, his wife brushes off Karen's arrogance.

Karen's eyes glide over her nails, admiring the glossy finish. She scoffs and rolls her eyes in disbelief. "I gotta run," she says with a pout as she sways her hips towards the door. The scent of her perfume wafts in her wake, leaving Samuel spellbound. Alice's lips curl into a sly grin as she observes the red flush creeping up his neck.

Samuel pours his coffee, the sound of the steaming liquid sloshing as it fills the cup. A smile of culpability pulls at the edges of his lips. Alice waits for the rhythmic clinking of the teaspoon to stop before she continues talking. Peering over her glasses, she fixes her gaze on Madison Granger. "Mrs. Granger, I am referring you to a psychiatrist, who also happens to be a good friend of mine, Dr. Ariana Schnitzer. She is—"

Madison interrupts Alice, her voice sharp and incredulous as she struggles to catch her breath. "This is ridiculous!"

Samuel's eyebrows raise with curiosity, and he looks at his wife. "Don't interrupt her, Madison," he says sternly. The tension in the room becomes palpable.

Alice clears her throat and explains. "Dr. Schnitzer and I are a team. We collaborate closely on our projects." She fidgets with her glasses, adjusting them on her face. "I shared a report and your letter with her. You know, the heartfelt one that Robert Quillen wrote?" A smirk forms on her face as she pops the question, and she can't help but notice Madison Granger flinch.

Alice takes a deep breath before continuing. "I have a high regard for Dr. Schnitzer in the psychiatric field. She has a unique understanding of the human mind and is well-versed in treating mental health issues. I believe she can help you find the answers you're searching for."

Madison and Samuel's voices blend in a frenzied duet, drowning the office in a cacophony of sound. The chaos reverberates through the space, creating a palpable tension that settles like a weight on the shoulders of everyone present.

Alice's eyes dart back and forth, trying to make sense of the tension between the couple. "You go first, Mrs. Granger," she says politely, motioning towards Madison.

Madison stares at the floor, her expression a mix of shame and defiance. She takes shallow breaths, her chest rising and falling rapidly. "Can you enlighten me about my condition, Dr. Laurier?" she sneers.

Madison's recognition brings a warmth to Alice's eyes and a smile to her lips. As she rifles through her notes, her eyes dart up to meet Madison's defiant gaze. Alice reads out loud, "I quote, 'I've been carefully reviewing your experiences and concerns, and based on my assessment, your client is experiencing a condition called delusional disorder.' She continues, 'Any person having delusional disorder holds strong, false beliefs that do not align with reality. It is within my ability to treat the condition with medication.'"

The distant sound of the doorbell echoes through the empty house, its chime reverberating off the walls. Alice meets Madison's gaze, seeing the sadness in her eyes as she wipes away her tears. She scribbles quickly, her pen scratching the paper as she writes 'overt manipulation' under her column name. Alice strains to hear the muffled commotion coming from the lobby, and can discern the sounds of laughter and chatter.

"I'm not sure who Robert is or what letter you're referring to," Samuel says, his confusion clear.

Alice gives him a sly grin. "As I am bound by a client confidentiality agreement with both you and your wife, Mr. Granger, I suggest you consult with her."

Samuel nods his head. "How will this psychiatric referral affect our divorce proceedings and hearing?" he asks, his tone worried.

Alice's eyes light up, and a thin smile spreads across her face. "First, it will inevitably delay the divorce hearing. Should Mrs. Granger be required to give testimony, her mental state may raise concerns about the credibility of her statements, particularly if her condition could impact her memory or interpretation of events."

Fury consumes Madison, and her face turns beet red with anger. "You got me this time, doc! Nice one," she says, her eyes flaring with rage. "But watch out because I'm coming for you!" She leaps up, slings her handbag over her shoulder and storms out, leaving behind a dark cloud of her dreadful scent.

Samuel raises an eyebrow at Alice. "That's decided, Alice," he says. "So, are you going to refer Madison to your friend?"

Alice's face lights up with sincerity. "I did it just to get her and her snake of a lawyer off my back," she comforts him.

Samuel stands, his chest heaving with relief as he exhales a long, satisfying sigh. "If she ever pulls a stunt like that again, give me a buzz."

He takes two brisk strides towards Alice, extending his hand with a warm smile. Alice takes his hand, feeling the rough calluses on his palm and the warmth of his fingers. She gazes up into his gentle eyes, taking in the sight of his rugged features and the mop of tousled hair on his head.

The scent of his masculine aftershave wafts over her, filling her nostrils with a heady aroma. As he pulls her close in a tight embrace, she can feel the heat radiating from his body and the muscles rippling beneath his shirt. She shivers with pleasure as his lips brush against her cheek, sending a wave of tingling sensations down her spine. "Alice, you're one of a kind.," he whispers huskily into her ear, his warm breath tickling her skin.

She closes her eyes, savoring the moment and the blissful feeling that washes over her. Her chest heaves as she tries to catch her breath, heart racing, as he pulls aways from the embrace.

Alice breaks the embrace and her hurried footsteps echo through the empty hallway as she rushes to the door. With a gesture towards the open door, she leads Samuel towards the front desk, where they unexpectedly run into the others. Natalie's face twists into a scowl as Mattia teases her, in a language she doesn't understand. James and Robert's eyes widen as they see Samuel Granger approaching, and they jump up from their seats.

Alice's smile broadens as she introduces Samuel, and her enthusiasm is palpable. "Mr. Granger, please meet my husband James and his business partner Robert," she says as she gestures towards them. "They're the famed duo responsible for installing the utility units in your hotel rooms."

A winsome smile spreads across Samuel's face. "Hey guys, nice to meet you. Good work!" he says, shaking their hands.

James's eyes twinkle with admiration as he gazes at the formidable Samuel Granger and enthusiastically shakes his hand.

"Here," says Samuel as he presents a pair of business cards. "Give me a buzz. Let's grab a drink. How about Mattia pick you up tomorrow night?" He places a reassuring hand on Mattia's shoulder.

Robert and James both nod vigorously, their wide grins refusing to fade.

"Where's Karen?" Alice asks, her brow furrowed in confusion.

Robert imitates a telephone by holding his hand to his ear. "So, she tells me 'bye' and bolts," he says. "But then Tiffany calls her up and says they've got to make up for lost time."

Alice follows Natalie's lead, trailing behind her as they make their way to see Samuel and Mattia out. At the top of the staircase, the cool morning breeze tousles her hair as she watches Mattia open the limo door for Samuel. She revels in her success as the limo disappears into the distance, her lips curling into a triumphant smile.

Alice finally finds a moment of peace with the house empty. She seizes the opportunity to tackle the dreaded task of administrative work. She opens the file cabinet and shuffles through the folders, trying to find the paperwork for Samuel and Madison Granger's divorce proceedings.

Her fingers brush against a thick manila envelope, and she pulls it out. Natalie marked it with the Granger's names. Her mind jogs as she remembers the events of the previous night. With a smile on her face, she hastily taps out a message to Fabian on her phone, feeling the smoothness of the touchscreen beneath her fingertips. She thanks him for the unforgettable night, hearing the soft clicking of the keys as she types.

In just a few moments, her phone chimes, and she immediately feels a rush of excitement as she reads the message. The words from Fabian's text make her heart flutter with joy as she remembers the amazing night before. "Your family is stunning," he writes, leaving her with a deep sense of satisfaction. The message continues, "Let's catch up again soon, okay?" and she can't help but grin from ear to ear.

Relief floods her face, and she lets out a satisfied sigh. She sits down at her computer and opens the transcribed document of the Granger's sessions, ready to compile the report. Alice works diligently, her fingers rapidly typing away at the keyboard, as the sound of her typing is the only noise that fills the room. Her eyebrows knit together in confusion. The rhythmic clacking of the keyboard fills the room as she types, but the words are appearing on the page at a sluggish pace. With each sentence she types, the lag seems to worsen, causing frustration to build.

She presses the button on her desk's intercom to buzz Natalie, but receives no response, assuming she must be out for lunch. To find a workaround, she attempts to compose an email to herself but experiences the same sluggishness. Despite her best efforts, the lag persists even after she saves her report and restarts her computer.

The sight of Natalie sauntering into the office with a tray of steaming coffee and sandwiches is a welcome relief. The rich, comforting scent of freshly brewed coffee envelops her as she takes a sip.

"Nat, have a look at this," Alice says, pointing to her laptop screen, her eyebrows furrowed in confusion. Natalie gets up from her seat and leaves her coffee aside. She walks around the cocobolo desk and intently gazes at the laptop screen. Alice's fingers move deftly over the keyboard keys, the clacking sound echoing in the room as she types out a long sentence that takes a while to appear on the page.

"Cher," says Natalie, her eyes wide as saucers, "we got ourselves a ghost in this here machine!"

With a look of concern, Alice furrows her brow and asks, "Do you have the contact information for that odd computer guy who fixed my computer?"

Natalie's footsteps reverberate through the room as she makes her way to her desk. She comes back holding a little black address book and flips through the pages, showing Alice the details.

Alice's fingers move over the intercom, dialing the number, and a shrill ringtone echoes from the speaker. "Liberty Leashes, Mare speaking. Good morning." A voice answers.

"Hi, good morning, Mare." Alice's voice is friendly, and she can't help but smile at the phone. "Please, may I speak to Leo?"

"Of course, one moment please," Mare replies, her voice slightly muffled through the speaker. Alice can hear Mare's footsteps fading away as she calls out for Leo. The sounds of birds chirping and dogs barking echo through the phone.

"Hello, Leo here," says the man in a pleasant tone. Alice and Natalie exchange a fleeting glance, their scowls deepening as the intercom crackles to life.

"Leo, it's Dr. Laurier," Alice says, her tone urgent. "Something's wrong with my computer. Can you come and look when you have a moment, please? I need your help urgently since I—"

"Excuse me?" the man interrupts, his tone filled with bewilderment. "I'm afraid you've got the wrong, Leo. This is a pet store, not a computer shop," the man points out and hangs up. Alice and Natalie stare in awe as the phone emits a soft, rhythmic beep, the hollow sound of a disconnected call echoing in the room.

With a look of concern etched on her face, Alice reaches for her phone and dials James's number. Her irritation grows as Natalie noisily sips her coffee and munches on her sandwich.

As soon as James answers the phone, Alice breathes a sigh of relief. In an affectionate tone, she asks, "Hey honey, do you know of a computer technician who could come and help me out? My computer is giving me trouble." She waits patiently for his response. "Sure, I'll hold," she replies calmly. Alice's smile spreads across her face as she holds the phone to her ear and says, "Great! Thanks, I'll take him out to dinner, whatever he wants. Thanks, love." Finally, she hangs up.

With a mouthful of food, Natalie fixes her gaze on Alice, waiting for her reaction

Alice's face breaks into a wide smile as she looks at her assistant, forgetting her irritation. "They're heading home, and Robert, who is supposedly a computer genius, will look." With a mouthful of sandwich, Natalie gives Alice a quick thumbs up, showing her approval.

Alice bites into her sandwich while she waits, savoring the aroma of fresh bread and deli meats. Sparky bursts with energy and lets out a series of barks, his nails scraping against the wooden flooring as he races towards the front door. His excited barking drowns out the voices of James and Robert.

The boisterous sound of laughter and the heavy thud of footsteps shatters the quiet of the office. Robert enters with a mischievous gleam in his eyes, causing Alice to clasp her hands together in a gesture of prayer. "Long time no see, Alice," he says with a chuckle. "Would you like me to look at your computer for you?"

Alice's heart races as she steps aside, making way for Robert. She can't help but notice the stale, malty smell of his breath and the overpowering scent of cigarette smoke and cologne that hangs in the air. Natalie stands nearby, looking on anxiously as Robert sinks comfortably into the plush leather office chair and inspects the computer.

The sound of rustling papers and tapping keys fills the room, and the dim light of the computer screen casts an eerie glow. The air is thick, the tension palpable as they wait for Robert's verdict. Alice can feel her nerves fraying at the edges as she watches him move nimbly over the keys, his fingers deftly probing the inner workings of the computer.

As he works, Robert occasionally emits a low whistle or hums softly to himself, lost in concentration. Alice can hear his breathing, deep and steady, as he leans in closer to the screen. Her body is like a blazing fire, emanating warmth from the inside out.

Finally, after what feels like an eternity, Robert sits back with a satisfied smile. Alice and Natalie breathe a collective sigh of relief, the tension in the room finally dissipating. Robert wipes his glasses clean, his gaze steady and focused. In her mind's eye, Alice can feel Robert's neck in her grip as she imagines shaking him, her jewelry clattering loudly. Robert holds his glasses up to the light, examining them carefully to ensure they are completely clean.

Taking a deep breath, he begins his explanation. "Someone has breached your computer's security," he says. "They have infected your computer with spyware. This suggests that the person has been monitoring your activity, recording every move and keystroke you make, and sending it to a remote location." He emphasizes his point by gesturing with his hands.

Standing up, he stretches his arms and his joints pop with a loud crack. "I can remove the spyware," he offers. "Or you could use it to your advantage," he suggests with a cunning smile.

Alice and Natalie share the same doubts, their eyes meeting briefly as they exchange knowing glances. "I'm confused. How exactly can spyware be useful?" Alice asks, fixing her eyes on Robert, silently begging for an explanation.

Robert raises an eyebrow suggestively and responds, "Your computer holds a valuable secret that someone will do anything to get their hands on. Can you think of anybody?"

Alice exchange inquisitive glances with James and Natalie, trying to read their expressions for any clues. The answer suddenly comes to her, and her face lights up with excitement. "Madison Granger, that deceitful reptile!" Her bouncing ponytail reflects the happiness she is feeling. Her excitement triggers a loud outburst of laughter in the office.

"Exactly Alice!" says Robert with a warm smile. "You can provide her with a substitute for what she wants. Do you understand?"

"Yes, I do." Alice sings the words with a high lilting alto. "She's desperate to get her claws on the psychological evaluation report." She nods her head and speaks with conviction to sway the onlookers.

Robert clears his throat, causing his voice to deepen and become more authoritative. "Write your evaluation report in a manner that highlights the benefits for her. Once you're ready to send the report, call me before sharing it. I have a trick to show you. Got it?"

"Gotcha!" Alice exclaims, snapping her fingers for emphasis. "I always email my reports to the court clerk." With a sneaky grin, she sinks into her plush seat, ready to tackle her work. The sound of shuffling footsteps fills the quiet office as her friends step out.

Alice's eyes grow tired as she waits for the computer to catch up, but she perseveres, fueled by the aroma of strong coffee. She feels a sense of relief and satisfaction wash over her as she finishes the report. With a critical eye, she reads it one last time, carefully checking for any inconsistencies and making sure it is believable. Her footsteps falter as the sound of rowdy men's voices from the lounge reaches her ears. As she cautiously peeks her head inside, the boisterous theme of an all-too-familiar sitcom blares from the TV—a melody that winds like a lost lover's lament played on a tuba, punctuated by clever staccato notes that echo like the rapid beating of her heart. The wooden floor beneath her feet shudders, trembling as if in tune with her own anticipation.

Their eyes remain fixated on the mammoth television screen, the flickering images casting a blue glow across the room as Robert and James eagerly expect the beginning of the story. Alice's knuckles rap a steady beat on the wooden doorframe, creating a resounding echo throughout the hallway. Sparky's high-pitched barks echo through the house as he rushes towards the door, his nails clicking against the wooden floor. James can't help but snicker at the dubious dog, his laughter echoing like a blissful melody through the lounge. Robert's eyes widen as Alice comes into view, and he jumps out of his seat. They traverse the hallway, the sound of their footsteps resonating off the cream-colored walls as they make their way to her office, the aroma of freshly brewed coffee wafting from the kitchen. James and Natalie follow closely behind, their footsteps falling in sync with the others.

Alice signals to Robert to take a seat on the black leather office chair. "I have finished the report," she declares, a mischievous grin spreading across her face. "All that remains is to attach it and send it."

The plush leather seat engulfs Robert, swallowing him as though it is a living entity with its own dark desires. He sinks into its luxurious embrace with a soft swoosh that echoes ominously in the silence. His fingers dance across the keyboard like a spider chasing its prey, the sound of the keys echoing throughout the quiet office. With a wide smile, he meets the eager looks of those gathered around him. "Okay, do you have the court clerk's email address?" he asks Alice.

Alice nods, her fingers tapping away on the keyboard as she leans over Robert's shoulder. "This is the one," she says, pointing to the screen.

Alice looks on eagerly as Robert's fingers move swiftly across his keyboard. "Great stuff," he says, turning to meet her gaze. "I've set up a temporary email that will self-destruct in an hour. And I've also made some adjustments to your email settings using a phony server that James and I put together for testing purposes," he adds, nodding with conviction. "Just send your report to the court clerk, and you're good to go. You will totally fool Madison and her cronies, thinking it's the real deal."

Excitement bubbles up inside Alice. She claps her hands and sinks into the plush, luxurious seat. The mouse moves in her hand, clicking like a typewriter, and she meets Robert's warm smile. "Done!" she exclaims, stepping aside to make space for Robert. With a cheer and a round of applause, Natalie and James urge Alice on. She sinks into a bow, her movements graceful and poised.

Robert takes over from Alice, settling into her seat and typing on the keyboard. His face lights up with a wide, joyful grin. "It worked!" He exclaims with excitement and quickly checks the screen. "We're good now, but let's keep the spyware for a bit, just in case. Got any pressing work to do?" he asks Alice.

"No," says Alice, jumping with joy and wrapping her arms around Robert. She raises her eyes to meet his serene gaze. "Thanks a million, Robert. I'll make it up to you!"

"My pleasure Alice," he says with a smile as they high five.

"We fooled and delayed Madison Granger and her legal eagle for a while," Alice says with a mischievous grin, crossing her fingers behind her back. The sound of cheers and applause fills her office as everyone celebrates their clever plan. Alice's shoulders relax, and her eyes glaze over as she daydreams about ways to celebrate her achievement.

Alice's feet pound against the wooden stairs, her breaths mixing with the boisterous laughter of the guys in the lounge. The feeling of triumph fills her chest, her heart pounding with pride. She gazes back down the staircase, hearing the echo of her own footsteps and feeling a sense of accomplishment.

Robert's voice echoes in her mind, his encouragement pushing her forward. Joy and satisfaction flood through her, the warmth of the emotions spreading from her heart to her fingertips. With newfound confidence, she strides forward, ready to face whatever challenges come her way.

Her phone chimes, the sound piercing the silence of her bedroom. With a sense of urgency, she rushes towards her phone. Her eyes grow wide in surprise as she notices the Wickr notification, causing a sudden flutter in her stomach. She taps on the message without hesitation, her curiosity piqued.

The message reads: *FYI: Hera. LOCATION: Confirmed. Tap pin to view. TIME: 07:30 pm. RSVP: Reply YES to confirm, NO to cancel. CLIENT: Mr. Vesper.* Her heart skips a beat at the sight of the familiar code name. Tapping the pin brings up a digital map that highlights the precise location of Hotel Grand Truss. A wave of nostalgia washes over Alice, tightening around her heart.

The realization hits her like a ton of bricks, and she nearly loses her balance. Her heart races as memories of her past with Samuel Granger flood her mind. It's almost as if a ghost from her past has come to life before her eyes. Suddenly, a veil lifts and she finds herself transported back to the hotel room with Samuel Granger. The memories surge back to Alice with a forceful intensity, filling her with emotions she had thought long forgotten. She's enveloped by the sound of raucous laughter and the warm, spicy scent of Samuel's cologne. The combination is intoxicating, hinting at the promise of new beginnings and undeniable chemistry. She feels as if she's in a dream because the moment is so intense that reality seems to blur around her. Alice can feel her face flush with a mix of excitement and apprehension.

The bright screen of the phone illuminates Alice's face, interrupting her daydream. She squints at the screen, her eyes adjusting to the light. Slowly, the message comes into focus; the words appearing crisp and clear. She takes a deep breath, trying to calm her nerves, but her hands tremble with anticipation as she types 'Yes' and taps send. A satisfying buzz echoes through the phone, signaling a confirmation message.

Alice sits lost in thought, a million questions swirling through her mind. The thought of spending time with Samuel again makes her anxious, knowing that it will bring up a lot of feelings she's not ready to confront. But despite her reservations, she can't help feeling a sense of excitement at the prospect of seeing him again. She knows that this could be the beginning of something new and exciting, and she can't wait to find out what the future holds.

The hot shower water cascades over Alice's body, and she feels a jolt of excitement that sends shivers down her spine. The sweet and earthy aroma of the shampoo reminds her of walking through a forest after a rainstorm, the smell of wet earth and greenery filling her senses. She moves to the raunchy pop tune playing in the background, swaying and singing to the beat. The song reaches its climax, and the sound of a wild wolf's snarl echoes through the bathroom. Her everyday routine is being interrupted by a moment of bliss as she feels alive. She turns off the faucet, wrapping herself in a plush towel. Glancing at her reflection in the full-length mirror, she admires the soft curves that enhance her figure in all the right places, feeling confident and beautiful.

Panic washes over Alice as she realizes she forgot to plan her outfit for the evening. She wastes no time and hurries to her wardrobe, the plush carpet muffling the sound of her bare feet. Her eyes scan the rainbow of colors in her closet as she rifles through her clothes, searching for the perfect outfit. The scent of freshly laundered fabric fills her nostrils as she pulls out various garments and lays them on her bed with precision.

The full-length mirror shows her every detail, including the way her damp hair falls in soft waves around her face. Dropping her towel, she quickly gets dressed, slipping into the form-fitting, sleeveless mini dress. She runs her hands over the fabric, appreciating its softness and stretchiness against her skin. The daring V-neckline draws attention to her elegant neck, and as she twirls on her heel, her gaze falls on the open back, revealing a glimpse of her smooth, sun-kissed skin.

In the softly lit room, the gentle glow of the vanity dresser accentuates Alice's features, giving her face a silky sheen. The sound of the brush against her hair is soothing as she styles her hair into a sleek, high ponytail, exposing her neck with grace, adding a touch of sophistication to her look. The fragrance of her makeup is subtle and elegant, with smoky eyes that pop and a hint of rosy blush on her cheeks. She finishes her look with a bold, deep red lipstick that complements the color of her dress perfectly.

With a delicate touch, she clasps a silver necklace around her neck, adorned with a sparkling pendant that catches the light with every movement. As she moves, the necklace glides along her collarbone, adding a touch of allure to her appearance. The necklace feels cool against her skin, making her feel even more elegant. Her mood is daring, and she opts for a perfume that leaves a trace of mystery and exoticism on her skin.

Alice slips on a pair of strapped stiletto heels in a matching burgundy shade to elongate her legs. She walks over to the full-length mirror and adjusts her dress, smoothing out any wrinkles. The sound of a camera shutter fills the air as she takes a selfie and sends it to Karen. With a last glance in the mirror, she adjusts her hair and smiles at her reflection, feeling confident and ready for the evening ahead.

The soft rustle of her tan overcoat fills the hallway. With each confident step, she glides down the stairs with poise, the sound of her heels tapping against the wooden steps. She hears the faint buzzing of her phone as she reaches the bottom landing and sees a message from Karen. She reads it and smiles as she sees the words: *Hey Spid! You look stunning. Your date won't be able to take his eyes off you.* She can feel the warmth of her friend's enthusiasm radiating through the phone.

The sound of the TV is barely audible, but she can make out the indistinct murmur of voices. Alice cautiously pokes her head into the lounge, the soft glow of the TV casting a warm hue over the room. The scent of popcorn wafts towards her, and she can't resist taking a deep breath. She blows the guys a kiss, and as she turns to leave, the feeling of James' gaze lingers on her. She can feel the weight of his admiration as he rubs the kiss into his heart and sends one back to her.

The bustling sounds of the city greet Alice as she steps out of the house. A warm golden glow envelops the metropolis as the sun sinks into the horizon. The air is thick with the aroma of sizzling street food emanating from the nearby carts, and the sound of people chattering and laughing fills her ears.

The cityscape transforms into a magnificent painting with hues of orange, pink, and purple that blend in the sky. A gentle breeze that brings a sense of calm and tranquility replaces the warmth of the sun's rays, making it the perfect time to take a leisurely stroll and enjoy the beauty of the metropolis. Alice notices a group of dancers performing a ballet in the park as she strolls along the sidewalk. She stops to watch them, mesmerized by their graceful movements and elegant costumes. They glide across the grass like swans on a lake, their limbs in perfect harmony. She envies their talent and passion, wishing she could join them in their artistic expression.

With a swift flick of her hand, she hails a cab. Each step Alice takes down the sidewalk turns the heads of the taxi drivers, all vying for her attention. The victorious driver screeches his cab to a stop beside her, the bumper of his car narrowly missing the curb. Alice takes a quick step back, her heart racing as the yellow cab halts. With a scowl, she shoots a glare at the driver, who responds with a cheeky grin. Another cab whizzes by, and she catches a glimpse of the bald-headed driver flipping off the driver in the cab next to her. Alice slides into the back seat and feels the crumbs from snacks crunch beneath her feet.

She informs the driver of her destination, and the cab zips away. The neon signs and street lamps blend together, creating a stunning, magical view as they zoom through the city. The radio crackles with the sultry voice of a female popstar who drags her ex-boyfriend through the mud. Alice leans forward, her nose almost touching the driver's seat as she tries to be heard over the deafening radio. "Can you please turn that off?" she yells, the pounding beat making her head throb.

The cabbie turns the music down, and his eyes flicker to the rearview mirror. "Man, that girl can really sing. Her voice is so sweet it's like honey for the ears," he says, gesturing to the car's roof. Alice's eyes widen in amazement as she looks up at the cab's headliner, featuring a larger-than-life poster of the popstar. The poster captures her stunning legs, looking like they go on forever. With a sigh, Alice rolls her eyes and shakes her head.

Alice basks in the newfound silence and looks out the window, feeling the excitement of the night ahead. The cool air from the air conditioning touches her skin, sending shivers down her spine. She can feel her heart racing as the cab takes her closer and closer to her destination. Suddenly, the cab screeches to a halt, and Alice steps out, ready for her night of adventure. The smell of the city hits her, and she takes a deep breath, enjoying the mix of fragrances. Sizzling samosas, spicy kebabs, and sweet jalebis—crispy, syrup-soaked spirals of fried dough—fill the air with their aroma from the nearby carts.

Approaching the entrance of the Sky Bridge Fusion cocktail lounge, Alice exudes poise and elegance, her steps confident and measured. Suddenly, a car whizzes past, sending water flying onto the sidewalk. She jumps back and flips the driver the bird, feeling a rush of anger pulsing through her body.

The usher, dressed in a striking mauve outfit, greets her with a smile and holds the door open as she approaches. She steps inside, and a strange familiarity washes over her as he escorts her to a secluded table. Soft music plays in the background, and the hum of animated conversations and laughter fills the air. With a polite gesture, the usher pulls out a chair and invites her to take a seat, the velvet fabric soft against her skin.

Alice scans the lounge, hoping to see Rick, the friendly server from her last visit. She had only been to this place once before, but Rick's warm smile and simple conversation had made a lasting impression on her. Suddenly, a server appears before her, interrupting her thoughts. He introduces himself as Mario, and his tone is gentle and caring. She eagerly scans the blackboard menu, her eyes dancing with excitement. "I'll have a lavender honey sour and some almond-crusted stuffed dates, please," she requests while pointing at the menu. Mario gives a quick nod of approval before making his way over to the server station.

Alice's gaze sweeps across the room, and she sees the couples moving to the beat of the music, their bodies swaying in perfect harmony. She hears the clink of glasses and the sound of laughter as friends and family toast to the night. The atmosphere is electric, and Alice's heart races with anticipation. She inhales deeply, the sharp, floral scent of the lavender in her cocktail tickling her nose. The sweet undertones of honey mingle with the aroma, sending a rush of excitement through her body. With each breath, the scent teases her senses, heightening her excitement for the night ahead.

Alice takes a bite of the almond date, feeling the satisfying crunch between her teeth. The smoky flavor of the goat cheese leaves a pleasant aftertaste in her mouth, and the blend of flavors creates a delectable sensation on her taste buds. She savors each bite, feeling a sense of satisfaction with every crunch.

Before departing, Alice makes a brief detour to the bathrooms. She checks her reflection in the mirror and adjusts her hair, feeling confident and ready to take on the night. Her eyes sparkle with eagerness as she takes a few steps towards the exit.

She settles the bill and adds a handsome tip to show her appreciation. The sound of the clinking coins as she places them on the table echoes in the quiet restaurant. "Could you direct me to the sky bridge that leads to the hotel, please?" she asks her server.

He gestures towards a revolving door. "Certainly. Advance through the doors, veer left, and follow the signs for the sky bridge."

Alice thanks him with a modest smile, feeling the warmth of the cozy lounge fade away as she steps outside into the chilly night air. She shivers slightly and pulls her coat tighter around her. She follows the signs for the sky bridge, feeling a sense of excitement building within her as she approaches her destination.

Alice walks towards the sky bridge, and the cool night breeze makes her hair dance around her face. The sound of a saxophone drifts to her on the breeze, filling her ears with a calming tune. She takes a deep breath, feeling the cool air on her face as the night sky twinkles above her. With her gaze fixed straight ahead, the sound of cars speeding by beneath the bridge makes her feel dizzy.

To steady her nerves, she grips onto the railing and moves slowly forward, one small step at a time. Alice looks out at the nightscape before her, mesmerized by the twinkling lights of the city skyline. The yellow and white lights of the streets below illuminate the skyscrapers, casting a warm glow over everything. She listens to the faint sound of a train in the distance, its whistle echoing through the air. It evokes memories of warm summer days spent chasing after colorful butterflies.

With each step down the stairs, she feels the tension in her body melt away, and she lets out a long sigh of relief. The staircase leads directly into the opulent foyer of the hotel. For a few moments, she stops to admire her surroundings, feeling a sense of accomplishment. Luxury surrounds her wherever she looks. Alice's footsteps echo throughout the lobby as she strides across the gleaming marble floors. Poised and patient, she stands in the short line leading up to the guest's clerk.

The line moves quickly, and before she knows it, she stands before the clerk. "Good evening, Vesper's the name," Alice says, and pulls out her phone to show the reservation details to the clerk.

"Welcome to the Hotel Grande Truss, Mrs. Vesper," greets the red-haired clerk with freckles. "Just a moment, please." She types into her terminal, extracts an envelope from the beehive behind her, and hands it to Alice. "Enjoy your stay with us," she says, her smile looking forced and artificial.

Alice shoves the envelope into her bag, her fingers trembling with anticipation. She takes a deep breath and strides towards the elevator, her footsteps echoing off the marble floor. A rush of excitement surges through her veins as the doors close. She slyly removes her wedding band and tucks it into her coat pocket, her eyes fixed on her fellow passengers in the mirrors.

The elevator doors open with a sharp ding, and the cool air-conditioned air rushes out. A stout cleaner, her face concealed by a visor and her ears plugged with a headset, obstructs the exit with her oversized cleaning cart. Alice gingerly shimmies through the narrow gap between the cleaner and the wall, her arms grazing against the cold metal, and sets forth down the dimly lit hallway. The scent of disinfectant and bleach fills the air, and the only sound is the soft swish of Alice's skirt as she glides down the seemingly endless corridor.

Alice takes a deep breath and straightens her skirt. She swipes the card key over the reader, the door unlocks, and she steps inside the quiet, empty room. Excitement wraps its icy fingers around her stomach and squeezes tightly, releasing a flutter of butterflies.

A faint scent of perfume infuses the air, a subtle yet alluring fragrance that fills the senses. The sudden squeak of the door startles Alice, causing her to jump in surprise as it slams shut with a loud click. Suddenly, a strange familiarity engulfs her. The jasmine scent, the surroundings, and the sound are all so eerily familiar. It is a surreal echo of a memory she cannot quite place, a sensation of Déjà vu that leaves her momentarily bewildered.

Alice tries to shake off the strange feeling, but her heart races faster. Her thoughts spin wildly as she considers the reasons that could have caused such a powerful response. Was it the scent of the perfume or the sudden noise that triggered the memory? She takes a deep breath, trying to calm herself, but the sensation of familiarity lingers, leaving her feeling both intrigued and unsettled. The hairs on the back of her neck stand up, and she can't shake the feeling that she's being watched. With her heart pounding in her chest, Alice turns around slowly, half-expecting to see someone standing there, but the room is empty, and the only sound is the faint hum of the air conditioner. She takes another deep breath, trying to steady herself, but the feeling of unease lingers, like a shadow that refuses to be dispelled.

With a deep breath, she gathers her courage and steps forward into the dimly lit hallway, squinting against the growing brightness at the end. "Mr. Vesper, I'm here!" Alice calls out, the eerie silence intensifies. As the icy chill runs down her spine, she wraps her arms around herself and rubs her skin to warm up. "Anyone home?" she asks, her voice shaking, the echo bouncing off the narrow walls.

Alice's heart thuds as she steps into the bedroom, the air thick with tension. She jumps with a start and gasps when she sees a stranger sitting before her. The exquisite, youthful creature stuns her. She squints at the young woman in the cane armchair and perceives the rhythmic tapping of her foot and the graceful way she crosses her legs. She styles her dark blonde hair in a tousled bun, with loose locks cascading down both sides of her face. The woman's loose-fitting dress shows off a pair of heavenly legs that seem to go on forever. Alice can feel the weight of shock settling in her bones as she sinks into an armchair.

Looking around the room nervously, Alice's eyes lock onto a beverage. She quickly snatches it up, feeling the cold condensation on her trembling fingers as she takes quick gulps.

The young goddess exclaims, "Just look at you!" as her eyes roam over Alice's figure. "Dressed to impress," she adds, sneering with emphasis on each syllable.

"How could this be?" Alice asks incredulously, her throat dry with tension.

Rising gracefully to her feet, the young woman approaches Alice with an air of elegance and extends a delicate hand in greeting. "I'm Blair," she says, a sly smile curling her lips, her deep blue eyes like pools, gazing at Alice.

"Where's Sam—Samuel?" Alice's voice quivers as she stammers nervously.

Blair stands and glides to the bar, her movements as graceful as a ballerina. Her arms move in an elegant motion as she pops ice cubes into the tumblers, the sound of their clinking echoing softly around the room. With the grace of royalty, she prepares two vodka sodas, her hands moving with practiced ease. Alice watches Blair with rapt attention, hanging on her every move

"Samuel, or Mr. Vesper as you refer to him, is not available". Blair says with a knowing smile as she places the tumbler into Alice's hand.

Alice lifts her glass and the ice cubes clink together, as she offers a silent toast to Blair's enigmatic presence. "You're not worried that Samuel might find out you're here?" She asks, her face contorted in bewilderment.

"Nope," Blair says, her lips curling into a mischievous grin, her eyes glinting with amusement, before she takes a sip of her drink.

Alice raises her eyebrows, her eyes widening with surprise. "Does he know I am here?"

"Nope," Blair says playfully, flashing a mischievous grin and taking a sip of her drink.

"Hold on, I'm curious. How did you manage to contact me?" Alice asks, her brow knitting together in confusion.

Blair fixes her gaze on the large window as she watches a passenger jet up close, being pushed back by a tug, its flashing yellow emergency light catching her attention. As Alice watches, she can see the pilots' faces clearly through the cockpit window. They share a comfortable camaraderie, and their eyes glide over their instruments as they chat and smile.

"Blair," Alice says again, her tone more insistent this time, "I need an answer to my question."

Blair's neck whips around, fixing Alice with a piercing gaze. "Being Samster's personal assistant means I have access to all the information I need in just a few clicks."

Alice tries to stifle a laugh as the sudden fierceness makes her grimace comically. "Samster?" she asks with a chuckle. Blair keeps her eyes fixed on the view outside the large window, feigning interest.

With a quick flick of her wrist, Alice finishes her vodka soda and sets the glass aside. She stands, slips out of her overcoat, and hangs it over the backrest of the chair. The bar counter is cluttered with empty glasses, but she carefully places hers among them before heading to the bathroom. She is washing her hands when a sudden chill runs through her body, and she turns around to see Blair standing behind her. Her hand instinctively goes to her chest, feeling the rapid thumping of her heart. "Wow, you scared me," she says, taking a deep breath.

Blair's coy smile is irresistible as she takes Alice's hand and leads her back into the bedroom. In a sudden rush, she hurries to the bar and hastily refills their drinks. The room falls into darkness as she stands before the utility unit, and the curtain closes with a soft whirr. A fire crackles gently in the hearth, the glowing embers dancing around like fireflies.

"Ah," Blair sighs contentedly, raising her glass in approval

Alice raises her glass and murmurs "Cheers" with a faint smile on her lips.

Blair chuckles. "Relax, I will not bite you!" she exclaims, rolling her eyes and biting her lip. Alice sits up suddenly and gives Blair a sharp look, noticing that Blair is copying her eye roll and lip bite.

A playful smirk crosses Blair's face. "What?" she asks with a feigned look of confusion

"You know, that thing where you roll your eyes..." Alice says before trailing off and stopping herself. Her words echo back to her, and she winces as she realizes she has just sounded like Samuel.

Blair leans in close and whispers, "Say it," her breath hot on Alice's face.

Alice feels an icy chill run down her spine, and she shivers involuntarily. Her eyes widen with surprise as she pulls her head back and glares at Blair. "Not a chance."

"Why did you screw my Samster?" Blair asks with an air of indifference.

The unexpected question startles Alice. "No, no, Sam and I did nothing like that!" she protests, throwing her hands in the air.

Blair's envy is clear in the blazing intensity of her eyes as she reacts with a sharp shriek and a sad expression, exclaiming, "He tried to kiss you!"

Alice winces as the sharp words pierce her ears. She stares off into the distance, lost in thought and barely aware of her surroundings. The flickering flames in the hearth create a mesmerizing display, casting dancing firelights on her face. A faint smell of burning wood fills her nostrils, reminding her of the stormy night when everything changed. Suddenly, a bolt of lightning strikes her mind, and she furrows her brow in confusion. The memory of the mysterious woman in the mirror rushes back to her, accompanied by a surge of apprehension. Alice's face brightens, and her eyes widen as she realizes the truth.

Her heart races as the realization hits her. She feels a surge of adrenaline, and her body tenses up in anticipation. She furrows her brow, trying to make sense of the jumble of memories in her mind. Her breath quickens as she realizes that the woman in the mirror was not just a figment of her imagination. Memories flood back, causing a chill to run down Alice's spine and goosebumps to erupt on her skin. Suddenly, she jumps up and clenches her fists, digging her nails into her palms. "Oh, my god! It was you!" she exclaims. Her cheeks flush a bright red, and she can feel her heart pounding in her chest. The room seems to spin around her, and she struggles to catch her breath, feeling suffocated by the intensity of her emotions.

Blair maintains a stoic expression, like a poker pro, but the slight curl at the corner of her mouth betrays her guilt. "Blair, how could you?!" Alice yells, her voice shaking with anger. The sound echoes off the walls, filling the room with a deafening roar.

Blair's cheeks flush a deep shade of red, her eyes glued to the floor in a mix of shame and defiance. Her hand plunges into her handbag and pulls out a sleek, stylish vape, perfectly fitting into her palm. She draws the vapor deep into her lungs, the sound of her inhale a low hiss. The sweet scent of strawberries mixed with the earthy smell of tobacco fills the air around her as she exhales a fragrant cloud. She lets out a deep breath and relaxes her shoulders, a guilty smile playing on her lips.

Alice's lips curl into a smile as she watches Blair, and she feels the tension in her body ease. She stands and fixes them both a double gin, the scent of juniper filling the air. Blair's hand trembles slightly as she takes a long, soothing gulp of the gin.

Blair speaks with a mix of nervousness and excitement in her voice as she gestures for Alice to follow her. "There's something I want to show you," she says.

Alice obediently follows Blair to the cramped space between the bed and the wall-to-ceiling mirrors. In the center of the row, a small red dot glimmers in the mirror's reflection. Blair holds her palm over the dot, and the two mirrors majestically slide open. Alice gasps at the sight before her as she steps inside. The mirrors slide shut behind them, and suddenly they are alone in the quiet room.

The hidden chamber leaves Alice in awe, with its lavishness taking her breath away as she enters. Her eyes dart around as she takes in the extravagant space. On either side of the room, luxuriously colorful couches adorn the walls. The plush cushions invite visitors to sink in and relax, while the vibrant hues of the upholstery add a pop of color to the space. Soft music plays in the background, filling the room with a melodious tune that creates a tranquil atmosphere for conversation or quiet contemplation. The private lounge exudes a warm and welcoming vibe, making it the perfect place to unwind after a long day.

The warm, flickering light of the scented candles fills the room, casting dancing shadows on the walls. At the sight of Alice's awed expression, Blair lets out a giggle that Alice recognizes as a shared understanding. "Pretty amazing, huh?" Blair asks. Blair becomes a blur in the background as Alice is captivated by what she sees.

"Hey, Alice?" Blair tries, and the sound of her snapping fingers echoes through the tranquil room. Alice is lost in thought until Blair's clicking fingers bring her back to reality. Blair leads Alice towards the next room with a firm grip on her hand, her excitement palpable. "It's pretty amazing, hey?" she exclaims, eager to show Alice what lies ahead

The sound of trickling water grows louder as they move on, urging them to follow the sound. The room is dimly lit, but the warm, orange glow of the Himalayan salt lamps casts a soft light on the hot tub in the center. A million diamonds seem to sparkle in the tub's shimmering water. A salty scent fills the air, creating a soothing atmosphere mixed with the steam from the tub. As they approach the tub, droplets of water fall from the salt lamps like stalactites, creating a soothing melody as they hit the tiled floor below. Alice's eyes sparkle with awe as she takes everything in. In the center of the hot tub is a small, tiled island with a bonsai tree growing from it. A mysterious alcove piques Alice's curiosity. She peers inside and admires the shelves stacked with bottles of pricey liquor and sparkling crystal glasses, all illuminated by the warm glow of recessed lights.

Alice looks up, her eyes widening as she takes in the breathtaking sight of the domed sunroof overhead. The night sky twinkles with stars, and she can almost feel the cold, crisp air outside. Blair takes her hand, sending a comforting warmth through her. She slides open the alcove with a soft rustle, and Alice can hear the faint click of the switch she reaches for. With a flick of her wrist, a hidden doorway opens, revealing the cozy living space. Alice's feet sink into the plush carpeting as soon as they step inside. The door closes behind them with a gentle thud, muffling the sound of the trickling water.

Alice gasps in amazement at the intricate details of the fish mosaic artwork that adorn the walls. The bright colors and intricate patterns seem to dance before her, mesmerizing her. "Did you spend the entire night in here?" she asks in amazement, her voice filled with curiosity. Without a word, Blair holds up a finger, signaling for Alice to wait. She hums a cheerful tune as she strolls down the hallway, her footsteps echoing softly on the polished marble floors.

Blair returns with a sly smile on her face, brandishing her room card key. She expertly swipes it over the fish's eye in the artwork, and Alice hears a soft click as the door unlocks. Alice can't help but feel a sense of excitement bubble up inside her as they step back into the hidden room. The mirrored doors loom ahead. Blair strides confidently forward, her movements graceful and fluid. Alice can't help but feel a sense of wonder and awe as she follows in her friend's footsteps.

From her vantage point, Alice can easily see the bed and other furniture in the bedroom through the one-way glass of the mirrors. Blair opens the door, and the smoky scent of the bedroom wafts towards them.

Blair struts around with a confidence that would put a sailor on payday to shame. She asks Alice with a telling smile, "Pretty cool, huh?" while crossing her arms. Alice, still reeling from what she just witnessed, stands motionless and struggles to regain her composure. She scratches her head and asks, "Yeah, I would think so, but why Blair?" Her mind seems to be elsewhere.

Blair's face contorts in disbelief, and she shakes her head. "Alice, can't you see? Sam is constantly showering you with praise and adoration. He's not satisfied with me because I don't have your skills." Envy twists her face, and tears threaten to spill from her eyes. She takes a deep breath, heaving her chest as she tries to hold back her emotions. "I watched and learned from you. Is it really so bad?" Her eyes fill with tears as she pleads, the flickering firelight casting shadows across her face.

Pity wraps its chilly fingers around Alice's heart, and she feels it squeezing tightly. She takes a step forward and pulls Blair into a warm embrace. Blair's body trembles with emotion as she struggles to control her sobs, moved by Alice's act of kindness. Alice whispers, "Shh, it's alright." She tenderly wipes Blair's salty tears away.

Blair gazes intently into Alice's eyes and makes a request. "Can you teach me your skills so I can impress the Samster?" Her face contorts with sadness and her eyes fill with tears.

Alice's heart races as she hears Blair's request, her eyes widening in disbelief. The woody scent of the old room fills her nostrils as she struggles to control the intense emotions flooding her mind. The sound of her own rapid breathing echoes in her ears as she realizes that her purpose for being here has been staring her in the face all along. A dark thought crosses her mind, causing her hands to tremble as she briefly considers ending Blair's life. She quickly glances at her bag, where she cleverly concealed a vial of Morpheus's tear among her weapons. Blair's life hangs in the balance because a single drop could send her into an endless sleep, undetectable in her bloodstream. She knows it is the perfect opportunity to remain unnoticed, since no one knows she is there. She wants to proceed, but without the agency's approval, she's at a standstill.

Alice cannot bring herself to harm Samuel's mistress and cause him pain. As before, she'll have to put on a facade and lie. She takes a deep breath and puts on a mask, disguising herself as a high-end escort for the agency. Her true identity must remain hidden. In a hushed tone, she replies, "I'm sorry, but these skills are exclusive to agency members."

A small, almost imperceptible smile graces Blair's lips. "I tried to contact them," she says, "but there is no number listed. Only a website."

Alice's heart pounds so hard that she can feel it in her ears. Her palms are slick with sweat, and her stomach is in knots. She tries to swallow, but her throat feels tight and dry. The warning sirens in her mind continue to blare, making it difficult to focus. She can feel her muscles tensing, ready for action if needed.

Alice leans closer, trying to catch Blair's eye. "What are you planning?" she asks, her voice low and steady. Blair's smile widens and Alice can see the glint of triumph in her eyes. The tension in the room is almost suffocating, and Alice struggles to keep her breathing steady. She tries to push down the fear that's threatening to overwhelm her and focuses on maintaining her composure.

Finally, Blair breaks the silence and speaks in a soft but menacing tone. "I have a proposition for you." Alice can feel Blair's intense gaze bearing down on her, making it hard to breathe. It's as if Blair's eyes are boring into her, trying to break her down. Alice knows she can't let that happen. She needs to stay strong and hold her ground, no matter what Blair has in store for her.

The tension in the room intensifies, like a storm gathering on the horizon. Alice senses the electricity in the air, the crackling energy of two strong wills clashing. She knows that whatever comes next, it will change everything. "What's the catch?" Alice asks, skeptical of Blair's proposition.

Blair responds with a sly grin, her voice carrying a hint of mischief, "Oh, nothing too steep. Just a little favor in return."

Alice shuffles her feet restlessly on the plush carpet, creating a soft, rhythmic sound. She pushes back, her tone firm. "I don't do favors for free."

Blair's eyes sparkle as she counters, "I wouldn't expect you to. Let's just say it's a mutually beneficial arrangement."

Alice's brow furrows as she inhales the familiar jasmine scent of Blair's perfume. She concedes, her voice laced with reluctance, "Fine. Let's hear it then."

A shy smile curls sensually on Blair's lips, and a soft shade of pink tints her flawless features. She walks up to the bar with an effortless grace, the fizzy sound of the soda filling the glasses as she pours two vodka sodas. Holding the glasses in her hand, she signals for Alice to join her and settles into a seat. Alice obediently accepts Blair's invitation, her curiosity piquing. She nestles into her seat, her senses heightened with anticipation.

Blair takes a long drag from her vape, and as she exhales, the room fills with a fragrant cloud of vapor, illuminated dimly by the light. "I am strapped for cash," she admits. "Being married to a wealthy man is challenging. Can I make extra cash if I join your agency?" she asks. Noticing Alice's stoic expression, she nervously takes a puff of her vape and quickly adds, "I can fill in for you or be your replacement when you need a break." Blair's trembling hand betrays her nervousness as she takes a long mouthful of her drink.

Alice flinches almost imperceptibly as Blair's proposition surprises her. With an unwavering gaze, Alice responds, "Without a vouch, you can't join the agency."

Blair's eyes plead with Alice as she whispers, "Can you vouch for me, please?"

With a charming smile lighting up her face, Alice tenderly runs her fingers through Blair's silky hair. "We can discuss the conditions later," she says, reluctant to get Blair's hopes up. "Let's set a date."

Blair's face beams with excitement. "Thank you, Alice," she says with a grateful smile. "I promise you won't regret it." Her steps are light as she makes her way to the bathroom. She stops at the minibar on her way back, the clinking of ice cubes echoing in the empty room as she prepares two vodka sodas.

"Here's your drink," Blair says, plopping into her chair. "How do I know if I'm eligible to join the agency?" she asks eagerly.

Alice's taste buds tingle as she takes a sip of her drink, relishing the sharp tang and the effervescence that tickles her tongue. She suggests, her voice tender, "Let's save the talk for our date." Then, motioning towards the bed, she adds, "But for now, why don't you take off your clothes?"

Blair sputters out a wet cough, her eyes watering as she looks at Alice incredulously. "Is this some kind of joke?" she asks in disbelief.

Alice's smile fades slightly as she notices the telltale signs of Blair's nervousness. She places a comforting hand on Blair's shoulder and says, "Relax, Blair. We'll take it one step at a time." She continues, attempting to persuade with a hint of desperation in her tone. "If you want to join, follow my instructions."

Blair gasps in awe, her jaw dropping as she sets her drink aside. She rises slowly, settling onto the plush carpet next to the crackling fire. She effortlessly slips off her shoes, her fingers trembling slightly as she unbuttons her dress. The fabric cascades to the floor, leaving her standing in her lingerie, striking a pose. The room is silent except for the soft crackle of the fire in the hearth. She appears almost ethereal, her skin aglow in the warm firelight. Her perfume lingers in the air, a sweet and heady aroma that suggests the sultry expression on her face. It feels as if the air is holding its breath, waiting for something to happen. Blair's beauty and grace mesmerizes Alice, and she gazes off into the distance, lost in her own thoughts, creating a suspended moment in time.

Alice grins playfully, and the corners of her mouth turn up. She gestures with her glass towards Blair and says, "All of it."

Blair's eyes widen with excitement, and she quickly turns away from Alice, fumbling with her bra strap until it falls to the ground. She swivels back, slowly, deliberately, and strikes a confident pose. Alice's eyes widen as she takes in Blair's exposed chest, her breath catching in her throat. The air is thick with tension as Blair smirks, enjoying the effect she's having on Alice. Blair's poses mesmerize her, and she's captivated by Blair's sensual prowess.

Alice gives a sly grin and then points to the delicate black lace thong. She says, "That too."

Blair protests with a sneer, daring Alice with a challenging gaze and exclaiming, "Oh c'mon!"

Alice smirks, her eyes glinting with mischief. "Don't forget who holds all the cards," she reminds.

Blair takes a deep breath, her chest rising and falling with each inhale and exhale, accentuating her curves. She slips out of the thong and strikes a pose, swaying her hips seductively. The dancing firelight casts shadows across her perfect curves, highlighting every inch of her body. Her movements are hypnotic and fluid, and every time she turns, the light catches her flawless skin, making it glow with a satin sheen.

A muffled sound catches Alice's attention and she turns her gaze downwards. Her eyes widen in surprise as she sees a small purple metallic object sitting snugly between Blair's feet. Alice can't take her eyes off the Kegel ball, its sleek and moist surface glistening in the low-lit room. Looking up at Blair, she raises an eyebrow in silent inquiry.

Blair gazes in amazement, and her lips part in awe. She shrugs and quips, "What? I'm just flexing my muscles," as she playfully sways her hips.

Blair looks on in amazement, and her lips part in awe. She playfully sways her hips and shrugs, quipping, "What? I'm just flexing my muscles."

Alice can't help but burst out laughing at Blair's pun, struggling to see through her watery eyes. "Can you move a little closer?" she asks.

Blair confidently strolls towards Alice, shooting her a smug look that oozes self-assurance. Alice's eyes roam over Blair's exposed figure, entranced by her beguiling elegance. With a sense of awe, she whispers, "Truly amazing." The fragrance of lavender-scented moisturizer wafts from Blair's skin, heightening her seductive allure. She signals Blair to turn around. Blair turns slowly, revealing every inch of her body to Alice. Alice's breathing hastens as she takes in Blair's firm buttocks and lengthy, slim legs. Their eyes meet briefly but intensely, increasing the palpable anticipation in the atmosphere.

The shrill ringing of the phone shatters the peaceful silence of the room. Startled, Blair and Alice exchange a quick glance. "That must be room service," Blair assumes, her footsteps echoing on the plush carpet as she approaches the phone. She lifts the phone from its cradle, pressing it to her ear. The sound of her voice is a practiced blend of professionalism and warmth, as she answers with a polite, "Granger suite, Blair speaking." Her eyebrows rise slightly and a spark of excitement lights up her face as she hears the response from the other end. "Uh huh... just for tonight."

Her mouth drops open in disbelief, and she covers it with her hand. "What!? But he is supposed to be in Oahu!" she exclaims incredulously. She casts a furtive glance at her watch, and her eyes widen in surprise. "How long do we have until he gets here?"

With a sudden motion, Alice jumps up from her seat, her face contorted with confusion and disbelief. Shooting a glance at Blair, she furrows her brow and silently mouths a "What?" in disbelief.

Blair presses her finger to her lips, signaling Alice to be quiet. She furrows her brow deeply as she strains to listen. "Uh-huh... uh-oh...please send a cleaning team up straight away." She slams the phone down on the cradle with a loud thud and Alice's questioning gaze. "Sam's en route! He'll be taking off for Oahu tomorrow morning." The feeling of urgency is palpable as the two women spring into action, the sound of their footsteps echoing through the suite. Blair hastily throws on her clothes, her fingers fumbling with the buttons.

"Holy cow!" Alice mutters under her breath. "I need to go. If someone catches me here, it's game over." With a determined look on her face, she swings her handbag over her shoulder and dashes down the hallway. The scent of cleaning supplies is overpowering as a pride of cleaners rush into the room while she approaches the door. Their fluorescent yellow uniforms are unmistakable against the neutral-toned walls. Alice quickly dives to the side, narrowly avoiding the clanging sanitizing arsenal of the cleaners. She takes a deep breath, and with a burst of speed, she darts past them and slams the door shut behind her.

The sound of hurried footsteps and excited chatter fills the previously calm hotel as soon as the news of Sam's arrival breaks. A group of housekeepers push a trolley of fresh linens down the hallway, their chatter filling the air and bouncing off the walls. The sound of jingling keys and static-filled two-way radios intermingle with the hurried footsteps of security guards as they quickly disperse.

A room door creaks open, and a disheveled security guard emerges, tugging at his rumpled uniform. As he walks by Alice, he wears a mischievous expression and gives her a sly smile. Alice smirks at him, a shiver running down her spine, as she heads towards the elevators. Not daring to wait, she takes the stairs, her footsteps echoing loudly as she gallops down. Her heart pounding in her chest, she feels the adrenaline coursing through her veins.

The delicious scent of cinnamon wafts through the air as Alice hurries through the lobby towards the exit. Stepping outside, a cold gust of wind hits her, and she instinctively wraps her arms around herself. For a moment, she stands frozen as she realizes she left her overcoat behind. She can feel the goosebumps rising on her skin, and she shivers involuntarily. She glances back at the hotel, silently praying that Blair could cover for her if Samuel notices the overcoat.

Alice hastily retrieves her phone from her purse and summons a ride. The ride-sharing app flickers with three blue dots, showing the pickup points. She follows the dot towards the back of the hotel, quickening her pace to avoid running into Sam. The narrow alleyway is dimly lit, and she squints to see her way through. The icy wind slithers through her dress, leaving her shivering and cold. She hears her high heels echoing against the walls, creating an eerie ambiance. An owl's hoot breaks the silence, causing her to jump in fright. She spots the owl perched on a lamppost, gazing at her. The yellow eyes of the bird bore into her like a predator.

She continues walking, her breaths echoing in the silence. Suddenly, a noise startles her, and she immediately turns, ready to face whatever danger lurks behind her. She sees a shady figure emerging from the shadows, and her senses go into high alert. With a deep breath, she turns and runs, driven by the fear of the unknown. Her high heels clack loudly as she runs, the sound drowning out the footsteps of the advancing figure. She spots a distant light and sprints towards it. The assailant's panting grows louder, making Alice more frantic.

Her heart pounds like a drum against the cage of her ribs, a wild, untamed rhythm that echoes the fear and determination coursing through her veins. With a deep, steadying breath, she gathers her courage, pulling it around her like a warrior's armor.

In an act of defiance, Alice whirls around, her movements as sudden as a summer storm. Her eyes meet those of the figure lurking in the shadows, a silent challenge hanging between them.

Alice's breath quickens as the figure approaches, her heart beating with both excitement and terror. She can hear his heavy boots thudding against the asphalt, sending tremors through the ground beneath her feet. She catches a glint of something metallic in his hand, and a chill runs down her spine.

Acting on instinct, she reaches into her handbag, her fingers searching for the cool, smooth surface of her stun gun. The scent of leather and perfume wafts up from her bag as she fumbles for the weapon.

The figure's footsteps grow louder, each one echoing in her ears like a thunderclap. His breathing is ragged and uneven, a sure sign that he's been running. He reaches her, and as he stoops down beside her, his breath mingles with the cool air in white, swirling tendrils.

But to her surprise, he presents her with her overcoat, holding it out for her to take. Relief floods through her, followed by a surge of embarrassment. She has been ready to defend herself against a would-be attacker, only to discover that he is a harmless stranger.

"Dang, you're fast!" he exclaims, a wry smile playing across his lips. "I had to hustle to keep up."

Alice feels a wave of relief wash over her as she lets out a deep sigh, causing her shoulders to relax. A sheepish grin spreads across her face as she recognizes the guard as the same one who came out of the hotel room earlier. She grabs her coat and excitedly puts it on, giving herself a warm hug against the chilly breeze. Struck with an overwhelming sense of gratitude, she struggles to find her words and stammers out a quick but heartfelt "thank you."

His eyes flicker to her in surprise, a faint furrow creasing his forehead. "What brings you out here all by yourself?" he asks, his voice echoing softly in the night's stillness. His gaze is inquisitive, slightly puzzled, as if he's trying to solve a mystery.

Alice narrows her eyes suspiciously, picking up on a tremble in his voice that gives him away. Straining her ears, she can make out the distant hum of machinery. Her mind drifts back to the day of her capture; the pungent odor of exhaust fumes from the van is still fresh in her memory. Instinctively, she clutches her bag tightly between her arm and side, feeling the rough texture of the fabric against her skin.

The security guard notices the shift in her demeanor and takes a step back, his hand hovering near his side. His eyes dart to her bag, and then he looks around, as if expecting someone to jump out and attack him. Alice disarms him with a charming smile. The soft glow of her phone casts an otherworldly light on his face. "Waiting for my ride," she says confidently, adjusting her bag on her shoulder.

He leans in closer, his eyes squinting at the screen. The faint blue hue from the screen washes over his face, accentuating the sharp angles and contours of his features. Her gaze lingers on the scar on his forehead, marveling at how it resembles the imprint of a shoe's heel. That's when it hits her—her mind drifts back to the moment she tried to escape through the opening in the wall, feeling the guard's firm grip on her shoe. She squints her eyes to get a good look at him, and the memory floods back, causing her stomach to flutter.

Her shallow breathing becomes more pronounced as the memory resurfaces, her chest rising and falling rapidly. She feels as if she's struggling to catch her breath, her chest tightening with each breath. Her mind becomes a whirlwind of thoughts and emotions, a chaotic storm threatening to consume her, like a thunderstorm raging inside her head. The fluttering sensation in her stomach intensifies, as if a swarm of butterflies has taken flight within her, their delicate wings brushing against her insides.

Her eyes remain fixed on the guard, studying every detail of his face. The lines etched on his forehead, the intensity in his eyes, and the firmness of his grip—they all become etched into her memory—a sketch on a canvas, every stroke precise and vivid.

She is trying to decipher his intentions, to understand why he is holding her back, but the answers remain elusive, like whispers being carried away by the wind. Despite her best efforts, she cannot untangle the web of memories that imprison her thoughts and prevent her from understanding his motives.

With each beat of her heart, she summons the strength to push forward, feeling the rhythm reverberating through her chest. It's as if her heart is a drum, pounding with determination. She knows she must overcome the ghosts that haunt her, the memories that threaten to pull her down. The memory, though haunting, becomes a catalyst for her unyielding spirit, like a spark igniting a fire within her soul, guiding her towards resilience and courage.

A long silence stretches between them as he nervously shifts his gaze between her face and the glow of the phone screen. The blue dot on the screen moves closer, inch by inch, with each passing second. They both know the truth about each other, their silence a heavy reminder of the event that has brought them together.

With no introduction, he suddenly straightens up and casually says, "Allow me to accompany you to your transportation." It's not a question but an offer, a silent promise to keep her company in this lonely hour. He steps forward, taking the lead with an air of quiet confidence.

Alice lets out a quiet, dramatic sigh of relief and matches his pace, feeling the gentle touch of the cool night air on her cheeks. The sound of leaves rustling in the wind fills the silence between them, a soothing lullaby that eases her nerves. She breathes in deeply, savoring the freshness of the air, the tranquility of the night.

The leaves crunch beneath their feet as they turn the corner, and suddenly her foot catches on something hidden beneath them. She stumbles, her heart leaping into her throat as she loses her balance. Fumbling for her phone in the dark, she turns on the flashlight and directs the beam towards the spot where she stumbled. The light illuminates two threadbare and worn shoes, with the toes sticking out. The man's tousled hair comes into view as she moves the beam upwards, framing his silver beard and rugged features.

"Evening, missy," he says in a voice, rough and raspy from a lifetime of vices, with a grin, revealing empty spaces where his teeth used to be. Alice notices the smell of cigarette smoke and alcohol on his breath, causing her to wrinkle her nose.

His piercing blue eyes catch Alice's attention, and she gasps. "Sorry, I couldn't see you because of the darkness," she says apologetically, fishing out some cash and dropping it into his lap.

With a swift motion, he grabs the money, crumples it in his hand, and stuffs it in his pocket. "Well, thank you, miss!" he says, smiling at the sky with a twinkle in his eye.

Alice's phone emits a cheerful melody, and she glances at the screen to see that her ride has arrived. Looking towards the blue dot, she spots the car parked just a few feet away. Accompanied by the guard, she rushes towards the car, the sound of her clicking heels resonating through the air. The guard kindly opens the car door for her. As she slides into the back seat, she sinks into the plush leather, relishing the car's heater, which envelops her in warmth. She rolls down the window, feeling the cold air against her face, and thanks her chaperon with a heartfelt "thank you."

"Take care of yourself," he says, his winsome smile spreading to his eyes as he playfully tousles her hair. With each stroke of his fingers through her hair, a soothing warmth spreads across her scalp, eliciting a pleasurable shiver down her spine. She can't help but feel a sense of comfort and affection radiating from his smile.

With amusement twinkling in her eyes, she teasingly pulls off her shoe and offers it to him through the open window. As she extends it towards him, she quips, "This one won't kick you in the face." His loud laughter overpowers the engine noise as the car drives off.

The security guard vanishes into the shadows as the car pulls away. The street is eerily quiet, with only the faint sound of the car's radio playing a news station. A chill runs down Alice's spine as she contemplates the old man, alone in the night, and the loneliness that must be tormenting him. A wave of sadness and regret sweeps over Alice.

Stepping through the front door, the tranquil silence of the house greets Alice, punctuated by the gentle ticking of the grandfather clock. The pendulum swings back and forth, its rhythmic ticking echoing the beat of her heart. She expertly slides out of her overcoat, the fabric whispering against her skin, and tosses her keys onto the dark console table. Out bounded Sparky, his Argus-eyed gaze locks onto her. His tail whips back and forth like a metronome set to the tempo of pure joy.

The feel of his fur under her fingertips is a sensation often overlooked in the rush of daily life, but now it feels like a balm to her frazzled nerves. Sparky's charismatic charm is infectious, his exuberance a stark contrast to the cold, calculated world she had just escaped.

A bright blue light illuminates the lounge, beckoning her forward. The silence of the empty lounge wraps around her as she peers inside. With a crisp clap of her hands, the lights gradually dim, and the familiar hum of the television set subsides with a quiet click. Darkness shrouds the room, and she feels the stillness and coolness of the air. She tip-toes up the staircase, the sound of the creaking wood a reminder of the house's age.

A single shaft of soft, warm light at the end of the long, narrow hallway cuts through the thick darkness like an ethereal beacon, guiding her forward. She cautiously pokes her head through the gap in the ajar door and sees James sleeping soundly on the bed with a book resting on his chest, the gentle sound of his rhythmic breathing filling the room. Sparky, his loyal furry companion, jumps onto the bed and lets out a contented sigh as he rests his head on his master's lap.

The scene before her evokes a deep emotional response and tears well up in her eyes. She tip-toes to her bedroom, the old wooden floorboards creaking beneath her feet like a rusty door. Before climbing into bed, she changes into her cotton nighties, feeling the soft fabric against her skin. Just as she raises her arms to clap, the soft hum of her phone on the nightstand breaks the silence, filling the air with a faint buzzing sound. The sight of Blair's name on the message preview fills her with a sense of excitement, her heart racing with anticipation. She eagerly taps the message to read what Blair has to say. *Wow, that was a close one! Samster is fast asleep and none the wiser. Counting down the minutes to our date! Hit me up whenever. Blair xx.*

Alice taps the reply button, her fingers hovering over the keyboard as she contemplates whether to send the message now or wait until after Samuel and Madison's divorce hearing.

The weight of her decision bears down on her, causing her fingers to tremble ever so slightly. Alice's mind is a whirlwind of conflicting emotions. She yearns to release the pent-up frustration and anger that has consumed her for months, feeling it boil inside her like a simmering cauldron. But a nagging voice of reason whispers in her ear, urging her to pause and consider the consequences of her actions.

The divorce hearing looms ahead, its presence intensifying the gravity of her choice. Her eyes dart between the send button and the clock ticking away on the wall. Time seems to stretch, elongating the moments of indecision. It is as if the entire universe holds its breath, waiting for her to make a choice that could alter the trajectory of her life.

In this moment, Alice realizes the power she holds with her decision. The timing of her message could have far-reaching consequences, both for Samuel and Madison's divorce proceedings and for her own relationship with them. The responsibility weighs heavily on her conscience, making it even more difficult to make a choice.

Her fingers tremble once more, but this time with a newfound determination. Taking a deep breath, she removes her hands from the keyboard and closes her eyes. The message could wait.

As she finally lets go of the reply button, a sense of relief washes over her. The weight on her shoulders lightens, if only momentarily, as she waits until after the divorce hearing to send her message. The journey towards healing and closure takes a detour, but Alice knows this pause allows her to approach the situation with a clearer mind and a more strategic approach.

Alice claps her hands twice, the sudden sound shrouding the room in a thick, velvety darkness, lulling her to sleep with a smile on her face, the soothing sound of James' breathing and Sparky's contented sighs echoing in her mind.

Acknowledgments

In the quiet corners of my heart, where words are born from whispers of inspiration, I owe an immeasurable debt of gratitude to two extraordinary souls.

To my wife, Marna, my Babalooba, who has been the beacon guiding me through the stormy seas of life. Her love is the wind in my sails, her faith in me is the compass that steers my course. She is the lighthouse promising safe harbor, even amidst the most tempestuous squalls. To her, I pledge my eternal love and gratitude.

Then there is Lettie van der Merwe, a woman of extraordinary strength and boundless love. She cradled my world in her seasoned hands, nurturing the seedling of my existence into the tree I am today. Her unwavering support and unconditional love have been my sanctuary, my refuge. In her honor, I strive to emulate her kindness and resilience in every line I write.

It is to these remarkable women that I dedicate my passion for writing. They are the ink that flows onto the parchment of my life, their love the tale that I yearn to tell. They are the heartbeat in every word, the soul in every sentence. And as long as my pen dances across the page, their spirit will live on in my stories.

Don't miss out!

Visit the website below and you can sign up to receive emails whenever Iwan Ross publishes a new book. There's no charge and no obligation.

https://books2read.com/r/B-A-ORLBB-SROQC

BOOKS 2 READ

Connecting independent readers to independent writers.

Milton Keynes UK
Ingram Content Group UK Ltd.
UKHW010939221123
433051UK00003B/210